BYLINE FOR THE DEAD

A NOVEL OF LABOR, CONSPIRACY, A BLOODY UPRISING AND TWO AMBITIOUS JOURNALISTS

RAY WELLING

Byline for the Dead:
A Novel of Labor, Conspiracy, a Bloody Uprising
and Two Ambitious Journalists

© 2025 Ray Welling

Cover design and cover art by Sonny & Biddy, WBYK.com.au
Interior design by Siori Kitajima, PatternBased.com

Cataloging-in-Publication data for this book
is available from the Library of Congress.
ISBN-13:
eBook: 978-1-958861-76-9
Paperback: 978-1-958861-77-6
Hardcover: 978-1-958861-78-3

Published by The Sager Group LLC
(TheSagerGroup.net)

MORE BOOKS FROM THE SAGER GROUP

BYLINE FOR THE DEAD

A NOVEL OF LABOR, CONSPIRACY, A BLOODY UPRISING AND TWO AMBITIOUS JOURNALISTS

RAY WELLING

This book is dedicated to everyone who has fought (and continues to fight) against greed and corruption and has tried to achieve fair outcomes for ordinary workers and citizens.

And to Roslyn, who always knew I had a book in me.

CONTENTS

1934

AUTO-LITE FACTORY, CHAMPLAIN STREET, TOLEDO, OHIO

They say history is written by the victors. I think history gets written by whoever survives long enough to file the copy. The rest just bleeds into the pavement.

I'm standing just off Champlain Street—notebook in one pocket, press card in the other, sweat on my neck, and the air stinking of smoke and men. It's not even noon, and the crowd already feels swollen—twenty, maybe thirty thousand bodies packed in like coal waiting to ignite. I count more baseball bats than lunch pails. More children than I'd like. And more tension than even the Guard seems ready for.

The factory gate looms like a fortress behind sandbags and bayonets. Guardsmen in dull olive wool, rifles at the ready, try not to meet our eyes. Half of them look younger than me. Some have that raw-lipped look of kids trying not to cry. You can see the rifles shaking in their hands. Bayonets fixed, boots planted—but they're barely out of high school.

A three-man crew has set up a machine gun tripod at the corner of Champlain and Elm, legs dug into the grass strip like it's France. One's squatting behind the barrel, another perched beside him, the third on the lawn like it's a Sunday picnic. I scribble a note: "deterrent or theater?"

Then Ralph Homer—all six feet and change of him, loose in the shoulders and already half-loaded on something brown—lumbers up to them, fists clenched.

"You know how to shoot this damned thing?" he slurs, loud enough to turn heads. "You might shoot yourself in the ass."

One of the Guardsmen shifts back slightly. Ralph grins, then kicks the machine gun hard enough to knock it off balance.

"There ain't even bullets in that thing," he mutters, walking away like a man who just won a bet with himself.

I hear a few chuckles. None from the Guard.

By early afternoon, it's hot enough that the pavement smells of tar and bodies. Someone near the gate starts chanting. Others join in. Then it breaks again—bricks, bottles, fists. The air goes sideways.

On the east side of the fence, a man in a fedora—clean-shaven, office type—tries to push through the crowd.

"I just need my paycheck!" he shouts.

A few of the women in the front rank turn on him like a murder of crows. There's no time for questions. They're on him in seconds. He's down on the curb with one shoe off, stripped to his shorts, arms flailing. I see someone slap him hard across the face with a handbag. Another yells, "To the Safety Building!" And then they march him like a prisoner, half-naked up the block. Later I hear the police had to step in. The next day *The Sword* runs a photo with a long, black necktie drawn on to preserve the man some dignity.

There was no necktie.

Across the street from the factory, a woman shouts down from her porch: "Take the bricks! Use the ones from the foundation!"

And they do. Not just from her house either. I watch three porches dismantled in under fifteen minutes. Brick by brick, they come down like altar offerings, passed forward hand to hand.

By now the Guard's formation is pulling tighter. Tear gas canisters arc overhead, popping and hissing across the street. The ones fired from rifles come fast and low. But the big ones—the "tin cans"—you can grab if you're quick. I see a group of ten young people rush into a corner store, come out with armfuls of work gloves. One kid shoves a pair on and hurls a gas can back, while another tosses one sidearm, like he's skipping stones.

A yellow smoke bomb goes off near the alley, rising high and sickly into the sky. It disperses a pocket of the crowd, but not for long. They're back before the cloud lifts.

Even though I'm still working as a stringer, I convinced the editor to let me use one of *The Times'* press cameras—surprisingly light and compact. I was given enough film to capture the full picture of what's going on today. As the smoke clears a bit, I take a few shots for atmosphere: the line of Guardsmen, the angry mob, the scabs and managers from Auto-Lite standing in front of the factory gate. One of them is a man in a tie holding a rifle, which looks out of place in a white-collar man's arms.

That's when I see him.

A young farmer. Looks about seventeen, though he carries himself like someone a bit older. He stands just inside the fringe of the crowd, jaw set, shoulders stiff. Sweat darkens the underarms of his plain but neat shirt. His hands are raw, cracked—the kind of hands that know fence wire and tractor grease.

He bends, picks up a brick.

Not wild. Not furious. Measured.

I snap a photo of him as he steps forward and lets it fly, shoulder low, arm straight—a motion practiced not in rage, but in rhythm. The brick arcs clean through the haze and strikes a Guardsman square in the head.

The man goes down hard. Helmet skips once, then rolls into the gutter.

Then the gunshots begin.

It happens fast—a single crack, then a volley. Screams. Not just from the crowd—from the Guardsmen, too. One drops to his knees, clawing at his face. Someone's shouting about being hit. I can't see who.

I can hear screams now—high, fractured. People scatter, slam into each other. Someone near me yells, "They're shooting!" as if we didn't know.

Across the street, a man crumples. I don't know his name. I never get it. He's maybe thirty-five, maybe more. He goes down holding his gut, folding inward like wet paper. The people around him scatter, then lunge back to grab him.

Someone else is down near the far corner of the fence—lying on his back, mouth open, eyes closed. I don't see blood at first. Then I do. It pools under his shoulder, sticky and black.

I snap a photo before I know what I'm doing. My hands are shaking.

Then I'm hit—not by a bullet, but the chaos around me. A tear gas shell whistles past and bursts ten feet from me. I drop, gasping, blind. My notebook flies out of my jacket. My lungs burn like they've been soaked in kerosene. I crawl toward the curb on my elbows, coughing bile, eyes streaming. My jacket rips. My pen falls out. Someone's shouting my name. I ignore it. I pick the pen up. Gas scorches my throat and makes my eyes feel like they've been scrubbed with steel wool. I cough and crawl and swear, half-blind, until I hit the back bumper of a delivery truck and stay there.

There's no line anymore. No clear sides. The Guard stumbles backward, then forward again, swinging wildly. The crowd splits like a wound and bleeds in every direction.

A woman goes down underfoot. A man pulls her up, dragging her by the arm like a sack of grain. A boy no older than ten is dragging his sister away from the street. Her face is raw with tears and smoke. They disappear behind a parked truck, and I never see them again.

Someone pushes me in the ribs and keeps running. I lose my hat. I don't even remember wearing a hat.

I make it to the curb near the printing warehouse and crouch behind a milk crate. My lungs burn. My eyes are streaming. All I can think is: I have to write all this down.

Eventually, the gunfire stops. The yelling doesn't. The Guard falls back toward the factory steps. I hear someone shouting for medics. Someone else is crying—a high, keening sound that I hope I never hear again.

The Guard retreats, then surges forward again, swinging batons and rifle butts. The line's broken. There is no line. Just bodies in motion.

I press myself behind a stack of crates near a lamppost and wait. After a few minutes, I venture back out into the street. I find my notebook three blocks away, soaked and covered in boot prints but mostly intact. My hands shake as I flip it open and gather my words.

"Two men confirmed dead. Possibly three. Scores injured. Tear gas deployed. Shots fired. Rumors of Communist agitation. Rumors of a federal response. Factory remains under protection of National Guard. Strikers vow to return."

But that's not the full story.

The story is in the girl's shoe in the gutter. In the porch bricks, the stripped man, the scared kid with the glove. In the boy who threw a brick that broke the day.

It's in the silence after. The way no one talks about what they saw. Not really. Not clearly.

Even I'm not sure what I saw. And I was there.

I write it anyway because if I don't, someone else will.

And they'll get it wrong.

PART 1

CHAPTER 1

1984

YOUR BALLROOM DAYS ARE OVER

I wake slowly, painfully, to a blur of fuzzy orange pile flecked with yellow and brown. My head dangles off the edge of the bed. I roll onto my back and blink again. Still fuzzy—now it's horizontal strips of brown. I shut my eyes and rub my temples, trying to ease the jackhammer behind my forehead. My mouth tastes like I've swallowed an old penny. When I sit up too fast, my stomach lurches.

Damn Craig's Beer Barrel and its two-dollar pitcher night.

I reach for my glasses and sit up. The wood paneling on the walls and the shag carpet on the floor come into sharper focus—autumnal shades in a shrine to 1970s suburban interior design. It reminds me of a recent article I read, an interview with TV producer Michael Mann about a new show he was creating: *Miami Vice*, about two uber-smooth cops in South Florida. When asked what set it apart from other cop shows, Mann replied, deadpan, "No earth tones."

Clearly, Michael Mann has never been to my parents' house.

The dream I was having—back in Chicago, walking down Rush Street, the smell of smoke and beer, the crowded streets alive and moving, the smiles on our faces as we sloshed through the snow toward the next bar—was just that: a dream. Instead, here I am, twenty-five years old, still—or rather, again—living in my parents' house in Walbridge, in a split-level that backs onto busy railway tracks ten miles from downtown Toledo, Ohio, also known as Rust Belt Central.

Thanks to the post–Oil Shock Recession in the early '80s, after graduating with a journalism degree from Northwestern, I couldn't find a job in journalism anywhere near Chicago, so I took an entry-level job at *The Toledo Sword*, my local paper, where I'd worked as a copyboy during summer breaks. While I've always had a complex relationship with my parents, you can't beat the price of free rent when you're trying to save money. I moved back into the basement room I had stayed in during summer holidays.

I can hear my mother upstairs. It's hard to tell if she's talking to my dad or to herself. She's pretty good at one-sided conversations, especially since my dad hardly ever replies even when he's there.

"You don't realize how hard it is to keep this place clean with men in the house—especially the bathrooms. No wonder I'm so tired."

I run a hand through my hair and glance at the alarm clock.

Shit. I'm going to be late again.

I trudge upstairs, my head still thick with last night's cheap beer and bad decisions. Mom is in the living room, rocking in her La-Z-Boy, a cup of coffee in her hand and that familiar look of quiet disapproval on her face.

"You got home late," she says.

"Ummph," I reply. Nothing like being twenty-five and feeling like you're sixteen again.

"I hope you weren't drinking. You'll end up like your Uncle Bill, dying of cirrhosis of the liver and letting your whole family down."

Mom's older brother, Bill, was an ex-soldier who moved out west after the war. I only have a vague memory of him—he only ever made the occasional appearance back in Toledo. I've heard this warning multiple times since I was a child, increasing in frequency once I became old enough to drink.

I don't bite. There's no point. She'll win the argument, even if she has to move the goalposts three times to do it. I pour a bowl of Cheerios. I focus on the sound of the cereal hitting the bowl and the splash of milk bouncing off the little O's.

After scarfing down breakfast, I head back downstairs to change. One of the few perks of the basement room—my own bathroom. Minor victories. A train rumbles past the house, rattling the basement windows. I hope it passes before I reach the level crossing on my way to work.

I pull on my usual—khakis, a pale blue button-down shirt, my navy pea jacket that's been with me since college—and head outside to my car.

The Green Hornet waits in the driveway, its avocado-colored paint job faded by years of Ohio weather. The car is old, a hand-me-down from my uncle, but it runs. Mostly. I turn the key, and the engine coughs before settling into a rough idle.

I pop in a cassette—*Morrison Hotel*, one of The Doors' best efforts. As soon as that deep, bluesy groove kicks in, my mood lifts a fraction.

"Keep your eyes on the road, your hands upon the wheel . . . "

Jim Morrison, poet and prophet. Not that I need a beer this morning.

I pull out of the driveway and at the end of the street turn onto Drouillard Road. As I approach the crossing, I can hear the deep whistle of another train drawing near. I push the gas pedal a little harder, heading toward downtown, toward *The Sword*, toward another day of chasing stories no one cares about.

I take the same route into Toledo every morning, but today the city feels particularly grim. The residual headache from last night's overindulgence doesn't help.

Like my folks, almost everyone I went to school with—and their parents—has moved out of working-class East Toledo to the suburbs. I'm reminded of this urban flight daily as I pass through the old neighborhood on the way to the newspaper office downtown. The Green Hornet rattles over the cobbled streets as I take a shortcut down Oakdale to avoid traffic on Woodville Road. I could've taken I-280, but it uses more gas to drive all the way out to the expressway and back. I've heard people get into knock-down arguments about the quickest way to get from point A to point B in Toledo, depending on the time of day, the likelihood of a train blocking the crossing, etc.

Can't they argue about something that matters? Thinking about that does nothing for my headache.

Passing through East Toledo, half the blocks look abandoned—like some slow-burning disaster hit years ago and nobody bothered to clean up. Weeds push through cracked sidewalks. Paint peels from old houses suffering years of neglect. A stray dog picks through trash in a front yard littered with rusted-out appliances. On one porch, an old man sits smoking on a rusty swing, wearing a white sleeveless T-shirt. I sigh.

I roll down the window, letting in the damp, metallic scent of the Maumee River, laced with the stink of industry—what's left of it, anyway. Once, Toledo was a city that thrived, a blue-collar stronghold of auto parts and glass production. Now, most of the factories sit empty, the only movement coming from wind-whipped plastic bags and the occasional homeless guy pushing a shopping cart down the middle of the road.

They began shuttering the Libbey-Owens-Ford glass factory while I was at Northwestern. The Jeep plant, where my dad worked before he retired, and the Sun Oil refinery—whose aroma is wafting through my window—are about the only industries left in town.

At a red light, I slap the underside of the cassette player, coaxing it into submission. The opening notes of "Ship of Fools" crackle through the car's speakers. Jim Morrison's voice, half snarl, half sermon, fills the car, and I let the music pull me out of my head.

"The human race was dyin' out. No one left to scream and shout. People walkin' on the moon, smog will get you pretty soon . . . "

I don't know what it is about The Doors, but something about their sound—Morrison's eerie baritone, the swirling organ—makes me feel like I'm somewhere else. Maybe that's the appeal. I'd rather be anywhere than stuck back in this underwhelming town.

I cross the bridge into downtown. The skyline is a mix of old stone buildings hinting at Toledo's prosperous past and newer, soulless glass monstrosities put up in the '70s. The skyline is still dotted with smokestacks and clock towers, but closer to the ground, the city sags under its own weight. Empty factories gape like broken teeth. Whole blocks sit boarded up and silent. People blame foreign competition, blame the unions, blame bad winters and bad luck. Nobody ever mentions the men who signed the papers, who traded jobs for contracts, who gutted Toledo from the inside out and called it progress.

The Sword's office looms ahead, a relic from when newspapers still mattered. Off to the side, the Portside retail development is a shiny new thing, built on the site of the once-famous Tiedtke's department store. It closed when I was in eighth grade and burned down two years later. I remember thinking at the time that it seemed convenient that a fire razed the six-story building, saving someone the cost of tearing it down. The plans for Portside, announced soon after, seemed to confirm my suspicions.

After years of businesses and residents moving from the city out to the suburbs, they realized they'd gone too far and were now trying to reverse things.

Good luck with that.

I park three blocks away from the office, kill the engine, and take a deep breath. Another day at the paper. Another day of trying to pretend I give a shit about Toledo.

Inside, the newsroom hums with the usual morning energy—a few phones ringing, reporters badgering sources, the clack of typewriters blending into the low murmur of conversation. I weave through the maze of desks, past the chain-smoking copy editors staring at their VDT screens. I wave my arm in front of me to disperse the smoke, holding my breath as I walk past. I have my vices, but smoking isn't one of them. I can't wait until they ban smoking in public buildings.

Jim, my editor, spots me as I step inside. He makes sure I see him checking his watch, shaking his head, then waves me into his office.

"Gray, I've got a story for you," he says, not bothering with small talk.

I drop into the chair across from his cluttered desk. "Yeah?"

"It's the fiftieth anniversary of the Auto-Lite strike coming up, and I want you to write a piece about the commemorations."

"The Auto-what strike?"

"Auto-Lite," he repeats, like I should already know.

"Biggest auto parts manufacturer in the Midwest after World War I. They had a factory over on Champlain Street. The 1934 strike was a landmark event. It led to the birth of the auto unions." He pauses, sizing me up. "Though, honestly, I'm not sure how big of a deal this anniversary is. What's interesting, though, is that Local 12 isn't supporting it. Could be worth chasing down."

That makes me sit up a little straighter. United Auto Workers Local 12 is the biggest and most powerful labor union in this part of the country. My dad was a member of Local 12 for years when he worked at Jeep. They helped pay for my journalism degree—I won a Gosser Scholarship, awarded to children of Local 12 members. It was one of the few things I ever did that seemed to get a rise out of my dad. I remember my mother took me shopping for a new suit to wear to the awards dinner. It was powder blue with wide lapels and a vest with big buttons—a product of its time. At least there were no earth tones.

UAW Local 12 traces its origins directly to the Auto-Lite strike. Back then, it was known as Automobile Workers Federal Labor Union Local 18384. If Local 12 officials are distancing themselves from this commemoration, something doesn't add up.

Jim gestures toward the open door. "You need to start in the archives. Learn some history before you go making calls."

"Sure," I mutter, standing up.

"Gray," Jim says, his voice less gruff now.

I pause in the doorway. "Put some effort into this one."

I nod, already feeling the weight of the assignment settling on my shoulders. Stories about industrial disputes normally make me yawn—Woodward and Bernstein didn't bring down a president by writing about fifty-year-old labor strikes. But the Local 12 angle has piqued my interest, which is saying something.

CHAPTER 2
JUNE 1931
THE TYCOON

From his office on the top floor of the Security-Home Trust Company building, the tycoon looked out at the gathering shadows cast by the nearby buildings—tall structures that reflected the boom times of the past two decades, when Toledo had established itself as an industrial force in the Midwest. Looking out at the skyscrapers, he could almost forget the chaos that had reigned in the city—and across the nation—since October 1929.

The nine-story Nasby Building, Toledo's first skyscraper when it was built in the 1890s, was now dwarfed by several newer towers, most of them occupied by banks. Dominating the skyline was the imposing silhouette of the Ohio Bank Building, its twenty-seven stories of Indiana limestone and granite rising above the rest. Completed just two years earlier, in 1929, it stood as a bold statement of Toledo's aspirations, its art deco details gleaming in the late light.

Further in the distance, the muddy Maumee meandered toward the lake, divided by the High Level Bridge, completed only months before. The two largest steel girders in the world helped the bridge span a wide section of the river. They also helped drive the project's cost past $2 million—and now the city was struggling to meet the payments.

Plumes of smoke rose from the many factory chimneys dotting the landscape, a sign that, despite the economic downturn, Toledo's industrial heart was still beating. The massive Toledo Edison steam plant near downtown belched white plumes into the sky, its towering smokestacks visible for miles.

Church spires—once the tallest structures in the city—still punctuated the skyline, rising above the modest residential neighborhoods that spread out from the downtown core. The twin towers of Rosary Cathedral, though not yet complete, were already making their mark. Rumor had it the cathedral's construction cost more than the High Level Bridge. The tycoon guessed the Catholics had more money than the city council.

Not so the rest of the city. Empty storefronts and quiet factories at street level told a different story. Toledo, like so many other cities, was grappling with the harsh realities of the Depression. Many would argue that the 1920s boom had caused Toledo's businesses and government to overextend themselves, hitting the city harder than most when the crash came.

The tycoon was painfully aware of this. He was trying to keep the Security-Home Bank—of which he was a director—afloat. Almost every bank in the city, apart from the conservatively managed Toledo Trust, was in deep trouble. Real estate values had plummeted. Mortgage defaults had decimated the bank's balance sheet. Although he hadn't gone into default himself, the tycoon had lost $5 million in the collapse of the Maumee Heights housing development.

At the latest board meeting, the story had been dire: Sixteen percent of Security-Home's loans were unsecured, many backed by worthless lots. Ten percent of its loans were in the hands of the bank's own directors.

Despite this, the board had voted to issue a substantial stock dividend—even though the bank hadn't turned a profit since January. In fact, it had lost almost $100,000 in the first quarter of the year. The tycoon knew a pending audit would uncover all the issues dragging profits down, so he and the other directors planned to close the bank and draw their money out while it was closed to ordinary depositors.

He didn't trust banks anymore. They were built on paper and promises—and promises snapped under pressure.

He didn't trust bloodlines much either. One frail daughter, no sons, and a son-in-law more eager than wise— that was the brittle branch his empire rested on.

If his legacy was going to survive, it would have to be built in stone, not flesh.

"I'm never going to be involved in banking—or real estate—ever again," the tycoon muttered, turning his gaze from the window to the items on his mahogany desk.

His eyes rested on a photo of the opening of the Electric Auto-Lite factory from twenty years ago.

He had founded the company, merged it with Willys-Overland, and then sold it to his partner in 1914—only to buy it back in 1918 when Overland went bankrupt. Since then, Auto-Lite had become his most consistent source of income.

The tycoon nodded to himself.

"I'll stick to my knitting and make as much as I can doing what I know."

The next morning, the tycoon strode into his office at Auto-Lite, determination etched into his features. He buzzed his secretary. Within minutes, the factory manager and the head of finance were seated across from him.

"Gentlemen," the tycoon began without preamble, "we need to increase our profit margins at Auto-Lite. Significantly."

The men exchanged uneasy glances.

"Sir," the manager ventured, "we're already running a tight ship. The workers are putting in long hours, and we've trimmed every bit of fat we could find in our operations."

The tycoon leaned forward, his voice low and intense. "Then we'll have to find new ways to cut costs and increase output. I want production quotas raised by fifteen percent across the board. And we'll need to reduce our labor costs."

The finance manager cleared his throat. "Sir, are you suggesting we cut wages? The workers are already struggling to make ends meet. Any further reductions could lead to unrest."

The tycoon waved a hand dismissively. "It doesn't have to be anything that obvious. We'll implement a piece-rate system for certain departments. The workers will think they have an opportunity to earn more, but in reality, we'll be getting more work for less pay."

The manager shifted in his seat. "Sir, with all due respect, that could be viewed as exploitation. The unions—"

"The unions," the tycoon interrupted, "are in no position to make demands. Not in this economy. They'll be grateful for any work we provide."

He stood, signaling the end of the discussion. "I expect to see a detailed plan for implementing these changes on my desk by Friday. That will be all, gentlemen."

As the men left the office, the tycoon turned to gaze out the window at the sprawling Auto-Lite factory below. He could hear the hum of the machines, the rhythmic clang of metal on metal. Not as scenic as the view from the bank window—but a scene he could control.

Soon, that hum would grow louder, the pace more frantic. And from that increased tempo, he would recoup his losses, dollar by precious dollar.

CHAPTER 3
1984
I'M JUST SECOND-HAND NEWS

The archive room is one of my happy places at the newspaper. I love trying to understand the context for stories, and the archive staff are efficient and friendly—asking plenty of questions before pulling a folder or two that give you just the information you're looking for.

The Sword's archive room always smells like old glue and fresh toner—like memory clashing with immediacy. I push open the door, expecting the usual silence—and get instead someone humming off-key to Fleetwood Mac.

A woman about my age is standing on a step stool behind the counter, arms stretched over her head, filing a stack of microfiche boxes. She's wearing a gray cardigan and dark jeans, her short red hair pinned back with a pencil. When she hears the door creak, she glances over her shoulder. I'd heard they'd hired a new head archivist, someone with an MS in library science from Ohio State. I hadn't expected someone so young.

"Can I help you, or are you just here for the concert?"

I blink. "Uh . . . I was hoping to dig through your Auto-Lite clippings."

She steps down and flashes a crooked smile. "Strike anniversary?"

"Yeah. I'm Gray. Gray Wheeler." I extend a hand.

She eyes it for a beat, then shakes it. "Kirby. Just Kirby."

Of course. Librarian with a one-word name. Has to be.

Kirby disappears into the shelves and emerges a few minutes later. "I've got three boxes on the Auto-Lite strike. One for 1934, two for the retrospectives over the years. But the good stuff's usually in the footnotes." She reaches beneath the counter and slides a box toward me. Her fingers are ink-stained, like mine. I like that.

"You're digging into Auto-Lite?" she says, thumbing through microfilm reels. "You know there was a rumor someone in the city tried to bury the original strike files back in the fifties?"

I raise an eyebrow. "Where'd you hear that?"

She smiles. "Librarians don't reveal their sources."

She points to a machine in the back. "You can use that reader. But fair warning: It's temperamental. Like my mother and most editors."

I chuckle. "That's fine. I've dated temperamental."

She raises a brow in amusement. "And how did that turn out?"

"Touché."

She gives a slight smile and goes back to her sorting. I carry the box to the machine but keep one eye on her. There's something about her energy—dry, efficient, unafraid to needle a reporter who's used to doing the needling.

I flip through the files. A 1967 anniversary piece. A feature on local labor heroes. A photo spread of the strike zone, looking eerie in black and white. She wanders over a few minutes later, holding a thin file.

"You might want this too," she says, handing it to me. "Clippings about the Auto-Lite Council—the so-called 'company union.' It's barely mentioned in the big stories, but it was a major wedge issue early on."

I take the folder, surprised. "Thanks. That's very helpful."

She shrugs. "History's in the things nobody thinks to ask about."

"You ever think about going into journalism?" I ask, flipping through the file.

"Nope." She leans on the counter. "I enjoy being the one who knows things. You guys come in chasing deadlines—I get to be the calm in the storm."

"Well, you might be seeing a bit of me while I'm digging into this story."

She grins. "I'm counting on it."

I dig in and soon become absorbed in the files. The 1934 Auto-Lite strike in Toledo was much more than a simple labor dispute. It began in February with a handful of workers— reports varied from twelve to fifteen—protesting for better wages and conditions at the Electric Auto-Lite Company. A few days later, the workers returned after the company agreed to consider improvements; however, the company's inaction prompted a larger, more organized strike, with hundreds of workers walking off the job in April.

By May, the situation had escalated. Fifteen hundred Auto-Lite workers joined the cause, and in a city devastated by the Depression, thousands of others—maybe with nothing better to do—joined the strikers. The streets of Toledo became a battleground as strikers and onlookers tussled with police and pelted the factory with bricks, etc.

The governor called in the Ohio National Guard, with thirteen hundred guardsmen attempting to quell the unrest. The confrontation, which newspaper reporters dubbed the "Battle of Toledo," resulted in two deaths and more than two hundred injuries. Auto-Lite management came to the table in the end and gave workers more job security and allowed them to unionize.

I'm stunned. Thousands of rioters taking over a factory for weeks? The National Guard? I could remember the widespread outrage over the National Guard being called to the Kent State Vietnam War protests in 1970 and four students being shot and killed. "Tin soldiers and Nixon coming . . . Four dead in O-hi-o," as Crosby, Stills, Nash & Young later sang. Kent State seemed such an unprecedented event, but thirty-five years earlier an even larger contingent of National Guard was called out right here in Toledo.

How had an event that completely reshaped labor relations in the United States escaped my attention?

Turns out the strike's impact extended way beyond Toledo; it sounded like it had national implications, influencing labor movements and leading to the establishment of unions across various industries. *The Sword* archives included clippings from *The New York Times* and other national publications—this hit the front page across the country.

Despite growing up here, despite being raised in a union household, despite having a high school history teacher who grew up in Toledo and told us to be proud of our local history, I had never heard of this event. As Cliff Clavin, the mailman on *Cheers* would say, what's up with that?

Reflecting on the dates of the strike, I realize my dad would have been around during that time. He was living on a farm twenty minutes outside Toledo when all this happened. Perhaps he had firsthand accounts or personal memories of the strike. I make a mental note to discuss it with him tonight when I get home.

While I'm gathering up my folders and notes, Kirby emerges from behind a stack of old newspaper clippings, brushing a stray curl from her forehead.

"Hey, this might be something—or maybe not."

"What's that?"

She slides a faded clipping toward me, one that looks older than the rest. The headline is dry enough: "Flanagan

Family Expands Toledo Influence." It's a business page fluff piece, decades old, showing men shaking hands at some ribbon-cutting event. I skim over the text.

"See that guy?" Kirby points to a smiling, younger man standing behind Clarence Flanagan, the president of Auto-Lite. "That's Owen Sinclair. Flanagan's son-in-law."

"Who?" I glance up, distracted.

"Owen Sinclair. Married Flanagan's daughter Charlotte, but there's not a whole lot else about him in these files. Looks like he preferred staying behind the scenes."

I peer at the photo again, noting the confident posture, the slight, knowing smirk Sinclair wears. Even in black and white, something about his expression feels calculated—like he knew a secret no one else did.

Kirby shrugs, returning to sorting the clippings. "Thought it was interesting. You never know, right?"

"Yeah." I nod, my attention already moving on to other documents. "Good catch. Can't hurt to keep his name in mind, I guess."

Determined to gather more information about the strike, I head over to the main Lucas County Library—another early twentieth-century stone edifice, just a ten-minute walk from the newspaper office. The staff there are used to *Sword* reporters digging deeper into their topics. A helpful librarian points me to the right section, and I pick out a few relevant books.

I discover that 1934 was a pivotal year for labor movements across the country. In addition to the events in Toledo—where several other auto-related companies, including Willys-Overland (which eventually became Jeep), went out in sympathy with the Auto-Lite workers— significant strikes also occurred in Minneapolis and San Francisco. Together, these collective actions highlighted the growing unrest among Depression-era workers and their demands for better conditions and representation.

What started as a routine assignment is turning out to be connected to a defining moment in Toledo's—maybe even America's—labor history. One of the reasons I pushed myself in school and won scholarships to attend an exclusive private university was to escape my working-class origins. But now, I find myself intrigued by the lives of the working poor during the Depression. The resilience and determination of those workers, standing up against formidable opposition, resonates with me. Like the protesters at Kent State, these workers wanted to stick it to the man. And in the middle of the Depression—with massive unemployment, wage cuts, and firings with no recourse—the stakes were arguably even higher than for students protesting government military policy.

Mom has set aside some dinner for me. My parents and I rarely eat together—Mom and Dad always have dinner at five o'clock sharp, no exceptions, and I never leave work until much later. When I get home, Dad is sitting in his recliner, pipe in one hand, *Time* magazine in the other. Mom sits next to him in a rocking chair, watching a game show with the sound turned low so it doesn't disturb Dad.

I sit at the chunky dining room table under the hum of the overhead fluorescent light. A plate of meatloaf and instant mashed potatoes sits before me—the kind of meal I could eat on autopilot.

"So, Dad," I start, cutting into the silence between the clinking of silverware, "you ever hear about the Auto-Lite strike?"

He doesn't look up from his magazine. "Sure," he mutters after a pause.

I wait for more, but he keeps reading, eyes fixed on the page like it holds all the secrets of the universe.

"Well, I was reading about it today at the paper," I continue, watching him closely. "Seems like a big deal—thousands of people in the streets, the National Guard called in, shots fired, people killed. How come we never learned about it in school?"

"Yeah, well," Dad says, finally looking up, his brow furrowed, "they don't teach you everything in school."

Mom makes a small noise in her throat—a nervous chuckle. I can't tell if she's listening to our conversation or laughing at Bob Barker on the TV.

Dad picks up his pipe, looks at it, then sets it back down on the little stand beside him. "Why you so interested?"

I shrug, keeping it casual. "It's the fiftieth anniversary. *The Sword* wants me to cover the commemoration. But UAW Local 12 isn't even backing it."

Dad shakes his head and lets out a dry chuckle. "Of course they're not."

That gets my attention. "Why not?"

He hesitates, then picks up his magazine again. "It's complicated."

Mom cuts in, her voice tight. "Gray, you should focus on writing what they tell you. No need to go digging around where you don't belong."

That's an odd thing to say. I frown at her. "It's just history, Mom."

She huffs and turns to Dad. "Tell him it's nothing, Fred."

"Did you know anyone involved?" I ask, keeping my tone light. "You would've been, what, twenty back then?"

His mouth opens like he might answer, but then he clamps it shut. His jaw tightens. "I don't remember much about it. A bunch of troublemakers making life hard for working men."

With that, he raises the magazine in front of his face. Conversation over.

Mom gives me a sharp look and shakes her head. "You know how he gets."

I set my fork down, appetite gone. "Yeah," I say. "I know."

I know my dad is closemouthed at the best of times, but something feels different. I'm not sure what or why, but I'm going to sort this out.

Later that night, I'm lying in bed, trying—and failing—to fall asleep. The only sound is the ticking of the clock.

Then I hear it: Dad's voice, low and frayed, drifting down from the living room, speaking to someone on the phone.

" . . . He's digging into it for some story he's writing about the fiftieth anniversary. Yeah, I told him to leave it alone . . . No, I didn't tell him everything. What do you want me to say—that I was part of it? That I watched it happen?"

My chest tightens. I stop in the hallway, heart thudding.

"No. He can't know. It'll wreck him. It'll wreck everything."

The line goes quiet.

I retreat a step, trying to catch my breath.

He never talks like that. Not about the strike. Not about me.

SUMMER 1933

THE BOYS FROM DEPARTMENT TWO

The boys from Department Two were sitting outside the front of the Auto-Lite building, enjoying the sunshine on their lunch break. They were glad to be out of the hot, musty press room for a bit. They were glad to have a job—as hard as it was—and glad that each of them still had ten fingers because the punch press was the most dangerous job in the factory.

A man walked along the other side of the street, giving the group sidelong glances. The punch press boys looked at each other.

"Do you know who that is?"

"I don't know him from Adam."

The man sat down on the ground at the edge of the parking lot. He called to the boys, and with nothing better to do, they sidled over.

"How are you fellows doing?" the man asked.

A few of the boys shrugged and raised their arms as if to say, "Okay, I guess."

The man asked about their job, teasing out the tough conditions they were working under. He mentioned the name of someone in Department Twelve who he said was his cousin. He seemed nice enough; some of them thought maybe he was angling for an introduction to the hiring manager.

When they came out for lunch the next day, the man was there again. This time, he took charge of the conversation.

"You know, there's a law now that means you can organize. You can join a union—you don't need to be afraid."

The federal government had suspended antitrust laws in 1933 to encourage industries to form alliances and write industry-wide codes of fair competition.

The boys looked at each other.

"Afraid of what?" one of them asked, raising his shoulders.

"Afraid of standing up for yourselves and earning what you deserve. Didn't you used to be making sixty cents an hour?"

The boys nodded.

"And what are you making now?"

"Forty-eight cents an hour," one of them said.

"And what's changed? Is your job easier or more secure than it was when you were earning more?"

The boys looked at each other. They knew their required piece rate for extra earnings had been increased, not decreased. If anything, their jobs were more insecure than ever. There were a few nine-fingered former press operators whose families had ended up on public benefits.

The organizer eyeballed them. "You don't have to say anything. I think I know what you're thinking. Say, you know you fellows oughta join a union and get organized.

You don't have to worry about getting fired. If you get fired, the union can back you up."

"Union? You mean the Auto-Lite Council?"

The man spat in the street. "That's no union—it's a mouthpiece for Auto-Lite management. I mean workers like you, in factories all over the country, working together to make things better."

The boys looked at each other. One of them spoke up. "Lunch break's almost finished. We better get back inside."

They shuffled back to the press room without turning to look at the man.

The man came back the next day. And the day after that. And the day after that.

He kept asking questions.

"How would you fellows like to have seniority rights and all that? How would you like to get a little raise?"

Every lunch hour, the man would be there, asking questions. One day he said to the boys, "There's going to be a meeting over at the Moose Hall."

The boys chatted among themselves, and decided it wouldn't hurt to go and see what the union people had to say.

After work, they all went to the Moose Hall. They sat there for a couple of hours, listening to the guy talking about getting organized and getting this and getting that.

One of the boys said at the meeting, "You know fellas— look, we run one thousand pieces, we get a dollar for it. We run two thousand, and we get thirty-eight cents for the second one instead of a dollar. Who gets the other? The boss and the big shots get it all."

CHAPTER 5

1984

I SEE A CLINIC FULL OF CYNICS

The Electric Auto-Lite Fiftieth Anniversary Commemoration Committee is meeting in the back room of a union hall that has seen better days. Yellowy-green walls surround a table with mismatched chairs. A few leftover flyers from past organizing drives litter the bulletin board. Dust and burnt coffee permeate the room.

A half-dozen people sit around the table—some straight-backed with arms crossed, others with hands folded like they're expecting a fight.

I'd called the committee's chairman, Mike Ferner, an official in the Toledo Public Service Union, and wangled an invitation to attend the meeting. Ferner sits at the head of the table, rubbing his temple like he's nursing a headache as bad as my recent hangover. I recognize him from other union stories I've covered, though I've never seen him this on edge.

"All right," he says, exhaling. "Let's get started. As you all know, we're only a few weeks out from the commemoration, and—"

"—and we still don't have Local 12 backing us," a woman cuts in. She's middle-aged, wiry, with sharp eyes that miss nothing. "In fact, they're telling their members to stay away. You believe that?" She looks my way to make it clear she's interjecting for my benefit.

A grumble goes around the table.

"Why?" I ask, lifting my notepad. "I mean, this strike is part of their history."

A man across from me, burly with a graying beard, lets out a bitter laugh. "History," he says. "That's exactly the problem."

Ferner holds up a hand. "Look, Gray's here to understand what's going on, all right? Let's keep this productive."

The woman shakes her head. "It's not complicated. The union doesn't want to touch this thing because of the damn Red Scare hangover. That's the truth."

"Red Scare?" I ask, intrigued.

Ferner sighs. "Look, back in '34, the Auto-Lite strike wasn't just a union strike. I mean, it started out that way, but it grew into something bigger. The American Workers Party was involved. A lot of radicals—Communists, Socialists, Musteites . . . "

"Muskie what?" That's a new one on me. "Any connection to Ed Muskie?"

"Not Muskie. Muste. A. J. Muste was a big mover in the labor movement in those days. A pacifist. Founded the American Workers Party. He showed up in Toledo. The AWP merged with the Trotskyites, the Communist League, but Muste went on to become an antiwar protester."

The burly man leans forward, arms on the table. "The UAW, as strong as it is now, doesn't want to be linked too closely with anything that could be construed as 'Communist influence,' especially not now, with Reagan's people watching. They've worked too hard to get into the mainstream. They don't want to dredge up anything that could make them a target."

"For crying out loud," I mutter, flipping back a few pages in my notebook. "Fifty years later and we're still afraid of Reds under the bed."

Ferner gives a short, humorless chuckle. "Some issues never go away."

A younger guy, no older than me, says, "This is bigger than just the union not showing up. There's pressure coming from somewhere else."

"Pressure from where?" I ask.

Ferner hesitates, his fingers drumming on the table. The others exchange glances.

The wiry woman speaks up, her voice quieter now. "Let's say there are people who don't want this commemoration happening the way we planned."

I glance around the table. They aren't just frustrated. They're nervous. I can feel the shift in the room—something heavy and unspoken hanging between us.

Despite the challenges, the committee still has plans for the commemoration. Ferner places his elbows on the table and steeples his fingers.

"Even without Local 12, we're going ahead with things. We've got speakers lined up—historians, two old-timers who were there in '34, and some labor activists who know what this fight meant. We'll have a march from the old Auto-Lite site to the courthouse lawn, retracing the route of the original strikers."

"We've also got some artists working on an exhibit," the wiry woman adds. "Photos from the strike, newspaper clippings, even a few relics people have dug out of basements. We're trying to make this real for people—not just another history lesson no one pays attention to."

After another fifteen minutes of discussing logistics, Ferner checks his watch and sits up. "All right, I think that's enough for now. We've all got things to do. Let's keep moving forward as best we can."

Chairs scrape against the floor as people gather their things. As I pack up my notepad, Ferner comes up beside me and claps a hand on my shoulder.

"There's more to this story," he says, his voice low. "But I can't tell you here."

I turn to him, raising an eyebrow. "Okay . . . "

"Meet me at the White Tower on Starr Avenue," he says. "Tonight. Ten p.m."

I frown. "You're making this sound like a spy movie."

He smiles, but there's no humor in it. "Just be there," he says. "And bring your notepad. But not your tape recorder."

As we step out into the gray afternoon, Ferner pulls his coat tighter around his shoulders and glances up and down the street. A battered delivery truck rattles past, backfiring once with a sharp crack. Ferner flinches so hard he almost drops his briefcase.

Then he walks out, leaving me standing there, notebook in hand, stomach twisting with curiosity.

CHAPTER 6

FEBRUARY 1934

THE TROUBLEMAKERS

As February 1934 began, the boys from Department Two decided they could no longer put up with the conditions they were working under. The factory floor had become an avenue of adversity, where men and women toiled for long hours under dangerous conditions for shrinking pay. Safety precautions were often an afterthought, and injuries were common.

The company's recent threats of further wage cuts had been the final straw.

As one of the boys—not a boy, but a seasoned punch press operator with calloused hands and a permanently furrowed brow—said to his mates over lunch, "We're not asking for the moon. Just a fair shake and a bit of respect."

The tycoon had long viewed unions as a threat to Auto-Lite's control and profitability. Management employed a variety of tactics to discourage organization among the workers. They planted spies throughout the factory to report any whispers of unionization. Those suspected of harboring prounion sentiments often found themselves assigned to the worst shifts—or laid off without explanation.

Over the autumn and into the winter of 1933, the meetings at Moose Hall had shifted from proselytizing to planning. A core group—mainly the boys from Department Two, with a few others—had formed Federal Labor Union 18384, affiliated with the American Federation of Labor. The union was still in its infancy, with only a fraction of Auto-Lite's fifteen hundred–strong workforce as members, but it represented hope to that core group.

On the morning of February 23, the punch press operators in Department Two decided it was time to take a stand. As they gathered in the predawn chill outside the factory gates, their breaths visible in the cold air, they knew the risks they were taking.

"This might cost us our jobs," said one man, who had a wife and new baby at home. "But if we don't do something now, what kind of future are we looking at?"

The small group refused to enter the plant when the whistle blew. Instead, they formed a makeshift picket line, holding handmade signs demanding better wages and working conditions. The sight of the strikers took many of their coworkers by surprise. Some hurried past, heads down, unwilling to meet the eyes of the men they'd worked alongside for years. Others paused, torn between the fear of losing their jobs and the desire to join their colleagues in protest.

As word of the strike spread through the plant, tension mounted. Foremen scrambled to keep production lines running, while management huddled in emergency meetings. The tycoon, upon hearing the news, was beside himself.

"This is nothing but troublemaking," he thundered to his executives. "We'll have this sorted out by lunchtime."

But the strikers held firm. Throughout that first day, they maintained their picket line, their numbers slowly growing as a few—but only a few—workers found the courage to join them.

The following days were a test of will for both sides. The company attempted to bring in replacement workers, but the resolve of those on the picket line turned many away. Local police were called in to maintain order, but they were reluctant to use force against workers who were their neighbors and friends.

By week's end, it was clear the strike would not collapse. If anything, the resolve of the press operators had inspired others across the factory. The smell of oil and sweat still clung to their clothes—but now so too did something rarer: solidarity.

And with it, the fragile beginnings of a broader resistance.

CHAPTER 7
1984
DAYS OF FUTURE PAST

There's no time to hunt down decent coffee, so like most underpaid reporters, I head to *The Sword*'s staff kitchen for the usual: scorched coffee and, if I'm lucky, a leftover cookie from the tea lady. Scratch that—no cookies today. Just a few empty wrappers on the counter. Vultures.

I pour myself a cup from the scorched communal pot and spot Sidney Feldman at the counter, stirring his coffee like he's got all the time in the world.

Sidney's one of the old-timers—more than forty years at *The Sword* and still working, well past retirement age. He writes light-hearted history pieces for the Apricot Section (named for the soft orange paper it was printed on to distinguish it from the hard news—the name stuck, and so did the color). Quirky local profiles, soft-focus stories about Toledo's past. Maybe a bit dull, but never controversial. I bet Jim's never told him to pull his head in.

"Gray," he says with a nod. "You look like a man with something on your mind."

I shrug. "Working on a piece about the fiftieth anniversary of the Auto-Lite strike."

Sidney's bushy eyebrows lift. "No kidding? That was the first story I ever covered."

I nearly choke on my coffee. "You covered the strike?"

He chuckles, shaking his head. "Hell, I was just a kid. Journalism student at UT. Got a gig as a stringer for *The Toledo Times*—not a real job, more like, 'write something good enough and we might throw you a few bucks.' "

"So you were there? Start to finish?"

"Started following it in February, when just a few guys walked out. Auto-Lite had seen small strikes before, but they always fizzled. This one, though? Something was different."

He takes a sip of coffee, eyes drifting toward the distance.

"Management gave the strikers their jobs back and promised to let them form a union. Instead, they created a company-run version—the Auto-Lite Council. Nothing changed. So in April, the workers walked out again. This time, it was better organized. Several hundred marched out."

He glances at me. "By May, it wasn't just Auto-Lite workers anymore. The whole damn city was watching. By late May, there were thousands in the streets. The police, sheriff's deputies—they couldn't control it. They begged the governor to send in the National Guard. I skipped classes that week. Wrote a dozen stories. That's when the *Times* offered me a job."

I try to picture a younger, more hirsute Sidney elbowing through crowds, scribbling notes while tear gas drifted overhead.

"You still have any of those old notes?"

"I might," he says with a faint smile. "I've always been a packrat."

"Would you be up for an interview?"

He chuckles. "Gray, I never turn down a chance to talk about the past."

CHAPTER 8

FEBRUARY 1934

THE STRINGER

The young reporter adjusted his tie as he stood outside *The Toledo Times* building, clutching a battered notebook and a fountain pen that leaked just enough to stain his fingers. The editor, a gruff man, had hired him as a stringer just a week ago.

Still a journalism student at the University of Toledo, this was his first proper assignment: writing "color pieces" on the Electric Auto-Lite strike. *The Times* had full-time reporters covering the facts; he was being given a chance to prove himself by following up on the stories they weren't covering. His job was to capture the human side—the lives affected, the struggles endured, the voices that might otherwise go unheard.

The editor barked out the stringer's name from behind his desk as soon as he entered the newsroom. "You're not here to write some bleeding-heart manifesto, got it? We've got real reporters covering the facts. I want you out there talking to people—workers, families, whoever's caught up in this mess. Give me something that'll make people feel like they're standing on that picket line." Unspoken was the reality that if the editor didn't like his stories, unlike the salaried reporters, the stringer wouldn't be paid.

"Yes, sir," the stringer replied, voice cracking slightly. He stuffed his notebook into his coat pocket and stepped out into the chilly February air.

The streets around the Auto-Lite plant were alive with tension. The houses near the factory leaned against each other like tired men. Paint curled from the siding. A porch sagged where the foundation had slipped.

The corner store kept its lights off now, even during business hours. The glass had been patched with cardboard and tape, and the bell above the door no longer rang when it opened.

The strike had begun just two days earlier, when a small group of press operators walked off the job to protest low wages and poor working conditions. Even though the group was small, the stringer could hear their chants before he even turned onto Champlain Street.

He approached with hesitation, unsure where to begin. Most of the picketers were men, wearing threadbare coats and caps pulled low against the wind. Determination and exhaustion etched their faces.

"Excuse me," the stringer said to one man holding a placard that read: FAIR WAGES OR NO WORK. "I'm with *The Toledo Times*. Can I ask you a few questions?"

The man looked him over with a wary eye, then gave a slight nod.

"Can you tell me a bit about your situation?"

"Been working at Auto-Lite for eight years now."

"And why did you decide to join the strike?" the stringer asked, flipping open his notebook.

The picketer let out a bitter laugh. "Why? Because I'm tired of breaking my back for pennies while those fat cats in their offices rake in profits! You ever been inside that plant? It's like hell on earth—hot as blazes in summer, freezing in winter. Machines so loud you can't hear yourself think. And if you get hurt? They toss you out like yesterday's trash."

The stringer's pencil dashed across the page. "What about wages?"

"Wages?" The man spat on the ground. "I make fifteen bucks a week if I'm lucky. Got three kids at home who need shoes and food. You tell me how far fifteen bucks goes."

The stringer moved along the picket line, speaking with more workers and jotting down their stories. One man displayed a jagged scar on his forearm from a press machine accident. Another described being laid off twice in as many years.

He spotted a woman standing near the factory gate, arms crossed tightly over her shivering torso. She looked out of place next to the rugged workers—her coat patched but clean, her hair neatly pinned beneath a scarf.

"Ma'am?" the stringer asked hesitantly. "Are you here supporting someone?"

She turned to him with sharp eyes that seemed to see right through him. "My husband's inside."

"Inside? You mean he didn't join the walkout?"

She looked down and shook her head. "No. He's too scared of losing his job. But I told him—we can't keep living like this! We're already behind on rent. What difference does it make if they fire him?"

The stringer hesitated. "Do you think more workers will picket?"

She shrugged, speaking as if ignoring the question. "You know what's funny? They tell us we should be grateful for these jobs—like they're doing us a favor by paying us starvation wages."

As the clock in the tower above the factory marked the end of the afternoon shift, the stringer's fingers were numb from taking notes in the cold. But he knew he needed more perspectives. He headed to a neighborhood near Stickney

Avenue, where many Auto-Lite workers lived—a cluster of small houses with sagging porches and laundry lines strung between them.

The streets were quiet except for children playing in alleys and women unpegging laundry. He knocked on a door at random. An older woman with tired eyes answered.

He smiled, trying not to show how awkward he felt. "Good evening. I'm writing about the strike for *The Toledo Times*. May I ask how it's affecting your family?"

After a pause, she stepped aside to let him in. The house was sparse but clean; a pot of soup simmered on the stove.

"My husband's out there," she said, pointing toward the window that faced Champlain Street. "And my son too."

"Do you support them striking?" the stringer asked.

She let out a deep sigh as she sat at the kitchen table. "I don't know what else they can do," she admitted. "But it scares me—what if things get violent? What if they lose their jobs for good? We've got nothing saved up; we're barely getting by as it is."

Her voice cracked. "But then I think about my youngest— he's only ten—and I wonder what kind of future he'll have if things don't change."

At day's end, the stringer returned downtown to file his story. His mind buzzed with everything he'd heard— the anger and frustration of workers, the quiet desperation of families trying to hold things together, the simmering tension that seemed ready to boil over.

Even though he couldn't afford it, he stopped at a diner for coffee and spread out his notes on the counter. The words trickled at first, then flowed:

"On Champlain Street today, amidst biting winds and bitter resolve, I met men and women whose lives are bound by hardship—and hope . . . "

He wrote until his coffee went cold, capturing not just facts but emotions: anger at injustice, fear of an uncertain future, and determination to fight for something better.

When he handed his piece to the editor later that night, the man skimmed it and grunted his approval.

"Not bad for your first assignment," he growled. Then, with a faint smirk: "Don't get too attached to these folks though—they'll be back at work before you know it."

But the stringer wasn't so sure. As he walked home through Toledo's darkened streets, he couldn't shake the feeling that this strike was just the beginning—that something bigger was brewing beneath the surface.

Despite his efforts to remain an objective observer—a journalist chronicling events from a safe distance—the stringer knew, deep down, that unforeseen circumstances had already invested him in this story.

CHAPTER 9

1984

MOONLIGHT DRIVE

That night, with time to kill before my 10 p.m. meeting at the White Tower with Ferner, I decide to stop at the old Auto-Lite factory. I want to see the place for myself—to stand where the strike happened, to absorb something of its history before sitting down with someone who's been fighting to keep that history alive.

A forgotten relic, the Auto-Lite factory on Champlain Street stands as a testament to a battle fought and lost, its skeletal remains a reminder. Most of the windows are gone, knocked out or sagging in their frames. Rust coats every surface that used to move. The roof on the far end has collapsed inward, and a cottonwood tree has taken root in the middle of the old assembly floor. There's a loading dock still visible under the debris. You can just make out the number stenciled in faded paint—Bay 4. The old factory clock still clings to the brick like it's waiting for a shift change. No hands. Just dirt and numbers fading into the sky.

Nothing here was built to last this long, and yet some part of it always does. The structures hang on even after the work, the people, the purpose are all gone. Rust and age mark the padlocked gates, the chain-link fence sagging from repeated breaches. The shattered windows, jagged glass catching the dim glow of the streetlights, are a stark contrast to their former gleam reflecting factory life. Graffiti snakes across the lower walls—a mix of crude profanity and desperate poetry left by kids who have no memory of what this place once was.

I park across the street, the engine of the aging Hornet ticking as it cools. I step out and take a long breath; the air is tinged with the scent of damp concrete and decay. It's quiet here—so quiet it jangles my nerves. The hum of machinery, the clatter of tools, the indistinct murmur of voices debating union politics—all of it is long gone. Now, the wind moves through the abandoned shell, rattling loose sheet metal and stirring up old ghosts. The whistle that once split the air every day at 3:45 is long gone.

I pace along the fence, fingers brushing against the cold links, and try to picture it as it had been in 1934. Thousands of workers, fists raised, standing shoulder to shoulder against the company, against the police, against the National Guard. I imagine the crack of gunfire, the sting of tear gas, the thud of clubs against bone. I picture the individuals who stood their ground here, fighting for something bigger than a paycheck—something they might never live to see.

I pull my notebook from my jacket pocket and flip it open to look over my notes. I try to picture more than ten thousand people flooding this street. A strike that started small but grew into an uprising. The Guardsmen firing into the crowd, bullets cutting down workers who had only rocks to throw. Two dead. More than two hundred injured. A city on the brink of war.

And now? Now it's an empty shell. A ruin. This ruin reminds us how things can disappear without you even noticing. The company was sold soon after the strike, and the factory had been closed since 1962—more than twenty years ago. Earlier this year, the company shut its doors for good, another victim of an economy that has abandoned places like Toledo. The jobs are gone. The fight was won, then lost again in slow motion over decades.

I sigh, snapping my notebook shut. I don't expect answers here, but I hope for something—a feeling, a connection, some lingering imprint of history that might help me understand what the hell is happening now. Instead, I'm left with silence.

I glance at my watch: 9:25. I still have time to grab a burger at the White Tower before my meeting with Ferner. I turn back to the car, my footsteps swallowed by the wind, the factory looming behind me like a monument to a forgotten war.

I pass blocks of boarded-up storefronts, their signs faded and windows punched out. On the east side, a vacant lot sags behind a crumbling fence where a labor hall used to stand—or so the rusted plaque says, half-buried in weeds. No one rebuilt. No one bothered.

Somebody got rich off the wreckage. That's how it always goes. The names change. The ruins stay.

I pull into the White Tower lot at 9:50 p.m., expecting to find Ferner already waiting in a booth, sipping bad coffee (note to self: someone starting a business that specializes in good coffee could make serious money!), and looking over his shoulder like some paranoid whistleblower. Instead, the place is nearly empty—a couple of truckers at the counter and a kid in a busboy uniform wiping down tables. I order a coffee and a few sliders, sit in a corner booth with a view of the front door, and wait.

At 10:10, I'm tapping my fingers on the table. 10:20 and I'm staring at the clock on the wall. By 10:30, I've finished my coffee and I'm thinking I've been stood up. This is starting to feel like my love life since returning to Toledo.

So much for cloak-and-dagger.

I drop some notes on the table and head back to my car. I sit behind the wheel with the door open, letting the night air roll in, giving Ferner a few more minutes to show up. He had seemed serious—agitated, even. So why bail? Cold feet? Maybe someone warned him off?

Or maybe I was chasing shadows.

Either way, I wasn't going straight home. The thought of another evening staring at that wood paneling and listening to my mom describe how the world has dealt her such a bad hand was too much to contemplate. If I'd already driven out here, I might as well make something out of the evening.

I turn the key in the ignition, the Hornet coughing and, after several turns, coming to life. The cassette deck clicks, and "Riders on the Storm" drifts through the speakers.

"There's a killer on the road, his brain is squirming like a toad . . . If you give this man a ride, sweet family will die."

So what now?

I could hit up a bar, but I'm not in the mood to drink alone. I decide to drive around for a while, let the city roll past the windows, see if anything catches my eye.

Starr Avenue isn't far from Lake Erie, so I take the long way, heading out toward Maumee Bay. The occasional truck rumbles past. Flames from the Sun Oil refinery in the distance glow in the dark, plumes of smoke rising into the night sky. Even with the window cracked, I can smell the mix of lake air and rotten egg gas.

I pull over near the state park, right on the water. A few boats, their masts creaking in the wind, are tied up at the docks. I get out and lean back against the hood. If this were one of those film noir movies I like to watch, I'd light a cigarette. Maybe I should take up smoking, just to appear more troubled and mysterious. Though I think my friends would say I already project "troubled" well enough without picking up a new bad habit.

The lake stretches out before me, dark and endless. Somewhere beyond that horizon is Canada—another country only a few miles away. Behind me, I can hear the flames being forced through the stacks.

I think about Ferner—why didn't he show up? About the Auto-Lite strike. About my dad at the dinner table, looking like he'd swallowed glass when I brought the strike up.

There's more to this story. I can feel it. Or maybe I just want there to be more—to make me feel like part of something bigger, something of substance, some story that will get me noticed so I can move on somewhere else.

I take a metaphorical drag from my nonexistent cigarette, flick it into the water, and listen to the embers sizzle out. Then I get back in the car and head home.

CHAPTER 10

FEBRUARY 1934

THE VICE PRESIDENT

The vice president's breath fogged the factory window as he stared down at the picketers circling Auto-Lite's gates. Their signs bobbed like tombstones in the gray February slush: "FAIR WAGES NOW" and "NO MORE SPEED-UP."

Behind him, the punch press floor lay silent for the first time in a decade, its skeletal machines draped in tarps. The strike had lasted five days—five days of stalled production, bleeding profits, and headlines that painted Auto-Lite as a tyrant. Five days too many.

He adjusted his tie, its silk slippery against fingers still calloused from the shop floor he'd risen from twenty years earlier. The union men called him a traitor to his class. The board called him a pragmatist. He called himself a survivor.

"They're ready for you, sir."

His secretary hovered in the doorway, her voice tentative. The vice president raised his hand in assent but didn't turn. Through the glass, he spotted the strike leader—a wiry man in a patched coat—marshaling workers into a ragged line.

Children, he thought. They think this is a game.

In the conference room, three of the boys from Department Two occupied one side of the table, their sleeves rolled up to reveal forearms mapped with old burns. Across from them, Auto-Lite's executives sat in their pinstripe suits and waistcoats, their faces grim. The vice president took his seat at the head, forcing a smile that felt like a crack in porcelain.

"Gentlemen," he began, "let's discuss solutions, not slogans."

The strike leader placed his hands flat on the table. "We've been discussing solutions for ages. Your 'solutions' got us here."

A murmur rippled through the union men. The vice president let it linger before raising a palm.

"You've made your point. The question is, what will it take to get those presses running again?"

The demands came rapid-fire:

- Rehire all fifteen fired punch press operators.
- End the speed-up system that docked pay for missed quotas.
- Raise wages by 10 percent.
- Recognize the union as the workers' sole bargaining agent.

The vice president steepled his fingers. Point one was manageable—the fifteen men had existing skills and a willingness to take on the most dangerous job at the factory. Point two could be fudged with creative bookkeeping. Point three was negotiable. Point four was non-negotiable.

"Reinstatement is . . . workable," he said. "As for production standards, we're open to reviewing them."

"Wages?"

"We can offer workers 5 percent."

The strike leader's eyes narrowed. "And the union?"

"The company," the vice president replied, "recognizes its employees' right to individual representation."

Silence thickened the air. Across the table, the workers exchanged glances. They knew this dance—knew that Auto-Lite would sooner shutter the plant than tolerate collective bargaining. The vice president watched the strike leader's jaw tighten, saw the instant when his resolve buckled. Hunger always won.

"Reinstate the fifteen. Review the quotas. We'll vote."

The vice president nodded. "Done."

After the handshakes—limp and wary—the vice president retreated to his office. February's weak sun sliced through the blinds, striping his desk with light. He poured two fingers of bourbon from the drawer he kept for emergencies and studied the agreement:

- Rehire fifteen workers with back pay.
- Form committee to "review" production speeds.
- Five percent wage increase.
- No union recognition.

A sham. A necessary sham.

He'd learned early that strikes were wars of attrition, and Auto-Lite had deeper pockets. Let the workers think they'd won a battle; Auto-Lite would win the war. He sipped his drink, the burn steadying him. Outside, cheers erupted as the picketers dispersed.

Fools, he thought. You've bought nothing but time.

That night, in the private dining room of the Toledo Club, the vice president met with the tycoon for dinner.

"A temporary setback," the tycoon grumbled, sawing his meat with unnecessary force. "We can't let this fester."

The vice president swirled his wine. "It won't. They'll be back at their stations tomorrow."

"And the union?"

"A gnat. We'll swat it."

He laid out his plan. Management would isolate the reinstated workers by changing their shift hours. The company would hire private detectives to tail the strike leaders. Management would also increase production quotas over time, department by department.

"Divide and conquer," the tycoon mused. "You're certain?"

The vice president smiled. "They're factory hands, not philosophers. They'll turn on each other by summer."

At dawn, the vice president stood at the factory gates as workers trickled back in. The reinstated punch press operators shuffled at the front of the line, their faces a mix of triumph and suspicion. The strike leader approached, hand outstretched.

"To better days," the man said.

The vice president gripped his hand—rough, ungloved, the nails blackened with old grease. "To moving forward."

As their palms parted, he imagined the man's fingers crushing to dust in his grip.

Back in his office, the vice president drafted a memo to the foremen:

"Monitor all reinstated workers. Report any agitation immediately."

He sealed it with Auto-Lite's crest, the stylized A taunting him. Let the workers have their victory lap. Let them think the speed-up would ease. In six months, a year, they'd beg for the old quotas. And when they did, he'd own them.

The presses roared to life—steady, obedient. The vice president tilted back in his swivel chair, bourbon in hand, and toasted the profits that would follow.

CHAPTER 11

1984

BLOOD IN THE STREET

Jim is in his go-to position—leaning back in his chair, feet up on his desk, chewing on a Bic pen.

"So, what've you got?"

I hesitate. "I met with the commemoration committee. They're pissed that Local 12 isn't backing them. Ferner pulled me aside after the meeting and wanted to talk later, off the record, but . . . " I scratch the back of my head. "He never showed."

Jim frowns, rolling the pen between his fingers. "Ferner?" He sits up straighter. "Wait a second—check with the police desk. Somebody got tagged in a hit-and-run last night. Name was something like that."

My eyes widen. "I'll check that out."

I make my way over to the police desk, where Tommy Schwartz, the cop reporter on day shift this week, is shuffling through his notes.

"Hey, Tommy, you got anything on a fatal accident last night?"

Tommy answers without looking up. "Yeah, some guy over on Nevada Street. Found him outside his duplex, DOA. Name was—hold on." He squints at his notepad, then flips a page. "Ferner. Mike Ferner."

My stomach tightens. "You sure?"

Tommy looks up, raising an eyebrow. "Yeah. You know him?"

"Sort of. He was supposed to meet me last night to talk about a story I'm working on."

That gets his attention. "No shit? What about?"

I hesitate. "Something to do with a union march."

Tommy narrows his eyes. "Well, he sure isn't talking now." He grabs a sheet off his desk and hands it over. "Initial report says it was a hit-and-run. No witnesses, no plate number. Just some poor bastard found crumpled outside his place."

I scan the report. No signs of robbery. No forced entry. Just a guy run down in the street.

"Cops think it was an accident?" I ask.

Tommy shrugs. "They don't know. Could've been drunk kids. Could've been some asshole in a rush. But I'll tell you something—there were no skid marks."

"No skid marks?"

Tommy shakes his head. "Whoever hit him didn't even try to stop."

I set the report down, a sick feeling gnawing at my gut. Ferner had been nervous. I remembered the way he jumped at the truck's backfire, how he kept looking over his shoulder.

Maybe it hadn't been nerves. Maybe he already knew he was living on borrowed time. He said there was more to the story.

And now he's dead.

Just my luck. An interesting lead goes and dies on me. How am I supposed to get that story now?

Remembering my upbringing, I check myself and say a prayer for Ferner and those who knew him. But my resolve to get to the bottom of this story only hardens with his death.

MARCH 1934

THE "UNHOLY THIRTEEN"

The stringer pushed open the creaky wooden door of a narrow diner on Bush Street, shaking the drizzle from his coat. A warm blast of air hit him, thick with the scent of grease and fried potatoes. In the farthest booth, under the glow of a single overhead bulb, sat one of the boys from Department Two, hunched over a steaming mug. His fingers were thick and calloused, and he looked weary beyond his years. He glanced up as the stringer slid into the seat across from him.

"You that reporter fella?" he growled.

"That's me." The stringer set his notepad down. "Heard you've got a story worth telling."

The man snorted, lifting the mug to his lips. "Yeah, but not sure how much good telling it will do." He nodded toward the counter, where the cook rested on his elbows, half-listening. "You never know who's got ears for the bosses."

The stringer lowered his voice. "That bad?"

The man shook his head and puffed his lips. "Worse." He leaned in, eyes darting to the doorway before he spoke again. "Now that the bosses know we're organizing, they've got spies all over the plant. You'd think they'd spend more time figuring out how to pay us a decent wage, but no—they spend it trying to root us out."

The stringer flipped open his notepad. "When did it start?"

Settling back, the man stared into his coffee like the answer might be buried at the bottom of the cup. "Last year. Spicers were stirring, and we saw what they were doing. We knew we had to do the same. There were nine of us at first, trying to organize under their noses, real careful-like. We'd pass union membership cards under the bathroom stalls. A buck a pop." He chuckled. "Hell of a way to run an underground movement, but what choice did we have?"

The stringer kept taking notes. "That was the Federation of Labor, right?"

"Yeah, back when it was all still just a dream." The man scratched at his unshaven chin. "We called ourselves the 'Unholy Thirteen'—not quite righteous, but we had to be. We knew the company was watching. They saw us whispering, taking too many lunches and smoke breaks together. It didn't take much to end up on their list."

His voice dropped lower. "Then came February. Spicer's workers had walked out, and we knew it was our time. Fifteen of us—thirteen plus two sympathizers—stayed out of Department Two like kids staying out after curfew."

The stringer glanced up. "That was the first strike?"

"Yep. We made our own picket signs out of scrap cardboard. Stood outside in the cold, walking in circles, chanting whatever came to mind. It wasn't much, but it was ours."

"And how did you survive?"

The man exhaled through his nose. "We stole bread. Bakery deliveries would leave boxes outside the grocery. We'd pry them open, grab a couple of loaves, slam the lid shut, and run. Otherwise, we begged. Went from store to store, hoping some sympathetic shopkeeper would slip us a can of beans or a sack of potatoes."

The stringer noted how the man's fingers curled around his coffee cup, white-knuckled. Hunger's mark lingered long after the stomach was full.

"The women in our section—some of them wanted to join us," he continued. "But they had families to feed. They couldn't afford to lose their jobs. Some stayed behind, kept working. But after their shifts, they'd slip over to my house, arms full of whatever they could spare. Bread, soup—once even a whole chicken. They never said much. Just left it on the stoop and knocked."

The stringer caught the flicker of something in the man's eyes—gratitude, maybe, or guilt.

"What about the company?"

"They brought in guards. Called 'em watchmen, but we knew what they were—hired muscle. They'd tell us to clear out, tried to call the cops." The man shook his head. "But the police, they didn't care. Not then. They came, took one look, and said, 'They're not hurting anybody,' and left."

The stringer leaned forward. "And what was the mood like?"

The man's smile faded. "Desperate. Angry. We knew we were up against more than Auto-Lite. We were fighting a system that had no problem letting men starve so long as the bosses stayed rich. But we also had hope. We weren't just fifteen guys standing in the cold. We were part of something bigger."

He looked the stringer dead in the eye.

"And that's why they're afraid."

CHAPTER 13

1984

SAID YOU'VE BEEN THREATENED BY GANGSTERS

First things first: I need to know more about what happened to Ferner.

I decide to call on a contact I have in the police department—a guy I went to school with named Danny Dombrovsky. Danny had been a solid point guard at Waite but never had the grades for college. He went straight into the academy after graduation, and now he's a homicide detective. We weren't friends in school, but we got along— enough for me to rely on him for a bit of extra information.

I make the trip over to police headquarters rather than call him. It's harder to knock someone back when they're looking you in the eye.

While businesses and residents have fled downtown, public services have remained. The Safety Building is a five-minute walk from the newspaper, over on Erie Street. I stroll over and catch Danny as he's finishing up a report.

"Gray," he says, setting his pen down. He hesitates. Speaking to the press is a bit of a double-edged sword for cops. "What's up?"

"I need some info on a hit-and-run."

Danny gives me a look. "I don't work traffic."

"This one's different," I say. "Guy's name was Mike Ferner."

Danny's face darkens. "Yeah. I know about it."

"What are you guys thinking?"

Danny sighs, rubbing his temple. "We don't have a lead on who hit him. No witnesses. No plate number. Could've been anything." He hesitates again.

"What? What else is there?"

"Paramedics said he stank of booze when they found him."

"So he might have wandered into the street?"

"Maybe . . . but there was also a 911 call."

"From who?"

"Unnamed caller, but he sounded inebriated. Might've been Ferner."

"Dispatch got a call from him about an hour before he was found. Said someone was after him. But he was wasted, Gray. Slurring his words, rambling. Said he was being followed. Officers checked the area, but they saw nothing. Figured he was just drunk and paranoid."

I hold my hands out in front of me, inviting him to tell me more.

Danny exhales. "Look, I get it. Sounds suspicious. But you know how many calls we get like that every night? Usually it's some guy pissed at the world, talking out of his ass."

I drum my fingers on my notepad. "Any chance the driver didn't even realize they hit him?"

"That's what we're thinking. They found him in the street. No skid marks, no debris from the car. Could've been some guy half-asleep at the wheel. Could've been drunk kids. Could've been anything. Anyway, why are you so interested? Was he a friend of yours?"

"Not a friend—a source." Danny raises his eyebrows, inviting me to elaborate. I decline the invitation and thank him for the info.

I don't buy it. Ferner wasn't some random drunk wandering into the street. He was a guy who told me he had more to say—right before he ended up dead.

Something about this stinks. But I need more to go on.

So I head back to *The Sword*.

CHAPTER 14
APRIL 1934
THE MACHINIST

The stringer tapped his notepad against his knee as he sat on the splintered bench under a bare bulb in the kitchen of the machinist's modest home near the factory. The Auto-Lite machinist sat across from him—a man whose hands bore the hardened callouses of years spent at a lathe, shaping steel for an industry that never gave much back.

"The thing about Auto-Lite," the machinist began, rubbing his palms together as if still feeling the chill of the factory floor, "was that they never let up. They'd take what you had to give and then find a way to squeeze a little more. Foremen were kings in that place—what they said was law."

The stringer nodded, scribbling notes. He'd heard this before, but he needed it in the words of those who lived it. Auto-Lite wasn't just a place of work; it was a battlefield of daily survival, with foremen wielding power over men's fates with minimal oversight. They could fire workers for arbitrary reasons—or worse, simply because they were disliked—instilling constant fear.

"They had guys in the employment office all the time," the machinist continued. "Kept us in line, knowing we were replaceable. Except for the toolmakers and the model shop guys—they had security. The rest of us? We could be out on the street any day."

The stringer had already spoken to some of those toolmakers, members of MESA, the unaffiliated skilled workers' union. Management tolerated their organizing efforts because they couldn't function without them. But the workers on the floor were another matter. Their attempts at unionization were treated like an act of treason.

"Piecework was the real killer," the machinist sighed. "You ever heard of the satanic cycle? That's what we called it. They'd set a quota, and if you got good at hitting it, they'd raise the standard. You'd work your body to the bone thinking you were getting ahead, then realize you'd just made it harder on yourself. No reward—just more work for less money."

The stringer imagined the factory floor: a cavernous, sweat-drenched space filled with the rhythmic pounding of presses, the screech of metal grinding against metal. He pictured men hunched over machines, moving with frantic precision, racing against an invisible clock—knowing that if their productivity exceeded expectations, the company would punish them with an even higher quota.

"Didn't even have time for a damn cigarette," the machinist added. "Not unless you wanted to risk your job. They'd be watching—even in the toilets. You sneak a bite to eat or a puff of a smoke, and if the wrong person saw you? That was it. You were done."

"Did you ever see people get fired for that?"

The machinist let out a humorless chuckle. "Not just fired. Humiliated. They caught a guy with a sandwich in the storeroom. The foreman made a big show of it—called him out in front of everybody, then told him to get his things and go. Over a damn sandwich."

It was a system designed to keep workers in line—constant surveillance, arbitrary punishment, the ever-present threat of losing everything. No wonder there was resentment. No wonder a strike had taken root.

Another anecdote encapsulated the company's indifference to its workers.

"My brother got me the job back in '28," the machinist said. "Sixty-five cents an hour. It wasn't bad—could just about live on it. Then the Depression hit. I still remember the supervisor coming around. 'Remind me, how much you making? Sixty-five? Tomorrow, fifty-five.' Just like that. No explanation, no discussion. A month later—forty-five cents an hour. You think they cared? We were lucky they didn't cut us to nothing."

The machinist leaned back, crossing his arms. "It's not that we didn't understand business. We knew the Depression hurt everyone. But we also saw how the tycoon and his kind always made sure they didn't suffer like we did. The factory didn't shut. They still made money. They just made sure we made less."

The stringer thought back to the stories of those who had tried to organize before—the Unholy Thirteen who had dared to stand up in February, slipping union cards beneath toilet stalls, passing them like contraband. That kind of secrecy was necessary because Auto-Lite had spies everywhere. As soon as they suspected union activity, they marked you.

"Guards were tough," the machinist said. "They'd watch us real close, looking for any excuse. They wanted us to be scared."

Fear had been their greatest weapon. It wasn't just job loss—it was the hunger that followed. Men with families to feed couldn't afford to take risks. Even so, a few did. A few walked out, knowing the odds but refusing to be broken.

The stringer closed his notebook. He had what he needed—evidence that the conditions inside Auto-Lite weren't just unfair. They were cruel. Designed to wring every drop of energy out of the workers while keeping them too afraid to resist.

But resistance had come anyway.

CHAPTER 15

1984

CONTACT IN RED SQUARE

If the UAW wasn't supporting the commemoration, maybe they had something to hide. Maybe they didn't want certain things coming to light—things buried for fifty years. Maybe they were desperate enough to kill over it.

I decide it's time to understand more about the political angles at play before and during the strike. Among other things, it'll help me prep for my meeting with Sidney.

I call out to Kirby as I enter the archive. I can't see her, but the strains of "The Chain" waft from the back of the shelves.

The microfilm machine whirs as I scroll through the pages of *The Sword* from 1932. The words flicker on the screen in stark black and white, headlines revealing the desperation:

THOUSANDS LINE UP FOR BREAD IN TOLEDO
RELIEF FUNDS DRY UP – NO END IN SIGHT
ANOTHER FACTORY CLOSES AS JOBS DISAPPEAR

I know the Depression hit Toledo hard—any Rust Belt kid who grew up in the shadows of shuttered factories knows it on an instinctive level—but seeing it unfold in real time through the pages of the newspaper is different.

By 1934, the city had been on its knees for more than three years. Unemployment hit 80 percent in some neighborhoods, with thousands of men crowding relief lines and families scraping by on what little charity could provide. The auto industry, once the engine of prosperity, had stalled. Auto-Lite, Spicer, Willys-Overland—they all slashed jobs, cut wages, or outright closed down. The lack of resources forced people who had once owned their homes into single rooms with relatives—or worse, into makeshift shantytowns on the city's outskirts.

But it wasn't just poverty. There was anger. Toledo's working class had watched the wealthy weather the storm with relative comfort while they starved. Bankers still drove their shiny Packards past men who hadn't eaten in days. Landlords still demanded rent from families with no income. And when desperate workers sought relief, the city government—focused on the interests of business owners— gave them scraps and told them to be patient.

I find a 1933 article about a protest at the county relief office. Hundreds of unemployed had gathered, demanding more help than the meager amount they were receiving. The police came down hard, cracking skulls and dragging people off. That same year, there was a riot at the Lucas County courthouse when the city tried to evict families who couldn't pay their rent. People fought back, hurling bricks and bottles. Toledo wasn't just suffering—it was seething.

And out of that anger, something else took root. A radical strain of organizing that went beyond the established unions. The unemployed councils—groups of the jobless who refused to accept their fate—began staging protests, fighting evictions, and demanding real help.

I read about the rise of the American Workers Party, the small but vocal socialist group led by A. J. Muste—the guy Ferner and his buddies had talked about at that meeting. The Musteites saw an opportunity. Workplace organizing wasn't their sole focus; they weren't content to negotiate—they wanted to mobilize the power of the streets. And the dispute brewing at Electric Auto-Lite was a significant test case to exercise that power.

The workers at Auto-Lite had it rough—even rougher than most factory workers. The pay was garbage, the hours brutal, and the factory a sweatbox. Guys were losing fingers in the machinery, coughing their lungs out from breathing metal dust. The company didn't give a damn. And the man at the top, Clarence Flanagan, was living like a king.

Flanagan was more than the boss of Auto-Lite. He sat on the boards of half the banks in town. And when the banks started collapsing in 1933, wiping out the savings of regular working stiffs, Flanagan and his pals had already pulled their money out. Ordinary people lost everything. Guys who'd worked their whole lives were flat broke. Meanwhile, Flanagan kept his mansion, his chauffeur, and his fat stock portfolio.

Despite all this, people viewed Flanagan as a good boss and an all-around nice guy. As the workers agitated for better pay and conditions, Flanagan and his VP of operations, Alf Punch, played good cop, bad cop. Punch would get angry and call striking workers names, while Flanagan would make it look like he cared about the workers and their conditions.

By 1934, Toledo's workers had reached a breaking point. Auto-Lite, one of the biggest remaining employers, was still paying starvation wages while its executives lived comfortably. In fact, they used the straitened times as an excuse to cut wages even further.

When the new AFL Federal Labor Union 18384 tried to organize the plant, the company refused to recognize them. The strike started small—a handful of guys in February walking out to demand better pay. After five days, Auto-Lite gave in to some of their demands to get the punch press operating again. They thought they could wait it out, appease those wanting a union by working with the management-run Auto-Lite Workers Council.

In April, more workers walked out. But the real story wasn't inside the plant—it was outside. When the American Workers Party stepped in, things got interesting.

The unemployed joined them. So did the radical organizers. What began as a strike became something much bigger—a citywide confrontation between the desperate and the powerful.

The anger simmered until it boiled over.

The Communists wanted full-scale revolution—workers taking over the factories, overthrowing capitalism. The Socialists wanted more government intervention, fair wages, and protections. The Musteites believed in militant, direct action. For all three groups, the strike at Auto-Lite was the perfect spark.

By May 1934, the picket line had swelled into the thousands. Auto-Lite hired scabs, and that set the entire city on fire. Workers weren't just striking anymore—they were rioting.

And that's when the National Guard came in. I run my finger down a faded newspaper article:

GUARDSMEN OPEN FIRE ON PROTESTERS—TWO DEAD, DOZENS WOUNDED

More than a thousand National Guardsmen in the streets of Toledo, firing rifles into a crowd of unarmed workers. I shake my head in disbelief, still unable to fathom something like this happening in my hometown.

It makes sense why the UAW might want to keep this quiet. Honoring the past is only part of it—it's also about controlling the narrative. In 1984, with Reagan decimating unions and Cold War paranoia running high, the UAW desperately needs to avoid reminding people that American labor's roots were intertwined with Communists and radicals.

But is that enough reason to kill Mike Ferner?

I'm not sure yet. But I'm starting to think I've been looking in the wrong direction.

The Auto-Lite strike didn't happen in a vacuum. It had been building for years—forged in the Depression's hopelessness, in the anger of the jobless, in the brutal tactics of a system that saw workers as disposable. And now, fifty years later, the city is trying to commemorate it—while others are trying to bury it.

I glance down at my notes, scrawled hastily in the dim light of the library basement. If I want to understand what's happening now, I need to determine how dangerous this history really was.

The deeper I dig, the clearer it becomes: the 1934 Auto-Lite strike wasn't just another labor dispute.

It was a war.

I rehearse in my mind my next conversation with Jim. I have to convince him that this story about the commemoration can't be just a single article. It needs to be an exploration of the complex history of the labor movement in Toledo— including how the war is still going on today, still racking up casualties. This could be the story that will get my journalistic career off to a rocking start. This could be my ticket out of Toledo, out of my parents' basement, into the wide world.

CHAPTER 16

APRIL 1934

THE COMMITTEE OF TWENTY-THREE

A fragile settlement ended the brief but bitter February strike after five days. The picket lines had held strong, bolstered by sympathizers from Spicer's and the promise of a fight bigger than one factory.

Auto-Lite, under pressure, had made concessions: a modest 5 percent wage increase and a vague commitment to negotiating a contract by April 1. The company had also agreed to discuss critical issues—seniority, union recognition, and an end to blacklisting known organizers. But the ink had barely dried on that so-called settlement before Auto-Lite made it clear they had no intention of honoring it.

It was a familiar story—workers lifted by a glimmer of victory, only to be dragged back down by broken promises. A pattern as predictable as the Auto-Lite punch presses hammering out their relentless rhythm on Champlain Street. For the stringer, still talking to workers as disappointment piled upon disappointment, the writing was on the wall. The February strike had been a skirmish. The actual battle was yet to come.

Through March, tensions simmered. The stringer listened to the murmurs on the shop floor, the grumblings of workers who had returned to their machines with the bitter taste of betrayal in their mouths. Local 18384 existed on paper, but Auto-Lite refused to negotiate in any meaningful way. The wage increase was a pittance. Management had recognized the still-fragile union in name only. And most damning of all, the company had continued its campaign of intimidation—singling out union men for harassment, cutting hours, and making it clear that anyone showing open support for the union was putting their job on the line.

Then April arrived, and with it, the company's ultimate insult. No contract. No agreement. No negotiations. Auto-Lite's response to the union's demands was a simple, unwavering "no."

On April 11, the workers struck again.

This time, however, not everyone was willing to walk out. The memory of those five bitter days in February still lingered, and only a quarter of the workers joined the second strike when it began on April 12. Still, there were people from departments across the factory taking part, joining the punch press operators in Department Two.

The numbers were discouraging. And to make matters worse, the AFL's Central Labor Council—the so-called "Committee of Twenty-Three"—had agreed to support the strike in principle, but this proved ineffective in practice. Without firm backing from the larger labor community, the walkout seemed doomed before it had even begun.

That first morning, the stringer walked the picket line, notebook in hand, observing the scattered groups of men and their handmade signs. The weak turnout dampened spirits. The February strike had been a show of defiance. This one felt like a slow, painful surrender.

CHAPTER 17

1984

LET IT BE

I don't have to wait long before the UAW makes its displeasure known.

As I head out of *The Sword*'s office to grab a burger after a morning sleeping with the microfiches (to paraphrase *The Godfather*), a familiar face steps in front of me.

"Gray."

I stop short and look up. It's Dan Krieger, a bigwig at UAW Local 12. I'd interviewed him before—he'd been friendly then. Today, his face is tight, his eyes hard.

"Got a minute?" he asks.

"Sure."

We step into a quiet alley beside the building. Krieger glances around, making sure no one's within earshot.

"I hear you've been asking questions about the Auto-Lite strike," he says.

"That's my job," I reply. "It's the fiftieth anniversary. An important event in labor history. Toledo history."

Krieger sniffs. "You need to be careful with that history."

I raise an eyebrow. "Since when is history dangerous?"

He takes a step closer. "Depends on which part you dig up."

I wait, letting the silence stretch. Krieger hesitates, then says, "There were a lot of people involved in that strike, not just the workers. Communists, Socialists, outside agitators. People who wanted to turn Toledo into another Moscow. Some folks don't want that angle getting too much attention."

I cross my arms. "The UAW was born out of that strike. You'd think you guys would want to celebrate it."

Krieger's jaw tightens. "We want to celebrate workers fighting for their rights—not some damn Red uprising. You connect dots where they don't need to be connected, and you'll piss off the wrong people."

I stare at him. "Really? Get off my back, man. I'm just trying to write a story."

He shakes his head. "I'm warning you. For your own good." He looks around again, then leans in and says, "You're not the only one asking questions. And some others have ended up dead."

My stomach drops. "Like Mike Ferner?"

Krieger doesn't answer. He strokes his chin and tilts his head. "Wheeler. Aren't you Fred Wheeler's son?"

"That's right."

"We helped pay for your college fees, didn't we? I would've thought you'd want to support the union that kept your dad employed and got you that degree from that fancy-pants university."

I'm taken aback. While journalism is all about pursuing truth—without fear or favor—he has a point. And I feel guilty. While I'm still trying to come up with a witty retort, Krieger turns and walks away.

I'm not sure what he thought would come of that conversation, but I'm more sure than ever that I'm going to sort this out.

That night at home, I'm still chewing over the conversation when my mom stops me in the hallway.

"Gray," she says, lowering her voice. "Have you been handing our phone number out to your 'sources'?"

I frown. "What?"

"There've been some strange phone calls," she says. "A few times now, late at night. The phone rings, your father or I pick up, and there's silence. Then they hang up."

"Probably just wrong numbers," I say, though I don't believe it.

"I don't want you dragging this family into whatever mess you find yourself in at work. The stress could give me and your dad a heart attack."

I nod slowly. Yep, make everything about you, I think to myself.

Mom shakes her head. "Gray, this started after you began working on that strike story."

Before I can respond, my dad appears in the doorway to the living room. His face is dark with anger.

"You need to drop it," he says, his voice sharp.

I blink. "What?"

"I said, drop it," he repeats. "Leave the damn strike alone."

I stare at him, thrown by the intensity in his voice. My dad wasn't the type to get worked up—especially not over something like this. The last time I saw him this angry, my buddy Dave and I had gotten busted trying to sneak out of my second-story bedroom to toilet paper houses in the neighborhood on a Saturday night. We were twelve, and the sheet rope we'd constructed ripped when Dave was halfway down. He scrabbled against the weatherboard and woke my parents. My mom thought someone was breaking in and started pounding on Dave's hands as he clung to the windowsill. The look on my dad's face that night? It's the same look he's giving me now.

Back then, I was frightened of him.

Tonight, I'm just annoyed.

"Why do you care?" I ask, eyes flashing. "You never gave a damn about my work before."

He opens his mouth, then shuts it, his jaw tightening.

"There's nothing good down that road," he says after a pause. "Let it be."

I look at my mom, who's watching Dad with concern.

Something's weird about this. Dad isn't angry—he's scared.

My brother Paul is a history buff, and he has been living in Toledo—and living with Dad—longer than me. Maybe I had checked out the day we talked about Auto-Lite in contemporary history class, but I bet Paul hadn't. The next day I call him up and tell him I want to pick his brain about a few things.

"How about tonight? No time like the present."

I agree, although my journalism teacher's voice appears in my head, saying, "Avoid cliches like the plague."

Paul answers the door in his socks, wiping his hands on a dish towel. He's still wiry and lean, but there's a calmness to him now that I don't remember from when we were kids. Maybe marriage did that. Or maybe just being the one who stayed put.

"Hey," he says. "You're early."

"You're surprised I'm punctual?"

He smirks. "No, surprised you're here at all."

I follow him inside. Their house is a modest two-story on a cul-de-sac in Rossford—suburban quiet, freshly cut lawn, wind chimes at the porch. Carole's at the grocery store. The place smells like brewed coffee and laundry detergent. Comfortable. Settled. The opposite of how I've been living.

We settle at the dining room table, and Paul pours two mugs.

"You said you wanted to talk history," he says.

"Sort of." I take a sip. "You remember how Dad never talked about the Auto-Lite strike?"

Paul raises an eyebrow. "You mean how he didn't talk about anything?"

I grin. "Fair. But I'm serious. I've been digging into it. There's more to the story than people know. And I keep thinking—he must've seen something."

Paul leans back. "Maybe. I was just a kid when we lived on Raymer, but I remember some of his friends coming by. They'd drink Stroh's in the backyard, talk late into the night. I couldn't always hear what they were saying, but every now and then I'd catch bits—Auto-Lite, 'thirty-four,' 'the Guard.' "

My ears perk. "They talked about it?"

"Not when I was around. That's the thing." He looks at me, steady. "Soon as I walked into the room, they'd stop. Or change the subject. Like it was sacred or shameful, or both."

I nod slowly, thinking.

Paul leans forward. "There was one time—different from the others. I think it was a wake. One of Dad's old friends had died. I must have been ten. You were still little. Mom was out somewhere with you and Elaine. The guys came over to toast the dead. They said he was one of the brave ones. A real fighter. That he never gave up, even when the Guard came in."

I can almost hear it—the murmur of voices, the clink of bottles, the rough edge of memory.

"They talked about the day it happened. About Champlain Street. One of them said, 'He stood his ground when they opened fire.' Another said, 'Hell, he was ready to throw hands with the Guardsmen themselves.' They laughed, but it wasn't happy. There was something tight about it."

Paul's voice lowers. "Then someone said, 'You-know-who was watching from the factory steps, probably thought he was God.' And another one muttered, 'Don't say his name. Even now. Don't.' "

"Did they?"

"No. Just called him 'that bastard' or 'Flanagan.' I didn't know who they meant. But they sounded afraid. Like saying it out loud might summon him."

I heard someone say, 'It was never supposed to go that far. We were just told to stand there. Until someone pulled the damn trigger.' Then a long silence. Then Dad said something low, like, 'We all saw it, but none of us are gonna talk about it.' "

I look up. "Wait—Dad said that?"

Paul nods. "His voice was tight. Like he didn't want to remember. After that, I stopped trying to eavesdrop. There was something in the air—like if I kept listening, I'd find out something I couldn't forget."

He swirls his coffee. "I never asked him about it. And you know him—if you pushed, he'd just shut down. But it was clear. That day mattered."

I run a hand over my face. "I keep thinking—what if he saw who fired the first shot? What if he knew more, and just carried it with him?"

"Maybe," Paul says. "But he was a watcher, not a joiner. He might've stood there and taken it all in, but I don't think he ever wanted to be in the middle of anything. That's the Wheeler curse. Stand back. Say nothing."

I meet his eyes. "You think I'm doing that?"

"No," he says. "I think you're doing the opposite. Which is why I'm a little worried."

The silence settles between us.

"I've been reading up," he says, shifting tone. "After you called, I dug through a few old history mags. You're right— the official version of the strike is . . . sanitized. There're gaps. People still argue who fired first. I couldn't find much, but it's there."

"Yeah," I murmur. "It's real. And it gets darker the deeper you dig."

Paul's eyes linger on me. "So why dig?"

I finish my coffee. "Because I think the truth is still under there. And if we don't tell it now, it's going to stay buried forever."

He doesn't respond right away. Then he gets up, walks to a small shelf in the corner, and pulls down a folder.

"I made some copies. A few articles, maps, that sort of thing. Might help. Or confuse you more."

I take the folder. "Thanks."

"You'll tell me if this gets dangerous, right?"

I shrug. "When hasn't it been?"

He rolls his eyes. "Still full of drama, aren't you?"

"Only way I know how to be."

We sit for another minute. Then I stand.

"Tell Carole thanks for the coffee."

"You'll come back?"

"Probably when I need more free research."

He laughs. "Anytime."

I leave feeling heavier and lighter at once. There's no revelation, no lightning bolt. Just another thread. But maybe that's how the web gets finished.

I file Paul's memory away in my mental filing cabinet. Not just for the article. For the man I'm trying to understand—the man who never spoke of 1934, but who raised us in its shadow.

CHAPTER 18

APRIL 1934

THE PACIFIST

At first, it wasn't clear how or why, but an additional force entered the strike: the American Workers Party. The stringer had heard of them before—a group formed in 1933 by a man known as "the pacifist." It was a collective of nondogmatic Marxists, men who had been organizing the unemployed for over a year. In Toledo, their offshoot, the Lucas County Unemployed League, had a strong foothold among jobless workers. They knew how to organize, how to command a street, how to shift the balance of power in a fight like this.

By the end of April, their presence on the Auto-Lite picket line was unmistakable. The pacifist and his offsider, the AWP's leader, had stepped in, and suddenly, the strike was more than a struggle for Auto-Lite workers. It was a movement. The unemployed—once a source of strikebreakers and desperate scabs—were now standing with the union, sealing off the factory in waves of bodies.

Auto-Lite responded with the most powerful weapon left in its arsenal: the courts. It sought an injunction, and a local judge obliged, limiting the number of pickets to twenty-five at each entrance. It was an absurd ruling, given the thousands now surrounding the plant. Enforcement would be another matter.

In the early days of the second strike, the resistance had been deflating—like a tire with a nail in it. But this was different. The picket line was no longer a handful of defiant men with cardboard signs. It was a mass of the angry, the hungry, and the determined. And it was growing.

As the stringer took notes, listening to the mix of union men, unemployed workers, and radical organizers exchanging stories, he realized something had changed in Toledo. The Auto-Lite strike was no longer merely about wages.

It was about power.

It was in this charged atmosphere that the stringer found the pacifist. The man held court in a corner of the strikers' makeshift headquarters—a boarded-up storefront near Auto-Lite's gates, its windows papered over with union broadsides and hand-drawn maps of the factory perimeter.

Inside, the air buzzed with new energy: men mimeographing leaflets, women stitching banners, teenagers ferrying coffee to the swelling picket lines. At the room's heart, the pacifist sat cross-legged on a crate, spectacles perched low on his nose, scribbling notes in a battered leather journal.

"You're late," he said without looking up.

The stringer blinked. "How'd you know it was me?"

"Typewriter ink on your sleeve." The pacifist snapped his journal shut and gestured to a stool. "Sit. You've got twenty minutes before the solidarity march."

"This isn't just about Auto-Lite anymore, is it?" the stringer asked.

The pacifist's eyes gleamed. "It never was. February was a rehearsal. This? This is the overture to a new labor movement."

He outlined how the American Workers Party and the Lucas County Unemployed League had transformed the strike's dynamics. "We've shattered the old divide between employed and unemployed. That's what terrifies men like the Auto-Lite owners. United, we're not fighting for a contract—we're fighting for a new social order."

"But the injunction—"

"Paper tigers," the pacifist scoffed. "The judge can limit pickets to twenty-five, but he can't limit the thousands who stand with them in spirit and in flesh. The law is being exposed for what it is: a tool of the powerful."

Outside, a cheer erupted as another group of unemployed workers joined the picket line. The pacifist watched through a crack in the boards, satisfaction clear in his smile.

"You see? This is how you build a movement that outlasts tear gas and court orders."

As the stringer left, a striker pressed a mimeographed pamphlet into his hand:

THE WORKERS' PLAN FOR PRODUCTION

He tucked it into his coat; the words burned against his chest.

That night, typing up notes in a rented room, the stringer paused at the pacifist's final warning:

"Tell your readers this isn't just Toledo's fight anymore. It's a battle for the heart of American labor. What's happening here will echo in every city where workers are realizing their true power."

Outside his window, searchlights swept the streets, illuminating picket lines that seemed to grow by the hour. Somewhere, the pacifist still organized, argued, and in his quiet way, rewrote the rules of a rigged game.

The stringer lit a cigarette and inhaled.

This time, he knew the story wouldn't end like a deflated tire.

This time, Toledo was ready to fight.

CHAPTER 19
1984
JUST THE FACTS, MA'AM

Jim settles back in his chair, scratching the back of his head as I lay out what I've uncovered so far.

"So, let me get this straight," he says, puzzled. "You think someone ran over Ferner on purpose? And the UAW is trying to bury the history of the Auto-Lite strike because of Communist involvement?"

I shrug. "It's weird, right? Why would Local 12—the direct descendants of the workers who fought for union rights—not want to celebrate this? Why warn me off? And then there's Ferner. The guy asks me to meet him, and a few hours later, he's dead? That's a hell of a coincidence."

Jim sighs and sits up, clasping his hands together on the desk. "Look, Gray. I know you're excited about this. And yeah, I'll admit, some of it sounds strange. But let's focus on what we know."

"We know Local 12 isn't supporting the commemoration," I point out.

"That's a fact," Jim says. "So write about that. But don't go down some conspiracy rabbit hole about the UAW assassinating people."

"I never said—"

Jim holds up a hand. "Gray. Stick to the assignment. The commemoration. Who's speaking? What events are planned?

Give me a solid news piece, not an exposé on shadowy labor conspiracies."

I slump back in my chair. "You want a puff piece."

"I want a news piece," Jim corrects. "Facts. Verifiable facts. If there's a parade, write about the parade. If there are seminars, write about the speakers. Cover who's there—not who's missing."

He's right: I understand the difference between journalism and sensationalism. A voice pops into my head, unbidden—my first newswriting class at Northwestern, taught by a grizzled crime reporter moonlighting from the police desk at the *Chicago Sun-Times*. I can still hear his voice, crackling from too many cigarettes, telling his spellbound students, "Always check your facts—always. If your mother tells you she loves you, check it out."

I sigh, running a hand through my hair. This isn't what I want to write. But I'm not stupid. I know what my job is.

"Fine," I say. "I'll stick to the facts."

Jim nods. "Good. And Gray?"

"Yeah?"

"Be careful."

I frown. "You think I'm onto something?"

"I think you're sticking your nose where it might not be wanted. And that can get you in trouble."

I leave his office feeling like I've just been told to sit down and shut up. Is the UAW putting pressure on Jim to get me to back off?

Jim's warning isn't easy to shake. If someone buried Ferner's story once, they could do it again. Or worse—bury the people still trying to tell it.

But like my conversation with Krieger, Jim's warning only deepens my determination to dig deeper.

I'll check the facts, all right.

I head back to the archives, the Fleetwood Mac soundtrack comforting after another dead-end morning. Kirby looks up from the desk, a small, playful smile forming.

"Back again?" she asks, chin propped in her palm.

I clear my throat. "Ran into another brick wall. Thought you might have something to knock it down."

She arches an eyebrow. "I live to serve."

"I need whatever we've got on internal UAW communications—around the time Ferner first proposed the commemorative event. Anything suspicious. Private meetings, pushback, anything that smells wrong."

Kirby sits up straighter, all teasing gone. "That could be a lot of digging."

"I can wait."

She gives me a thumbs-up and vanishes into the back.

I pace, tapping the metal shelves with the flat of my hand. Minutes drag by. Ten. Fifteen. Twenty. I think about leaving, coming back later. Then I hear a soft curse from the stacks.

Kirby emerges, arms full of file boxes, a faint smudge of dust across her sleeve.

"I pulled three different years' worth of internal memos," she says, already flipping through one. "Most of it's about bake sales, grievance committees, election endorsements. Normal stuff."

"Anything off?"

She shakes her head. "Not yet. But . . . "

She trails off, frowning at a folder marked: Local 12—Internal: Sensitive Correspondence.

"What's that?" I ask, crossing to her.

She slides the folder onto the desk. "Found it misfiled behind a stack of grievance reports. Almost like someone wanted it forgotten but didn't quite manage."

We open it together. The usual junk: meeting minutes, reminder memos about monthly dues, a flyer for a Labor Day picnic.

And then—tucked between two blank letterheads—a torn sheet, yellowed at the edges, ripped as if someone had yanked it out mid-thought.

Kirby peels it apart with care and lays it flat.

Half a page missing. But what's left stops me cold:

" . . . critical that this stays buried. Ferner's stirring things up. We can't afford another scandal, especially with the Reaganites sniffing around. Deal with this quietly and—"

The rest of the page is gone.

I meet Kirby's eyes. They're wide, stunned.

"Where's the rest of it?" I whisper.

She shakes her head. "No idea. But someone didn't want it found. This was crammed in behind the wrong files."

A chill crawls up my spine.

"Who had access to these?" I ask.

"Editorial. Maybe a dozen people," she says. "Including Jim."

I exhale, heart pounding.

Kirby lowers her voice. "I'll keep digging. On the quiet."

I squeeze her arm without thinking. "Be careful."

She smiles—tight and resolute. "You too."

CHAPTER 20
MAY 1934
THE TEACHER

The teacher stood before her colleagues in the cramped faculty lounge of Woodward High School, her eyes blazing with determination. The room was thick with tension as she spoke about the ongoing Auto-Lite strike.

"We can't stand idly by while our neighbors fight for their basic rights," she declared, her voice resolute. "These workers are struggling to feed their families. We have a moral obligation to help."

The head of the English Department, a respected figure among the staff, nodded in agreement. "She's right. As union members ourselves, we understand the importance of solidarity."

"Exactly," the teacher said. "And now it's time to use that unity to help others. I propose we organize food drives for the strikers' families and join them on the picket lines after school hours."

The room buzzed with a mixture of excitement and apprehension.

"I saw the violence firsthand yesterday," the math teacher added, his voice grave. "It's not pretty out there. Thousands of strikers facing off against the police and deputies. They're using tear gas."

A collective gasp filled the room.

The teacher glanced around, a solemn look on her face. "All the more reason for us to show our support. Who's with me?"

Slowly, hands rose. The English Department head was first, followed by the math teacher. Soon, almost every teacher had volunteered.

The stringer adjusted his tie and swallowed twice as he approached the picket line outside the Electric Auto-Lite plant. His eyes scanned the crowd, and he stopped in surprise when he spotted a teacher from his alma mater—Woodward High School—holding a sign.

"Ma'am?" the stringer called out, notebook at the ready. "I'm from *The Toledo Times*. I was hoping I could ask you a few questions about your involvement here."

The teacher turned to him, her eyes bright with determination despite the fatigue clear on her face.

"Weren't you in my English class a few years back?" she smiled. "Of course. What would you like to know?"

The stringer cleared his throat. "Well, to start, what brought you and your fellow teachers out here to support the strike?"

The teacher smiled. "It's simple. We're union members ourselves—part of the American Federation of Teachers. It's important to support each other."

"But isn't it unusual for teachers to be involved in a labor dispute like this?" the stringer pressed.

"You might think so," the teacher replied, "but we've come a long way. Back in '31, when the banks closed, teachers were desperate. The federation looked pretty good to us then. Now, almost every teacher at Woodward is a member."

The stringer made notes in his pad. "And how have people reacted to your presence here?"

The teacher's expression turned serious. "It hasn't all been positive. There's still a lot of anti-union sentiment out there. Many people think union members are all thugs and uneducated troublemakers. They don't think teachers belong to 'that class of people.' "

"How do you respond to that perception?"

"We show them they're wrong," the teacher said. "As educated professionals, we're standing up for what's right. Unions aren't for one class of people—they're for all of us who believe in fairness and dignity."

As they talked, the chanting grew louder. The stringer stole a sideways glance at the growing crowd.

"It seems pretty tense out here. Aren't you worried about the potential for violence?"

"It's not pretty, that's for sure. But that's why we need to help out here."

The stringer finished jotting down her words, then looked up at her with a grin. "I have to say, your dedication is impressive. Do you think your efforts are making a difference?"

The teacher's eyes sparkled. "I know they are. We're not just providing material support—we're changing perceptions. We're showing that solidarity can cross class lines. And in doing so, we're not just supporting this crucial struggle— we're transforming ourselves in the process."

As the stringer thanked the teacher for her time and walked away, she called out:

"Don't forget that book we studied in senior English— Upton Sinclair's *The Jungle*. You might want to reread it before you write your article."

CHAPTER 21

1984

ENJOY YOURSELF (IT'S LATER THAN YOU THINK)

I push through the heavy door of Tony Packo's and the air hits me—thick with grease, onions, paprika, and something sweet turning over in giant steel pots. The walls are jammed with framed celebrity photos and faded clippings, and the booths are packed tight.

The long wall along Consaul Street is covered with hot dog buns autographed by famous people who've visited the restaurant, starting with Burt Reynolds in 1974 and including Jimmy Carter, Walter Mondale, and my favorite, Led Zeppelin's Robert Plant.

In the corner, I spot Sidney sitting alone, nursing a coffee that's gone cold. His cap sits folded on the table in front of him, his fingers drumming a slow rhythm I can almost feel through the tabletop.

I slide into the booth. We order a couple of Hungarian hot dogs each, and I ask him about where he grew up and how he ended up at *The Sword*. We chat about Tony Packo's and the publicity generated by the actor Jamie Farr, whose crossdressing character Corporal Klinger on *M*A*S*H* mentioned it no less than six times on the show. When Sidney mentions that Farr attended Woodward High School, his alma mater,

I tell him my cousin was at Woodward at the same time. "There you go—small world," he nods.

Sidney then starts in as if we're picking up a conversation started long ago.

"OK, you wanted to talk about Auto-Lite. You want the long version or the short?" he rasps.

"Start short," I say. "We can stretch it if we need to."

He chuckles, dry and humorless.

"It wasn't about pay, wasn't about hours. It was about dignity. About not letting some sonofabitch tell you that you were less than him just 'cause he held the pen and you swung the hammer."

The plates clatter down between us—bright red sausages so thick with paprika it stains the air. I watch as Feldman's hand trembles reaching for a napkin. I pretend not to notice.

"By the time May rolled around, there were thousands in the streets. The police, sheriff's deputies—they couldn't control it."

I try to picture it: a tide of grim-faced workers pouring through downtown Toledo, boots splashing through puddles, fists wrapped around picket signs made from scrap wood and fury. It's a different city than the one I know—raw, electric, half-desperate, strong-willed.

Sidney bites into his hot dog, unconcerned by the images he's conjuring.

He talks while we eat, giving me the broad strokes—the picket lines, the hunger, the fear. The way the city turned its back until blood hit the cobblestones. Names I've already heard float between bites: Flanagan, Auto-Lite, National Guard.

But it's the smaller stories that stick.

"First day they walked out, the sheriff brought the cops on horseback. Beat a boy half my age 'cause he'd spat near the wrong foreman. Soon, they had set up a machine gun placement. Imagine that, machine guns on the streets of

Toledo! After that, the strikers started carrying bricks. And then, of course, they called out the National Guard."

Sidney takes his time stirring his coffee, as if the memories thicken it.

"I was there when they fired. Right there," he says, voice low. "You never forget that sound. Doesn't matter how many years you pile on top."

My eyes widen. "You were there when the Guard fired into the crowd?"

"Front and center," he says. "You know how all the papers spun it? 'Mob attack forces Guard to act.' That was bullshit. I wrote it as it happened, but the editors overrode me and changed the tone. Damn editors—and politicians. Some things never change."

I sit back and let him talk, feeling the words settle over the Formica and chipped mugs. Outside the window, the world feels thinner somehow, like the past could punch through if you leaned too hard.

"We thought we were building something," Feldman says after a while, staring into his empty cup. "A better life. A better town."

He shakes his head.

"Funny thing about building something . . . you're never the one who gets to live in it."

I glance around the restaurant—the cracked seats, the bad lighting, the kid at the counter staring at something, not looking up. Outside, a man leans against a parking meter like it's the only thing holding him up.

Everything they fought for feels like it's crumbling around us.

Sidney sighs. "Look, I talked to everybody—strikers, strikebreakers, cops, National Guardsmen, reporters from national newspapers. Even the lawyer who represented the union. Some of them might still be around. Toledo's the type of place people never leave." That line feels like a short, sharp jab in my heart, but I say nothing. He's been happy enough to stay in Toledo all his life, and I don't want to sadden or anger him.

He hands me a folded piece of paper. "That's a list of folks I interviewed. No idea if they're still kicking, but if you wanna find the truth, start there."

"Appreciate it," I say, slipping the paper into my notebook.

Sidney wipes his mouth with a napkin. "I've got more. Boxes of notes from back then, stored in my attic. Haven't touched them in years. Why don't you come by tomorrow night and pick 'em up? I'll even make you dinner."

Another night without leftovers or meat loaf—jackpot! "Sounds good," I grin.

"Come by around seven. Let yourself in. Doorbell doesn't work, and my hearing ain't what it used to be."

As I close my notebook, Sidney sits back in his chair, studying me with a look that's half amusement, half warning.

"You be careful, kid," he says, voice low. "Stories like this . . . they don't like being dragged into the light. Got a way of dragging the reporter down with 'em."

He taps the ash from his cigarette and looks toward the door, his eyes narrowing.

"Some folks around here don't forget. And they sure as hell don't forgive."

CHAPTER 22

MAY 1934

THE TOOLMAKER

The air on Champlain Street crackled with tension as the Auto-Lite strikers gathered in growing numbers. What had started as a small group of disgruntled workers had swelled into a sea of angry faces, their determination fueled by weeks of frustration and hardship.

A toolmaker who had worked at Auto-Lite for eight years felt his heart racing as he surveyed the scene. The company's refusal to negotiate, the hiring of strikebreakers, and the heavy-handed tactics of the police had pushed them to the edge. Now, with thousands of supporters flooding the streets, something had to give.

"Catch!" called out his friend—unemployed, but standing with the strikers—tossing him a brick pried loose from the sidewalk. The toolmaker hefted its weight, his mind flashing to the countless hours he'd spent hunched over machines, his body aching, his pay barely enough to feed his family. With a grunt, he hurled the brick through a factory window. The crash of shattering glass was drowned out by cheers from the crowd.

All around him, workers and their supporters followed suit. Men, women, even teenagers ripped up bricks from Champlain Street's cobblestones and nearby porches, using anything they could get their hands on as projectiles. The air filled with angry shouts as windows throughout the Auto-Lite plant shattered under the barrage.

A young mother, whose husband worked at the plant, had come to bring food to the picket line. Now she was passing bricks to the men on the front lines.

"Give 'em hell, boys!" she shouted, her voice hoarse from days of chanting.

The crowd swelled as word spread through Toledo. Unemployed workers, union members from other factories, and curious onlookers poured into the streets. What had started as a strike of Auto-Lite workers had become a citywide uprising against injustice and oppression.

Among the newcomers were unfamiliar faces. Men with intense eyes and fiery rhetoric moved among the protesters, their words stoking the flames of rebellion. The toolmaker overheard snippets of their speeches:

"Workers of Toledo, unite! This is your moment to break the chains of wage slavery! The bosses think they can starve us into submission, but we'll show them the power of solidarity!"

These were the outside agitators the company had warned about—Communists, Socialists, members of the American Workers Party. But to the toolmaker and his fellow strikers, their words rang true. They weren't outsiders. They were allies in a common struggle.

As the day wore on, the violence escalated. A group of people overturned a police car, and within minutes it was ablaze, black smoke billowing into the sky. The sight of the burning vehicle seemed to ignite something in the crowd. People flipped more cars, smashed windows, and erected makeshift barricades from whatever they could find.

The police and deputies, overwhelmed by the sheer numbers, fought back with tear gas and clubs. But for every striker they knocked down, two more seemed to take their place. The air grew thick with gas and the smell of burning rubber.

One of the local leaders of the American Workers Party climbed atop an overturned truck to address the crowd. His voice carried over the chaos:

"Brothers and sisters! The time for peaceful negotiation is over. The bosses have shown us their true faces—the faces of greed and oppression. But we will not be cowed! We will not be broken! We stand here today for more than ourselves—for workers everywhere who are exploited and abused!"

A roar went up from the crowd, drowning out the police sirens. The toolmaker felt a rush of pride and purpose. This wasn't just about a wage increase. It was about dignity. About asserting their worth as human beings.

As night fell, the area surrounding the Auto-Lite plant had become a war zone. Fires burned, illuminating the faces of thousands of strikers and their supporters. The air was thick with smoke and tension. Everyone knew this was only the beginning.

Rumors spread that the National Guard was being called in. Fear gripped some; others remained defiant. The toolmaker overheard a group of young men vowing to stand their ground no matter what.

"Let them come," one spat. "We've got nothing to lose but our chains!"

The quote, which the toolmaker recognized from somewhere, seemed to sum up the mood. The situation had pushed them to desperation, and now they were fighting back with all their might.

As midnight approached, the crowd showed no signs of dispersing. If anything, it seemed to grow. Workers from the night shifts at other factories were arriving, bringing fresh energy and determination.

The toolmaker stood next to a man he didn't recognize—likely one of the out-of-town agitators. The man was passing out leaflets and rattling off his prepared speech to anyone who would listen.

"This is about more than Auto-Lite," he was saying. "This is about the whole rotten system. We're fighting for a world where workers control the means of production—where we all share in the wealth we create!"

Some of the words went over the toolmaker's head, but the passion behind them was infectious. He nodded along, feeling part of something much bigger than himself.

As the night wore on, the strikers braced for what the morning might bring. More police. More deputies. More tear gas. And with them, a proper test of their resolve.

But looking around at the thousands of faces lit by firelight, hope swelled within the toolmaker.

They had found their strength in numbers. In solidarity.

Whatever came next, they would face it together.

CHAPTER 23
1984
WATCHING THE DETECTIVES

At 7 the next night, I pull up outside Sidney's house on a quiet West End street. Once the bastion of Toledo's nineteenth-century nouveau riche, this part of the West End has become run-down—meaning even an impoverished reporter can afford to live in a three-story Victorian house. Like most homes in the neighborhood, the house is now dilapidated, though the lawn is tidy. A light glows from a front window. I can also see a faint glow through a tiny attic window at the top of the house.

I knock out of courtesy. No answer.

I turn the knob and step inside. "Sidney?"

The place smells of roasting meat. I follow the scent to the kitchen, where a baked dinner sits in the oven, still warming. Two places are set at the kitchen table.

"Sidney?" I call again, louder this time.

No response.

I wander through the house, checking the dim rooms. A stack of old magazines—*New Yorkers*, maybe—sits next to a faded, overstuffed chair in the living room.

I continue calling out as I work my way from room to room. When I reach the third floor, I see the attic ladder hanging down, a faint glow coming from above.

My stomach tightens as I climb the ladder, one careful step at a time. Dusty boxes and stacks of yellowed newspapers line the cramped floor space beneath the steep, sloped roof. A single bare bulb casts flickering shadows across the floor.

And then I see him.

Sidney lies sprawled on the wooden planks, motionless. His eyes are open, staring at nothing.

I crouch beside him, but I already know he's gone.

The floor beside him is covered in dust—except for two clean spots. Some boxes Sidney had been looking through have not long been removed.

Someone has been here before me.

And they've taken what they needed.

The ambulance has long since pulled away, its siren off—no rush when there's nothing left to save. Now it's just me and the cops, standing under the porch light while the neighborhood watches from behind their curtains.

Officer Landon, the older of the two, flips his notepad shut. "So, you say you arrived here and found him like that?"

"Yeah," I say, arms crossed against the night chill. "He invited me for dinner. I knocked, got no answer, let myself in. Found him up there." I point toward the house.

Landon exchanges a look with his partner, a younger guy named Bishop. "And you didn't touch the body?"

"Nope."

Bishop frowns. "Did he have any health problems?"

I shrug. "He was in his seventies, but he didn't seem frail or sick."

Landon sighs. "Could've been natural causes. Heart attack, stroke. We'll see what the coroner says."

"Maybe," I say. "But it's funny, don't you think?"

He glances at me. "What's funny?"

I shift my weight. "Mike Ferner, a guy I was talking to about the Auto-Lite strike, gets run down in the street. And now Sidney Feldman, who covered the strike firsthand, ends up dead the same week. Both of them were about to give me information on the same story."

Bishop's expression tightens. He shoots a quick look at Landon.

Landon clears his throat. "Listen, why don't you come down to the station tomorrow? We can go over everything in a more . . . formal setting."

"Am I under suspicion for something?"

"Not at all," Landon says. "We like to be thorough. You understand."

"Yeah," I nod. "I understand."

As I walk back into the house, I can feel their eyes on my back.

Something is going on. And I'm right in the middle of it.

I decide to dive in. I climb back into the attic to see if there's anything the killer—and I'm sure now that Sidney was killed—missed. In a dark corner, behind some old trunks, I find a couple of boxes. When I open them, I find files and photos dating back to the '30s. Maybe I disturbed the killer before they could do a thorough search.

I carry them one by one down the rickety pull-down stairs, load them into the Hornet, close up Sidney's house, and drive away.

CHAPTER 24
MAY 1934
THE DIVIDED FAMILY

It took the stringer fifteen minutes to find the house—a squat brick duplex off Earl Street with a sagging porch and a yard full of weeds. One window was cracked and stuffed with rags. He knocked twice. No answer.

Inside, a woman's voice rang out, sharp and bright with fury.

"I said the biscuits are burning because I'm trying to do three things at once!"

The door opened a moment later. A man in his thirties—rail-thin, pale in the cheeks—looked out as if expecting a landlord with an eviction notice. His gaze softened when he recognized the young man.

"You the newspaper fellow?"

"I am," the stringer said.

The man nodded, stepped aside, and let him in without further comment.

The stringer was hit with a heady mix of coal smoke, boiled potatoes, and burnt flour. The kitchen and living room bled together, a single space with blistered paint and a corner stove glowing faint orange. A photograph hung crooked above the table—younger versions of the couple now standing in silence.

She stood at the stove, sleeves rolled, apron dusted with flour. A pot boiled over behind her. A biscuit tin smoked beside the sink. She slammed the oven door shut with her hip and muttered, "You can sit or get out of the way."

The men sat.

"Ma'am, you were on the line this morning?" the stringer asked, flipping open his notebook.

"Every morning," she replied, not turning around. "Before and after the shift bell."

Her husband added, "She doesn't even work there anymore."

"I do so," she snapped. "Just ain't been paid for it in three weeks."

"She was in final inspection," he clarified. "Wiring, seals. She left when the walkout started."

"Quality control," she corrected, stabbing a spoon into the stew. "And half the problems came from folks like you rushing the line to meet quotas."

He didn't respond. Just clasped his hands tighter in his lap.

"They took him on after," she said to the stringer. "Said they needed hands."

"I didn't ask for it," he muttered.

"You didn't say no, either."

The stringer watched them—the space between them not wide, but sharp.

"It's just temporary," the man said. "I'll be done when the strike's over, and then you can go back, and maybe there'll be something else there for me."

"They're lying to you," she said. "And you believe it because it's easier."

She turned, set plates on the table harder than necessary.

"They tell you it's about money," she continued. "But it's more than that. It's about being treated like something more than broken machinery."

The man rubbed the back of his neck. "It's not like we ever talked about unions growing up. You were lucky to have work. If you didn't like a job, someone else would be happy to do it."

She looked straight at him. "You still believe that?"

He didn't answer.

The stringer paused his pencil. "When did the talk of organizing begin?"

"Late last year," she said. "Some of the girls brought flyers to the washroom. Said we deserved clean gloves. A lunch break. Not to be laid off with no warning. Said we could win something if we stuck together."

"I didn't think it would turn into this," the man said.

"No," she said quietly. "You didn't think. That's the problem."

A crash of shouting from up the street made them all pause. The stringer leaned toward the window—a line of officers had moved into place near the factory gates, forming a quiet, rigid wall.

He turned back. "Do you ever think about walking out?" he asked the man.

"Every damn day."

She glanced up. "Then maybe you still can."

The stringer closed his notebook. Some stories didn't need pushing.

As he stepped toward the door, the man followed. Neither of them spoke.

At the threshold, the man looked back at his wife, then down at the stringer.

"She's right," he said.

And closed the door.

Behind it, the sound of a single chair scraping against the floor, and a woman eating dinner alone.

CHAPTER 25

1984

I AM THE LAW

The police interview room is smaller than I expected. No two-way mirror, just a plain metal table, three chairs, and a buzzing fluorescent light that hums in the back of my consciousness like the murmur of a crowd.

Detective Landon sits across from me, his notepad flipped open. Bishop leans against the wall, arms crossed. All we need is some rising jazz music in the background, and this could be an episode of *Hill Street Blues*. I guess cop show stereotypes have to come from somewhere.

Landon taps his pen. "Alright, Gray. Let's start with how you knew Mike Ferner."

"He was a news source. I met him through the Auto-Lite Fiftieth Anniversary Commemoration Committee," I say. "He was the chair."

"And Sidney Feldman?"

I shrug. "We worked together at *The Sword*. I didn't know him well. I found out he covered the Auto-Lite strike back in '34, and I figured he'd be an excellent source. He had some notes from his time covering the strike and had invited me to his house to pick them up."

Landon nods, scribbling something down. He looks up and makes eye contact. "So let's get this straight: you talk to

Ferner about the strike, and he gets run over. Then you talk to Feldman, and he drops dead. That about right?"

I meet his stare. "That's about right."

He leans forward, eyes narrowing. "See, here's my problem. Two men die right after speaking to you. That's an enormous coincidence, wouldn't you say?"

I frown. "Are you saying I had something to do with it?"

Bishop, still standing against the wall, smirks. "We're just asking questions, Wheeler."

I exhale, feeling my frustration rise. The shift from using my first name to my last makes me nervous. "Listen, I think the UAW is involved in this. They don't want the commemoration happening. They're trying to bury the past. Ferner had something he wanted to tell me about that, but he died before he could."

Landon and Bishop share a glance. Landon asks, "The UAW? Why would the union go around knocking off old men?"

"Because they don't want people dredging up the Communist influence in the strike. You've seen what's happening in America now. With the air traffic controllers' strike, Reagan's got unions on the ropes. If the public starts associating the UAW with Communism, it could be a disaster for them. What better way to keep a lid on things than to make sure the people who know too much suddenly aren't around anymore?"

Landon shakes his head, a wry smile on his face. "You've been reading too many dime-store spy novels, Wheeler."

Bishop chuckles. "Yeah. You think the UAW's out there running a hit squad?"

I clench my jaw. "Then what do you think happened?"

Landon moves forward in his chair. "We think Ferner was drunk, wandered into the street, and got hit. We think Feldman was an old man who had a heart attack in his attic. That's what we think."

I shake my head. "And what about his missing notes?"

Bishop shrugs. "Maybe his family took 'em. Maybe he threw 'em out years ago. Maybe the attic's just dusty, and you're jumping at shadows."

I sigh. "Am I a suspect? Are you going to read me my rights? Do I need a lawyer?"

Landon doesn't answer right away. Then he says, "You tell me, Wheeler. Two people talk to you, and then they're dead. Maybe you're working for the crowd who don't want people to talk. Maybe you're the one trying to bury the past."

That floors me. "You can't be serious."

Bishop grins. "Let's just say we're keeping our options open."

I sit back, stunned. Something isn't right here. They're either blind—or they're being pressured to look the other way. Does the UAW's influence extend to the Toledo police?

Landon slaps his notepad shut. "You're free to go, Wheeler. But if I were you, I'd find another story to work on."

I don't reply. I look at the two cops and slowly shake my head.

As I walk out of the station, something catches my eye.

Two men are standing near the front door. Dark suits. Sunglasses. One old, one young.

They're not cops.

Feds.

They don't speak to anyone. They don't need to. Their presence alone sets off alarm bells in my head.

What the hell are federal agents doing here? Are they in on this? Are they working with the union to take down the commemoration? Are they there to make sure the union toes the line?

I force myself to look away and keep walking.

I'm probably being paranoid.

Probably.

As I head back to the office, I turn over everything that's happened. I feel like I've taken a step out of the kiddie pool and plunged into the deep end. Union officials are easy to understand. But a possibly complicit police force—with federal aid?

I need help navigating these deeper waters.

CHAPTER 26

MAY 1934

THE UNEMPLOYED LEAGUE

The stringer found them in the back room of the Lucas County Unemployed League's headquarters—a former butcher shop still reeking of lye and blood, its tile walls plastered with handbills declaring "JOBS OR INCOME NOW!" and "SMASH THE COMPANY UNIONS!" Two men hunched over a map of Auto-Lite's perimeter, fingers tracing patrol routes and police barricades. One wore a railroad worker's cap pulled low over sharp eyes; the other, younger and skinnier, had sleeves rolled to reveal forearms inked with faded tattoos of anchors and stars. Between them sat a coffee can overflowing with cigarette butts—and a revolver with its firing pin removed. A prop for intimidating scabs, the stringer guessed.

"You're the reporter," the first man said without looking up. "Make it quick. We've got an injunction to violate."

The stringer pulled out his notebook, pencil poised. "Let's start with the basics. What brought the Unemployed League into this fight?"

The first man lit a cigarette, the match's flame illuminating a face weathered by years of hard living. "Same thing that brought the rats into Noah's Ark—necessity. Auto-Lite's got fifteen hundred workers inside, forty thousand unemployed outside. You think those bastards in suits don't know they can replace every striker ten times over? Our job's to make sure the unemployed ain't the enemy."

The second man tapped his ash into the coffee can. "Capitalists breed division. Employed vs. jobless. Union vs. nonunion. White vs. Black. We're here to weld it all into one fist."

"How?" the stringer pressed.

A grin spread across the first man's face. "Ever seen a scab cross a picket line when five hundred hungry men are chanting 'We'll remember your face'? The League's the muscle. We patrol the perimeter, keep the factory sealed. Auto-Lite tried busing in strikebreakers last week—we tipped their drivers, redirected 'em to our soup kitchen instead."

The stringer noticed the first man's hands—calloused, scarred, with a slight tremor as he lit another cigarette. "How long have you been organizing?"

"Since the crash. October '29. I was working the railroads then. One day you're shoveling coal, next you're in a breadline with doctors and bankers. Funny how a depression levels things."

The second man nodded, eyes distant. "I came up through the docks. Watched good men jump off piers when their savings evaporated. That's when I knew—the system wasn't broken. It was working as intended."

"We started the League in '31," the first man added. "Thought it'd be temporary. Now?" He gestured to the bustling headquarters. "This is the new normal."

The stringer tried to capture the sense of history in these men's words. "Walk me through a typical day for the League during this strike."

The first man leaned back and exhaled a plume of smoke. "We're up at 4 a.m. First shift heads to the factory gates, sets up soup kitchens. Not just for strikers—for anyone hungry. You'd be amazed how many scabs change their minds over a hot meal."

"By 6, we've got patrols out," the second man continued. "Teams of ten, rotating every two hours. They watch for strikebreakers, cops, company thugs. We use a whistle system—one blast for warning, two for reinforcements, three if there's violence."

"Noon's when it gets dicey," the first man added. "Shift change. We form human chains, hundreds deep. Sing so loud the machines inside can't drown us out."

The second man's voice took on a note of pride. "Evenings are for education. We run classes on labor history, public speaking, even first aid. Knowledge is ammunition, brother."

"And the families? How do they survive with no paychecks?"

The first man grinned, a flash of triumph in his eyes. "That's the beauty of it. We've got a network—farmers sympathetic to the cause, small shopkeepers who extend credit. We organize barter systems, childcare collectives. Auto-Lite thinks they can starve us out? We're building a whole damn economy without them."

A commotion outside drew their attention. Through the grimy window, the stringer saw a group of men in suits—AFL representatives—arguing with League members. The second man sneered. "Here come the bureaucrats."

They stepped outside. The League organizers gave the red-faced, gesticulating AFL men icy stares.

"You're jeopardizing everything!" one AFL rep shouted. "Wildcats, mass pickets—you'll bring the military down on all our heads!"

The first man exuded calm. "And your strategy? Beg for table scraps while workers starve?"

"We negotiate! We build relationships!" the AFL rep insisted.

The second man stepped forward, voice cold. "With who? The same bosses who hire Pinkertons to crack skulls? Wake up. This isn't about contracts—it's about power."

"You'll destroy everything we've built!" the AFL rep cried.

"Good," the first man shot back. "It needs destroying. Your 'American Plan' is just company unionism with a fancy name. We're here to tear it all down and build something that works for the people who break their backs in these factories."

The argument escalated, League members forming a protective circle around their leaders.

Back inside, the tension lingered. The second man paced, agitated. The stringer sensed an opening. "This seems bigger than just Toledo," he ventured.

The second man nodded. "It's a powder keg, coast to coast. San Francisco's waterfront is ready to explode. Minneapolis teamsters are mobilizing. And don't forget the textile workers down South—they're planning the biggest strike in American history."

"FDR thinks he can patch this system up with his New Deal," the first man added. "But it's too late. Workers have tasted real power. The genie's out of the bottle."

"How does Toledo fit into all this?" the stringer pressed.

The second man's eyes blazed. "We're the test case. If we win here—higher wages, but more than that, real worker control—it'll spark a prairie fire. That's why they're fighting us so hard. This isn't just about Auto-Lite. It's about the future of American labor."

Shouts from the street interrupted their conversation. All three men rushed to the window. A truck was attempting to break through the picket line, escorted by police.

"Time for a practical demonstration," the first man said, grabbing his coat.

They raced outside. The scene was chaos—strikers linking arms, police swinging batons, the truck inching forward through a sea of bodies. The first man climbed atop a parked car, his voice booming through a bullhorn:

"Brothers! Sisters! Hold the line! No violence—but no retreat!"

The second man organized a flying wedge of League members, their bodies forming a human barricade in front of the truck. The driver revved the engine but faced a wall of grim, determined faces.

The stringer watched, heart pounding, as the standoff stretched into minutes. Then, slowly—improbably—the truck backed up. A cheer erupted from the crowd, louder than the curses of the police.

As the picketers regrouped, the first man turned to the stringer, eyes blazing with triumph. "That, my friend, is how you win a class war."

Back at headquarters, adrenaline still coursing, the conversation turned reflective. The stringer, still processing what he'd witnessed, asked, "After what I saw, I have to ask again—what are you aiming for?"

The second man's voice was solemn. "A world where no one starves while food rots in warehouses. Where machines serve people, not profits."

"We're not naïve," the first man added. "We know it won't happen overnight. But every battle like today's, every worker who realizes their true power—that's a step toward something better."

"And if you lose?" the stringer pressed.

The first man lit a final cigarette, the flame casting shadows across his weathered face. "Then we dust ourselves off and fight again. Because the alternative is accepting a world where men like those Auto-Lite bosses decide who eats, who works, who lives in dignity. And that, brother, is no world at all."

The stringer returned to his rented room. The nighttime streets hummed with tension—small groups huddled around barrel fires, police prowling in patrol cars, the distant thrum of idled factories.

He thought of the two men—the fire of the first, the cold calculation of the second. He thought of the faces on the picket line, the desperation and hope mingled in equal measure. And he thought of the forces arrayed against them—the wealth, the power, the machinery of state and capital.

In his mind, Toledo became a microcosm of a nation at a crossroads. Would the fire lit here sputter and die, or spread to engulf a system long overdue for change?

As he sat down to type, sirens wailing in the distance, the stringer knew one thing for certain: Whatever happened in the days to come, the story of the Auto-Lite strike—and the unlikely alliance forged in its crucible—would echo far beyond the borders of this embattled Ohio city.

The future, uncertain but pregnant with possibility, was being written in the streets of Toledo.

PART 2

CHAPTER 27

1984

I FOUGHT THE LAW

I know how it looks. Two people, both tied to the Auto-Lite strike, dead within weeks of each other. But no one's buying that it's anything more than coincidence—not even the local police, whose job it is to question coincidences.

I pick up the phone and call the one person who might help me make sense of this.

The hospital room is as bleak as you'd expect—beige walls, linoleum floors, and that faint antiseptic smell that clings to everything. A boxy TV flickers near the ceiling, tuned to a muted baseball game.

My best friend Larry is flat on his back, neck immobilized in a thick brace. His arms, though, are free—and already gesturing wildly when he realizes it's me on the phone.

"Far out. About time someone called me with something interesting," he says the moment he hears my voice. "You realize I've been stuck here for two weeks? Two damn weeks. I've watched the nurses change the IV bags four hundred times. I've memorized the entire hospital menu. I—"

"Yeah, yeah, you're suffering," I cut in. "I get it."

"You do not get it. You get to walk places. I have to use a damn bedpan. If I ever break my neck again, shoot me."

Larry and I have been friends since fifth grade, when we both had Mrs. Pearson and started an amateur detective agency. We uncovered plenty of crime in our neighborhood—real and imagined. His dad was older, silent and distant like mine, and we both dreamed of growing up and getting out of Toledo. After high school, Larry studied criminology at Wayne State and joined the Detroit police force. Unlike my boomerang career, Larry thrived. He made homicide detective in near-record time. Then came the car chase across a bumpy field, the wrecked cruiser, and the broken neck. Now, phone calls are the only thing keeping him sane.

"OK, noted. Shoot you next time you break your neck," I say.

"Thanks. So what's up?"

"I need your take on something. Two guys I interviewed about the Auto-Lite strike? They're both dead. One was hit by a car. The other—heart attack, supposedly. But it doesn't add up."

"You talked to both of them right before they died?"

"Yeah."

"Then congratulations, dumbass. You're officially a 'person of interest.' "

"I know. TPD already brought me in for questioning."

Larry barks a laugh. "Of course they did. You're lucky they didn't plant a needle in your pocket and call it a day."

"Real helpful, buddy."

"I aim to please." His voice softens. "So, let's assume you're onto something. You think someone's tying up loose ends?"

"Yeah. But here's the thing—the UAW isn't backing the Auto-Lite commemoration. They don't want it happening."

"Why?"

"I think it's because of the Communist and Socialist involvement in the original strike. The UAW doesn't want that dredged up. Makes them look bad."

"So you think it's the union doing the cleanup?"

"I think so. But not everything adds up. One of the guys wasn't even union. And when I was getting grilled by the cops, they weren't pushing the union angle. They were treating me like I'd stepped on something bigger."

Larry is quiet for a beat. "How much bigger?"

"I don't know. The feds, maybe? I saw some of them hanging around the station."

"Oh, good. Fantastic. Let me update my calendar so I know when to attend your closed-casket funeral."

"You're not taking this seriously."

"Oh, I am. Trust me, I am. I also know that if the feds are tying up old cases, you're either gonna find yourself in a padded room or a shallow grave."

"So what do I do?"

"Alright, first things first—who in Toledo PD is leading the investigation?"

"Guy named Landon."

"Never heard of him. That's probably bad."

"Why?"

"Because if he were clean, I'd have heard of him. You need to figure out who he takes orders from."

"You mean like, who his boss is?"

"No, I mean who his real boss is. If the Bureau's pulling strings, this guy's not running his own case. He's waiting for orders."

I feel a prickle at the back of my neck. "So how do I find out?"

"You get in his face. Make yourself a problem. If he tries to back you down, he's dirty. If he drops the case altogether, he's scared. Either way, you learn something."

Silence stretches between us.

"Have you ever considered that maybe you were always meant to be a criminal instead of a cop?" I mutter.

"Oh yeah," Larry says. "But I like my guns legally registered."

I crack a smile. "Thanks."

"Anytime. Now go bother a corrupt cop for me." He pauses. "And hey—if you get yourself shot, at least have the decency to get airlifted down here so I have some company."

I laugh, but it fades fast.

"Hey, Larry."

"Yeah?"

"You remember that time we got into it with those guys on the overpass when we were kids?"

There's a long pause. "You mean the time you got your ass kicked trying to save me?"

"I mean the time I should've done more before they laid into you with that one-wood and threw your damn bike off a bridge."

Larry snorts. "Well, you're making up for it now—except this time, they might throw you off the bridge."

CHAPTER 28
MAY 1934
THE JUDGE

In the judge's chambers, a half-empty bottle gleamed amber in the thin morning light slanting through barred windows, its neck tilted toward him like an accusation. Outside, the chants of the Auto-Lite strikers rattled the glass—*"No contract, no peace!"*—a metronome to the throbbing behind his temples.

The judge massaged his forehead, fingertips tracing the spider veins that mapped his cheeks, and stared at the stack of contempt petitions crowding his desk. Two hundred and thirty-seven names. Two hundred and thirty-seven souls who'd dared cross his injunction.

He'd meant it as peacekeeping.

A few weeks earlier, he'd signed the order in this very room, fountain pen scraping like a scalpel: a limit of twenty-five picketers at the Auto-Lite gates. No shouting. No obstruction. The strikers called it tyranny. The newspapers called it prudent. He'd called it law. Now, with the city on the edge of anarchy, he wasn't sure what to call it anymore.

The first defendant of the day slouched into the courtroom, hands cuffed, shirt streaked with soot. A boy—eighteen, maybe nineteen—with the defiant slouch of someone who'd never been told no until this strike. The judge squinted at the paperwork: Contempt Charge 184: Violation of Injunction.

"You understand why you're here, son?" the judge drawled, voice graveled by last night's whiskey.

The boy lifted his chin. "For standin' on a sidewalk."

"For *blocking* a sidewalk," the judge corrected. He'd rehearsed this script dozens of times already. "My order permits peaceful assembly, not mob intimidation."

"Ain't no mob. Just workers askin' for bread."

The judge's gavel trembled in his grip. He'd heard variations of this all week—the same hollow-eyed faces, the same righteous anger. Toledo's jail cells were bursting with them. He brought the hammer down. "Thirty days. Next case."

As the bailiff dragged the young man away, the judge reached for his flask. The silver was warm from sitting in his breast pocket, the bourbon inside bitter and familiar. He drank without looking. The burn steadied his hands for a moment. The court officials looked the other way.

By noon, he'd processed forty-seven cases. Forty-seven gavel strikes. Forty-seven men and women shipped to cells already crowded with the previous days' arrestees. The strikers' lawyers protested—"Cruel and unusual, Your Honor"—but the judge waved them off. The law was the law.

Yet the law didn't explain the tear gas, the smashed windows, the thousands of people now massing outside the factory each day.

His clerk slipped in, face ashen, clutching a fresh stack of petitions. "They're saying there are machine gun placements set up on the roof of the factory," she whispered.

The judge didn't look up. "And?"

"They're saying your injunction made it inevitable."

He scrawled his signature with a flourish that splattered ink. "They'll say worse before this is over."

The whiskey fog lifted briefly that evening as he trudged home, the streets quiet under a militia-enforced curfew. His house—a looming Victorian with peeling paint—felt colder than the courthouse. In the parlor, his wife's portrait watched him from above the mantel, her smile frozen in 1923, the year the gin took her liver and his patience.

He'd been sober then. Or near enough.

Now, he poured three fingers of bourbon into a teacup and unfolded his copy of *The Toledo Times*. The headline blared: JUDGE'S EDICT FANS FLAMES OF VIOLENCE. Below it, a photograph of a striker's widow clutching a child, both faces streaked with dirt and despair. He slammed the cup down, sloshing liquor onto the newsprint. The ink bled, turning the widow's tears black.

Back in court the next morning, the contempt cases bled together:

- A grandmother fined $50 for "inciting" by singing union hymns.
- A veteran of the Great War sentenced to sixty days for throwing a tomato.
- A pregnant woman released on "compassionate grounds" after fainting in the dock.

The judge's head pounded. His flask was empty.

When the strikers' lead attorney—a sharp-suited firebrand who'd switched from defending Auto-Lite to supporting the workers—stormed into the courtroom demanding an injunction repeal, the judge stifled a laugh.

"On what grounds?" he sneered.

"On grounds that your order violates the First Amendment!"

"The First Amendment doesn't protect trespass."

"It protects *assembly*," the lawyer shot back. "Or does the Bill of Rights mean nothing in Toledo?"

The judge leaned forward; the wood creaked beneath his elbows. "It means less than my gavel in this room. Bailiff, remove him."

As the lawyer shouted about appeals, the judge motioned for the next case. His hand shook.

That night, the bourbon didn't help.

He sat in the dark, listening to distant sirens, and thought about the strikers. Not the ones in his courtroom, but the ones he'd seen as a young attorney—the 1919 railroad men who'd frozen to death on the picket lines, the coal miners coughing up black in '22. He'd believed in the law's power to temper chaos. Now, he wondered if the law was simply another kind of chaos—slower and more polite.

A gunshot echoed somewhere north of downtown. He poured another drink.

By the end of the week, the jail was so overcrowded that the sheriff started paroling convicts to make room. The judge signed the releases like an automaton, his signature reduced to a jagged scrawl. When the last defendant—a girl no older than sixteen, charged with "gesturing provocatively" at strikebreakers—pleaded for mercy, he gave her ten days anyway.

"You'll thank me," he muttered, though he wasn't sure who he meant.

CHAPTER 29

1984

PHOTOGRAPHS AND MEMORIES

I sit cross-legged on the floor of my basement room, the boxes from Sidney's attic open in front of me. The musty scent of old paper fills the air as I shuffle through the contents: yellowed newspaper clippings, handwritten notes, and scattered photographs.

It turns out Sidney was not only a budding reporter in those days—he had the makings of a photojournalist, even before the term entered the lexicon. Either that, or he was working closely with a photographer from *The Times*. Either way, it's an impressive collection of photos for fifty years ago.

The first photo I pick up is of a picket line outside Auto-Lite—people in patched-up coats standing shoulder to shoulder, their faces etched with defiance. Another shows homeless people sprawled across the courthouse lawn, wrapped in threadbare blankets, their eyes hollow with exhaustion.

There are more: crowds crammed into a courtroom, heads turned toward the front as strikers stand before a judge; policemen swinging billy clubs at retreating workers; a man in a truck under a sign that says "Buddy Box Lunches," standing behind a steaming coffee urn, smiling as he hands out cups of coffee to the picketers. I flip it over. "Grant Vincent," it says on the back. I'm sure I've heard that name somewhere. Is that on Sidney's list? Is he still alive? Worth talking to if he is.

There are a few images of a man in a suit, surrounded by workers, speaking to reporters on the courthouse steps. "George Slaughter," the back reads. I make a mental note to follow up on this one as well.

I let the images wash over me, flipping through them one by one. Four men pulling back an inner tube stretched between two houses, ready to launch a brick at the factory. Strikers with gardening gloves gripping tear gas canisters, their faces covered with handkerchiefs as they prepare to hurl them back at the police. Young National Guardsmen—not men, but boys—staring at the crowd with wide, fearful eyes as they point their rifles.

I pick up a photo that seems to epitomize the crowd's involvement as well as the strikers'. A young man is frozen mid-motion, arm cocked back, a brick clenched in his hand. He's ready to launch it toward the Guardsmen, jaw tight with determination. I study his face—the curve of his nose, the line of his jaw. Something about him tugs at me.

My gut tells me there's something I'm not seeing yet. I set it aside and reach for the old list of interviewees Sidney gave me. Most of the names are unfamiliar, but I recognize a few surnames from my research—former Auto-Lite workers, community organizers, and sympathizers who had spoken out in the past. Along with them: Grant Vincent and George Slaughter.

I grab the White Pages from my desk and start cross-referencing names. Most of the entries are long out of date, the numbers disconnected. Some of these people no doubt passed on decades ago. But I'm not giving up yet.

That night at dinner, I broach the subject with my parents. The dining table is small and cluttered, the air thick with the smell of Mom's meatloaf and instant mashed potatoes—again.

"So, Dad," I start, spearing a green bean with my fork, "what do you remember about the Depression?"

Mom stiffens. She glances at me, then at Dad, and tries to change the subject. "You should focus on your job, Gray. Didn't you say you had an article due?"

Dad sets his fork down. He stares at his plate, then exhales. "Times were tough back then," he says, sighing. "No one had a job in the city. No one had food. Except for the rich."

"What do you remember about the strike?" I know I've asked before, but Dad seems more receptive tonight.

He pushes his potatoes around with his fork. "I never worked at Auto-Lite," he says, "but I knew people who did. Everybody knew about the strike. It kept going, dragging on, and more and more people joined the picket lines. Some of us . . . " He hesitates. "Some of us went to watch."

My ears prick up. "You went down there?"

"A couple of times. When I wasn't working the farm with Grandpa and Uncle Hal."

I wait for more, but he stops there.

"So, what was it like?" I press.

He looks at me, his face unreadable. "The Depression was something you wouldn't wish on your worst enemy."

That's it. No details. Nothing about what he saw, who he talked to, what he might have done. Only that cryptic, frustrating statement.

I want to push, but Mom shoots me a warning glance. I sigh and drop it.

Later that night, I lie in bed staring at the acoustical tiles on the ceiling, listening to a freight train rattling past the yard.

Where the hell was I headed? With this story? With my life?

I remember a snapshot from my childhood. When I was eight, I built a soapbox racer out of scrap wood and old wagon wheels. Mom didn't tell me I was clever, or brave, or bound to win. She stood on the porch wringing her hands, whispering to herself that I was going to break my neck.

She didn't hope for the best. She prayed to avoid the worst.

It's not that she didn't believe in me—it's that she believed in bad luck more. I was always so frustrated with that attitude.

Maybe she had a point?

CHAPTER 30

MAY 1934

THE ORGANIZER

His heart pounded in his chest as the organizer stood before the judge. The stuffy air pressed against the bodies of the striking workers who packed the courtroom to the brim. The tension was palpable—a living thing that seemed to permeate the crowd.

As he approached the witness stand, he could feel the eyes of his fellow workers boring into his back. He knew what he had to do. Meticulous planning had led to this moment, and now everything hinged on his performance.

The judge's voice boomed through the courtroom. "How do you plead to the charge of breaking the injunction?"

The organizer took a deep breath, his gaze steady as he met the judge's eyes. "Your Honor, I am guilty. I am guilty of breaking that injunction."

A murmur rippled through the courtroom. The organizer could feel the energy in the room shift, coiling like a spring ready to release.

The judge's brow furrowed. "You admit to disobeying a court order with deliberate intent?"

"Yes, Your Honor," the organizer replied, his voice clear and unwavering. "I am guilty."

As he spoke, he reached into his pocket and removed a handkerchief. He brought it up to his face, making a show of wiping his nose. It was the signal they had agreed upon.

Suddenly, as if a dam had burst, the entire courtroom erupted. Workers leapt to their feet, their voices joining in a thunderous chorus.

"Your Honor!" they shouted, the sound deafening in the confined space. "If he's guilty, we're all guilty! We were all there!"

The cacophony of voices drowned out the judge's banging gavel. The organizer stood still, watching as the judge's face cycled through shock, anger, and then resignation.

The judge waited until the noise died down. When he spoke, his voice was tinged with a mixture of frustration and grudging respect.

"I can't put you all in jail," he said, his eyes sweeping across the sea of defiant faces. "And I will not find this man guilty because he isn't any more guilty than the rest of you." He paused, then added with a sigh, "Case dismissed."

The crowd cheered, and the organizer felt a surge of triumph. They had done it. They had faced down the court and won. As he stepped down from the witness stand, he knew this was not simply a legal victory—it was a turning point in their struggle.

Their spirits high and resolve strengthened, the workers left the courtroom. The organizer knew the fight was far from over, but for now, they had shown the power of solidarity.

The Auto-Lite strike would continue.

CHAPTER 31
1984
DON'T FORGET TO REMEMBER

I didn't expect to care much about the Auto-Lite strike beyond a single article for the anniversary. It was supposed to be a quick historical piece for the commemoration—another obligatory salute to the past. But the more I dig into it, the more I realize how pivotal it was in both local and national history—and how little I actually know. And if I, a journalist in this town and the son of an auto worker, don't understand what happened, what does that say about the average Toledoan? About the UAW guys working the line? The factory foremen? The cops patrolling the same streets today?

This story also appears to be important enough to kill for. That has to be worth more than a simple news piece.

I knock on Jim's door and plop down in the chair opposite his desk.

"How's that article going, Gray? You seem to be spending an inordinate amount of time on it, and I haven't seen a draft yet."

Instead of one article, I pitch him a series. "This will be an in-depth dive—interviews, archives, first-hand accounts. The retrospective is only part of it. It'll also be an autopsy on labor history, a dissection of an event that shaped this city and the people in it."

Jim tilts his head and screws up his face. "It's fifty years ago, Gray. Who's gonna care?"

"Some people who were there are still alive," I say. "People who fought in it. People who bled for it. Some of them still live here. I think that matters."

He sighs. "Give me a draft of the first one. We'll see."

I walk back to my desk and start making calls.

The first person I interview is a retired cop who worked in the 1930s. He's blunt about it.

"When I went into the department, the only training you got was you went out with a policeman three nights, and from then on you were a policeman and on your own," he says. "In 1933, Mayor Solon T. Klotz cut our wages. We were up to $200 a month, which was pretty good money in those days. Then they cut us back to $150. Then $135. Then they paid us in scrip for almost a year, and we had a terrible time."

"Scrip?" I ask.

"City-issued money. Worthless, unless you found someone willing to take it."

So the system screwed even the cops. That was something.

A former machinist at Auto-Lite talks about the Great Depression that led up to the strike.

"In 1929, I heard rumors that officials were pulling their money out of the Security Bank," he tells me. "My father rang the branch manager of our bank in East Toledo, and they said there was no reason to worry. A week went along . . . so my father went down to draw his out, and they said, 'Well, you can't draw. We can't give it to you for 30 days.' Then they closed their doors. And every bank in Toledo was closed."

"How'd people survive?" I ask.

He laughs, but there's no humor in it. "You just did."

Lynn Waters, another policeman, describes the war zone the strike became.

"Houses up there were close together, little houses. Strikers cut inner tubes in half, nailed them between two houses, and used them as slingshots to launch bricks. If you were in the way, it'd take your head clean off. They broke every streetlight. Once they ran out of bricks, they'd tear them out of the foundations."

He shakes his head. "Some of those houses had next to no bricks left after that strike was over."

John Toczynski never worked at Auto-Lite, but he was there.

"I'd say most people were spectators," he admits. "I know because I was one of them. I'd get off work, head down, and watch. And after a while, you'd feel it—you'd feel like you were part of it. Like you were fighting for a cause. So yeah, I threw a few bricks myself."

The interviews keep piling up. Each one adds another layer, another contradiction. The strike was more than workers versus bosses. Teachers, police, lawyers, radicals, and everyday people got involved. It was chaos. It was desperation. It was a city grappling with something bigger than itself.

The Toledo Sports Arena looms ahead, its weathered façade still carrying a certain pride. Inside, echoes of skates on ice and the distant cheers of past games seem embedded in the walls. I follow directions through dim corridors until I reach a door with a small brass plate: Grant Vincent—Executive Office.

I knock.

"Come in," says a voice from the other side—warm but clipped.

Inside, the office is simple but solid: an old oak desk, walls lined with photographs of hockey teams, a Toledo Mercurys pennant, a framed ticket from the first game ever held at the arena. Grant sits behind the desk, silver hair slicked and combed back, sleeves rolled up, reading glasses resting on a notepad. He looks up, sharp-eyed but not unkind.

"Gray from *The Sword*?" he asks, standing to shake my hand.

"That's me. Thanks for making the time."

"Of course. You said this was about the Auto-Lite strike?"

I pull out my notebook. "I heard you were there. Not just there—but involved."

Grant chuckles, settling back in his chair. "You could say that. I was twenty-five. Ran a lunch truck called the "Buddy Box." One van, a few coolers, and a lot of hope. In those days, food service was as close to job security as a working man could get."

"And you fed the strikers?"

"Free coffee and doughnuts. I parked near the gates at Champlain Street. Every morning like clockwork. I knew most of them by name. Hell, I grew up with some of them."

I glance at a black-and-white photo on the shelf behind him—Grant shaking hands with a hockey player in full pads, an American flag draped in the background.

"What made you do it?" I ask. "Giving away food during the Depression wasn't what you'd call a sound business plan."

Grant folds his hands. "Because I was raised right. Because my father broke his back for twenty-five cents an hour and never once got the respect he deserved. And because I knew—if those guys won, we all stood to gain."

"Is it true Auto-Lite asked you to cater to the workers inside?"

Grant's jaw tightens. "They did. Came to me with a solid offer. Said they'd pay cash, no questions asked. Wanted boxed lunches for the scabs. I told them to take their money and shove it."

"You didn't worry about the fallout?"

"Of course I did," he says. "But there's a line. You don't cross it. I would not feed the men helping to break the backs of my neighbors."

He gets up to refill his mug from a coffee pot near the window, motions if I want one. I shake my head. He sits back down.

"You think people remember that today?" I ask. "What you did?"

Grant shrugs. "Most don't. And that's fine. I didn't do it for a plaque. I did it because it was right."

I glance around the office again. "From one lunch truck to co-owning the Mercurys and building this arena . . . that's quite a leap."

Grant laughs. "After the war, I saw Toledo needed more than factories. We needed places to gather. Places to be proud of. Sports, music, community—that's what I invested in. We opened the arena in '47. Sold hot dogs out of the same coolers I used in '34."

"And now?"

"Now I watch games from the box seats and hope some kid in the crowd learns the same lesson I did: stick by your people."

I close my notebook and look Grant in the eye. "If there's one thing you'd want Toledo to remember from that time, what would it be?"

He looks out the window toward the rink, silent for a beat.

"That sometimes the smallest gestures—like a cup of coffee on a frosty morning—mean more than we think. Those men felt seen. That mattered."

We shake hands again. As I step into the hall, I hear the faint sound of skates echoing from the arena below. I consider all the untold stories—how people on the margins often shape history by doing the right thing unnoticed.

CHAPTER 32
MAY 1934
THE SET-UP MAN

The stringer sat across from the man in the cramped kitchen of a narrow Toledo boarding house, its walls yellowed from years of tobacco smoke. The scent of machine oil lingered on the man's work clothes, even though he hadn't set foot in the Auto-Lite factory since the strike began.

The man leaned forward, elbows resting on the table, fingers clasped together as he studied the stringer with a weary gaze. Though not yet old, years of setting up machines—now operated by unskilled strikebreakers—had lined his face and thickened his knuckles.

"Of course they called a strike," he said, his voice flat, as if the words themselves carried weight. "People got hungry. Needed money. But then they got rough, started destroying things. More and more, it's gotten dangerous to walk around the streets near Auto-Lite. Everyone figures we're potential strikebreakers."

The stringer jotted down notes, the man's sharp eyes never leaving him.

"Do you ever think about crossing the picket line?"

The man let out a dry chuckle. "Hell no. The company's dominated us for too many years. 'We'll never give in,' they're saying. 'Let 'em starve; they'll come crawling back.' That's their attitude."

He shifted in his chair, the wood creaking beneath his weight. "You don't know who you're talking to half the time. Is it an Auto-Lite worker? A Young Communist? A guy looking to break the picket line? You're afraid to say too much. Speech isn't free—not now. Everybody's a potential enemy. Even management has guys out there, sniffing around, feeling you out."

The stringer glanced up from his notebook. "So there are Communists involved?"

"Oh yeah. It's much more than Auto-Lite workers and interested locals. Over time, we figured it out. There are Communists and Socialists from Detroit, Cleveland, Chicago—traveling the country, organizing factories. They started holding meetings, open ones. At one, this guy gets up and says, 'I'm a Communist.' Introduced himself like that! They passed around pamphlets, talked about why it's good to be a Communist. But I don't think it's taking hold. No one's been going to their meetings—more nonbelievers than believers."

The stringer scratched a note in the margin. He'd heard this before—working men who distrusted Communists as much as they distrusted the company.

"What about the women in the strike?"

The man chuckled again, shaking his head. "You ever seen a bunch of women get together? During the strike, they've been out there cutting wood, bringing food, making suppers, cussing up a storm. Oh, they'd do things a man wouldn't even think of. Women are the toughest ones out there. We've had more women on the picket lines than men. Don't know how their homes looked during the strike because they're always out picketing. They're militant—more outspoken than any man."

"What about the strikebreakers? Where are they coming from?"

"Southern states," the man answered without hesitation. "Company brought in a truckload of them. Professional strikebreakers, some of them. But from what I hear, the company's been losing money on them. No one to train them. They've ruined more equipment than you can imagine."

The stringer tapped his pen against the table. "Has the Depression made the strike more intense?"

The man's face darkened. "Not sure what you mean by 'intense,' but it's sure made it worse. People are getting thrown out of their homes. Can't pay rent. Cops come, toss all their furniture onto the street. Then, when the cops leave, the union comes and puts it all back. It's near to a general strike. I can see it coming. And that? That will be vicious."

He shifted again and pointed a finger at the stringer. "If Toledo goes into a general strike, it sure won't stop here. It'll spread—Ohio, Michigan, Illinois. I don't know what could happen. I don't even want to think about it."

The stringer let the silence stretch between them. He clicked his pen and flipped his notebook shut. "I appreciate you sharing this with me."

The man waved a hand, dismissing him with a smirk. "Don't make me sound too damn old."

The stringer grinned. "I'll do my best."

CHAPTER 33

1984

FUNERAL FOR A FRIEND

It's an overcast Saturday morning when I stand outside St. Joseph's Church in downtown Toledo, collar up against the wind. The streets are slick with last night's rain, and the stone steps leading up to the doors are damp and dark—like the eyes of the handful of mourners already gathered. The lot is full, and cars spill over onto nearby side streets, a testament to Mike Ferner's influence—or at least the size of the shadow he's left behind.

Ferner's funeral isn't open casket. The obit didn't mention a traffic accident, so there's some confusion among the mourners about what happened. They whisper in corners: *"He was too young,"* or *"Mike wasn't the type to keel over."* I've heard the same speculation enough now that it doesn't feel like gossip. It feels like consensus.

Inside, the church is cold. The stained-glass windows bleed pale light across the pews. The acoustics muffle quiet conversations. People cluster in groups, voices subdued, faces drawn and pale beneath the harsh fluorescent lights. I scan the room, noting familiar faces—union reps from the UAW, local politicians, activists from various labor groups around Toledo. They've come to mourn, yes, but something in their manner feels guarded.

I spot Ferner's widow up front. She looks like a statue carved from exhaustion—rigid posture, black veil, hands clenched around a folded tissue. Next to her is a young man I assume is their son, awkward in his suit, staring straight ahead like he's trying not to cry or punch someone. Maybe both.

The priest drones on about service, about justice, about how Ferner cared for his community. I try to listen, but my mind is already spinning. The union hasn't made a statement. I heard someone mention on the way in that Local 12 didn't even send flowers. If they didn't love Ferner's politics, couldn't they at least pretend?

When the service ends, I linger at the back of the church while people file out. I hear snippets of conversation.

"He was stubborn."

"Had his enemies."

"Not just the company, either."

As I hang back, a familiar face emerges at my side—Dave Breck, an official from UAW Local 12. He offers a firm handshake, eyes sharp despite his mournful expression. His grip feels calculated, like he's sizing me up.

"Gray," he says in a low voice, with practiced solemnity. "Didn't think I'd see you here."

"Wouldn't miss it," I reply, sensing something beneath his casual greeting. "Mike deserves to be remembered."

Breck glances around the room. "A real shame, losing him like this." He lowers his voice. "He was one of the good ones."

"One of the good ones?" I raise an eyebrow. "That implies there are some 'bad ones.' "

Breck's eyes tighten. "Not bad. I mean people who try to hide things. Mike, on the other hand, had a habit of . . . digging up old battles better left buried."

"What battles?" I ask, sensing an opening.

Breck's eyes flicker with something close to annoyance. "Look, the past is the past. It's painful enough as it is. Mike kept bringing up issues better left alone."

"Like the Auto-Lite strike?" I press, voice dropping.

Breck stiffens and glances around before responding. "You think everything ties back to that strike. Sometimes, a car crash is just a car crash."

"And sometimes it isn't," I reply.

Breck's jaw sets. His expression turns stony. He steps in closer, lowering his voice even further. "Listen, Gray. I understand you've got a job to do. But be careful you don't start seeing things that aren't there. People around here won't appreciate you kicking up dust."

I start to respond, but he claps my shoulder—hard. A gesture meant to seem friendly to anyone watching.

"I'll catch you later, Gray," he says, stepping away. His smile doesn't reach his eyes.

I'm left alone, the hairs on the back of my neck standing on end. Was that a warning, a veiled threat, or just advice from someone who thinks I'm pushing too hard? Breck clearly wanted me to back off—and his discomfort only fuels my suspicions. But is this about the union trying to bury uncomfortable history, or is it something more?

Outside, I watch the hearse crawl down Summit Street. A few cars follow. Not many. The rest of the mourners shuffle toward their own vehicles or light cigarettes, speaking in hushed tones. Nobody's crying. Nobody's shouting. It's quiet in that chilling way—like the city itself is holding its breath.

I spot Ferner's widow again. She's standing alone now beside the curb, as if waiting for someone who never showed. I consider going over, saying something—"I'm sorry," or "He was a good man"—but the words feel hollow.

Then she turns and sees me. She holds my gaze for a long second. No tears. Just weariness. Recognition. Maybe even expectation.

She nods once.

And I know.

There's more she wants to say. Just not here.

I step outside into the cold again, pulling my collar up against the icy wind. The sky has released its grip, sending a fine drizzle down onto the pavement. Across the street, Breck watches me carefully as he climbs into his car.

Maybe I am chasing ghosts—or maybe I'm on the verge of uncovering something much bigger. Something worth killing over. Either way, Mike Ferner's funeral hasn't closed any doors.

It has opened new ones.

And I'm more certain than ever I want to find out what's waiting behind them.

After the funeral, I stand in the cramped living room of Mike Ferner's house, the air heavy with cigarette smoke and a lingering undercurrent of unease. His widow, looking tired, motions me toward a box resting on the dining table.

"This was Mike's," she says. "He'd been working on it for weeks before . . . before it happened. He mentioned your name. Said if anything ever happened to him, you'd know what to do."

She doesn't linger. Gives me a tight smile and disappears down the hallway, leaving me alone with the box.

I pull it closer. It's not large—maybe the size of an old file storage box, worn and covered in dust. Inside, it's a jumble of folders, manila envelopes, and a few legal pads with Ferner's looping handwriting. A scent of paper with a metallic hint hits me—maybe old staples. Or bloodied ink.

I sift through it, piece by piece.

There are newspaper clippings from the 1930s—photos of the Auto-Lite strike, headlines about National Guard deployments, factory shutdowns. Ferner had annotated some of them with a red pen: *"Unanswered questions," "What about this guy?"* and in one case: *"No way this was random."*

Tucked into a folder marked *Misc.* is a letter on faded company letterhead. Most of the content is boilerplate corporate PR speak, but a handwritten note at the bottom catches my eye: *"Continue pressure—Champlain and Central must remain 'quiet' through spring."* It's unsigned.

Another envelope contains photocopies of land transfer documents from the 1950s and '60s, highlighting how certain lots changed hands several times—always passing through one particular shell company before ending up under a well-known real estate holding group. There's a sticky note attached: *"Follow the money. All roads lead back to this network."* No specific names, but a web beginning to form.

The legal pads are full of scribbled timelines. Dotted across the margins are initials, events, and cryptic connections. *"F. F. and S. F. both dead within 6 mos. Why now?"* *"Who benefits from silence?"* One margin note reads: *"G. W. link?? Check with* Sword *archives librarian."*

Toward the bottom of the box, I find a cassette tape labelled *Toledo 1934–?* but it's blank. Either never recorded—or wiped.

No one name leaps out. No smoking gun. But a pattern emerges. A shadowy figure—or perhaps a group—preserving a legacy that started in blood.

And Ferner was getting close.

As I load the box into my car, I glance back at the house. I see that someone has drawn the blinds. She's not watching.

I don't have answers yet. Just questions. But if Ferner was willing to risk everything to uncover this— whatever "this" is—then I owe it to him to follow the trail.

Even if it gets me killed.

CHAPTER 34

MAY 1934

THE SHERIFF

The tycoon paced back and forth in his opulent office at the Electric Auto-Lite Company, his face etched with worry and frustration. The strike that had begun in April was spiraling out of control, and he could feel the situation slipping through his fingers. He glanced out the window, watching as the growing crowd of picketers chanted and waved signs, their voices carrying even through the thick glass.

A sharp knock at the door interrupted his thoughts.

"Come in," he barked, turning to face his visitors.

Auto-Lite's vice president and chief enforcer entered the room, the Lucas County sheriff following close behind. Both men looked haggard, their clothes rumpled from long hours of dealing with the escalating crisis.

"Gentlemen," the tycoon said, gesturing for them to sit. "I think we all know why we're here. This situation has become untenable."

The sheriff, grim-faced, said, "Sir, I've got to be honest with you. My deputies are outnumbered and overwhelmed. We can't contain this crowd much longer."

The vice president leaned forward, pointing at the sheriff, his voice tense. "The strikers are getting bolder by the hour. And we've got unemployed rabble-rousers from all over the city joining in. It's a powder keg out there."

The tycoon sighed, sinking into his leather chair. "Gentlemen, I believe we have no choice but to request help from the governor. We need the National Guard."

A heavy silence fell over the room. Under Ohio law, the governor could call in the Guard to respond to domestic emergencies—disasters, civil unrest. But it was a drastic step, one that could have far-reaching consequences.

The sheriff was the first to speak. "Sir, I understand your position, but are you sure that's wise? Bringing in the Guard could escalate things even further. We've already got reports of violence breaking out. If we add armed soldiers to the mix . . . "

"What choice do we have?" the tycoon snapped. "Your deputies can't handle this, and I'll be damned if I let these agitators destroy everything we've built here."

The vice president joined in. "Sheriff, with all due respect, we're past the point of peaceful resolution. These people aren't just striking workers anymore. They're a mob, plain and simple."

The sheriff's face hardened. "Now wait a minute. Many of these folks are decent, hardworking people trying to feed their families. They're not criminals."

"They became criminals when they defied that court injunction," the vice president retorted. "The judge limited the number of picketers, and they've ignored the ruling. There are thousands out there right now!"

The tycoon held up a hand, silencing them both. "Gentlemen, please. We need to make a decision, and we need to make it now. Sheriff, I understand your reservations—but can't you see we're out of options?"

The sheriff stood and walked to the window. The crowd had swelled even in the short time since he'd arrived, filling the streets around the plant. He could see the strain on his deputies' faces as they struggled to maintain order.

"You're right about one thing," the sheriff said. "This is beyond my men's capabilities now. But bringing in the Guard . . . it's a big step. There will be consequences."

The tycoon's voice was bitter. "The consequences of inaction will be far worse. My plant is being held hostage by a mob of Communists and malcontents. I won't stand for it."

The vice president added, "If we bring in the Guard now, we can end this—and fast. Show these people we mean business."

The sheriff turned back to face the room, his expression troubled. "And what happens when shots are fired? When people get hurt—or worse? Have you thought about that?"

A tense silence followed. The tycoon walked to a cabinet and pulled out a bottle of whiskey. He poured three glasses, handing them to the vice president and the sheriff before taking one himself.

"Sheriff," he said, his voice softer now, "I know you're worried about the people out there. But what about the people inside? My workers who want to do their jobs, who are being threatened and intimidated? Don't they deserve protection too?"

The sheriff took a long sip of his whiskey, considering the tycoon's words. "You're right, of course. We have a duty to protect everyone—not just the loudest voices."

The tycoon nodded. "Exactly. And right now, the only way to do that is with the National Guard. We need to restore order before someone gets seriously hurt."

He set down his glass and picked up the phone. "So, are we agreed? Do I make the call to the governor?"

The sheriff hesitated, then sighed. "Okay. Make the call. But God help us all if this goes wrong."

As the tycoon dialed the governor's office, the three men exchanged grim looks. They all knew that whatever happened next would change Toledo forever.

Outside, oblivious to the decision being made, the crowd continued to grow. The chants rose louder, the tension thick in the air.

As the sun set, the die had been cast. The "Battle of Toledo" was about to begin—and none of the men in that room could have predicted the consequences of their decision.

The phone call completed, the tycoon turned to his companions. "It's done," he said. "God willing, this will all be over soon."

But as the three men looked out at the seething crowd below, they couldn't shake the feeling that this was not going to end well.

CHAPTER 35

1984

A SILK PURSE?

I pull into the parking lot at Portside, easing the tired Hornet into a space near the entrance. I dig out coins to pay for parking, grumbling to myself. Why would people pay to park downtown when they can park for free at the mall?

The air is cold and damp, the Maumee River sluggish and dark beyond the new complex. Across the promenade, the glass on the new hotel still shines like it belongs somewhere else. You can smell the river if the wind shifts—diesel, fish, the sour edge of something industrial.

Two blocks inland, the storefronts are empty again. A sandwich board advertises a business that closed last fall. Someone's spray-painted over the logo, but the outline still shows through.

Portside was supposed to be a sign of Toledo's rebirth, but all I see is a slick, corporate facelift on a city that's still crumbling underneath.

Inside, Il Porto is busy with the after-work crowd, and I spot Pat and Mark already seated at a corner booth. Pat waves me over with her usual bright enthusiasm. She's always smiling, always hopeful—one of the few people I know who truly believe in Toledo's future. Mark, quieter but steady, nods as I slide into the seat across from them.

I like to paint a picture of myself as broody and mysterious, with no strong connections, but I do have some firm friends who stand by me. Pat and Mark are my oldest friends—we met in Sunday School when we were three. They ended up getting married, and they both try hard not to make me feel like a third wheel when we get together.

"I'm starving," Pat announces, flipping through the menu. "I was telling Mark, we need to come here more often. It's nice, isn't it? Feels like Toledo is turning a corner."

I smirk. "Willard Scott showing up for a ribbon-cutting doesn't exactly signal a renaissance." The avuncular *Today Show* weatherman had broadcast live from the opening a few weeks ago, celebrating the consumption habits of middle America.

Pat rolls her eyes. "You're impossible."

Mark chuckles, glancing at the menu. "Gray's upset he can't find a way to turn this into a conspiracy."

I smile. "Give me time." I pick up a menu and glance at the options. No meatloaf, thank goodness. "Don't you think it's convenient that the old Tiedtke's building 'burned down'"—I waggle my fingers in air quotes—"so Portside's developers didn't have to pay to tear it down?"

Pat shoots me a look. "Gray, you are one of my dearest friends, but sometimes your cynical attitude is too much."

The waitress arrives and takes our orders. Pat turns her attention back to me.

"So, are you seeing anyone?"

I sigh. I know where this is going. "No."

"Three years back here and you haven't had a steady relationship. You should call Julie Hopkins," Pat says. "Remember Julie? From Waite? She got divorced a few months ago."

I raise an eyebrow and cock my head. "Julie? Didn't she marry that linebacker? What was his name?"

"Steve McCleary," Mark interjects. "Two years ahead of us."

I shake my head. "Nothing against Julie, but I'm not looking to date anyone in Toledo."

Pat gives me a look. "Why not?"

I hesitate, choosing my words carefully. "Because with my luck, I'd fall in love, get comfortable, and end up stuck here forever."

Pat sighs. "Is Toledo really that bad, Gray?"

I'm ready to let my true thoughts slip out, but I catch myself. Pat and Mark are happy here, building their life together. I have no right to rain on that. I don't need to impose my biases on other people.

"No, but it's not the right place for me," I say instead. "I feel like I already left once, you know?"

Pat doesn't press further, sensing none of us would end up happy if she pushed the point. Instead, she switches gears.

"So, tell me about this Auto-Lite thing. You said there's going to be a commemoration? I'm sure we'll be covering it at the station." Pat works as an event manager at the local CBS affiliate.

I smile, grateful for the change in topic. "Yeah. It's the fiftieth anniversary of the resolution of the strike on June 3. There's a push to recognize what happened, but not everyone's thrilled about it."

"Why not?" Mark asks.

"Well, for one, the union leadership isn't exactly jumping to celebrate a strike with clear Communist ties. And I think some people want to keep the past buried."

Pat frowns. "It's strange, isn't it? I mean, our parents grew up here. You'd think we would've heard more about this."

"Right?" I say. "Remember Mr. Mack's history class?" Mr. Mack had grown up in Toledo and was always telling us to be proud of our local history. "He never mentioned it in twentieth century history."

Mark shakes his head. "Just goes to show, people remember what they want to remember."

I fill them in on my recent activity, including the deaths of Ferner and Feldman and my interviews with Auto-Lite survivors.

"There's that conspiracy you were looking for," Mark says at one point.

Our food arrives, and for a while, the conversation drifts to lighter topics—work, house-hunting, with Pat and Mark planning their own move out of the city. I listen, chiming in once in a while, but my mind keeps circling back to what Mark said.

People remember what they want to remember.

What is it they remember?

CHAPTER 36
1934
THE NEIGHBOR

The neighbor stood at her window, eyes wide with disbelief as she watched the scene unfolding before her. It was 4:30 in the morning, and her street—two blocks from the chaos of the strike—had come alive with activity.

The National Guard had arrived.

Young men in uniform poured out of trucks, their faces a mix of determination and uncertainty. Her heart raced as she realized the gravity of the situation.

"Oh my goodness," she whispered. "The army's in town."

She watched as they unloaded their equipment, breath catching in her throat when she saw machine guns being lifted with care from the vehicles. These weren't toys or props. These were real weapons, meant for real conflict. And they were being set up right in front of her home.

As dawn broke, curiosity got the better of her. Despite the tension in her chest, she stepped out onto Michigan Street, wanting to see the guardsmen up close. What struck her most was their youth. These weren't hardened soldiers, but boys—barely older than her younger brother. Their uniforms hung loose on some of them, as if they hadn't quite grown into the role they were now expected to play.

Throughout the day, her feelings bounced between fear and fascination. The strike that had been brewing for weeks had escalated overnight into something she could never have imagined. Auto-Lite—a place she passed every day on her way to the market—had become a battleground.

After dark, the real horror began.

Chaotic sounds echoed through the streets as windows in the plant shattered under a hail of bricks. The pungent aroma of tear gas seeped into her home, forcing her to close all the doors and windows. Still, the noxious fumes found their way in, making her eyes water and her throat burn.

From her house, she could hear the chaos unfolding—shouts, more breaking glass, the popping of tear gas canisters. In her mind's eye, she saw the strikers—her friends and neighbors—catching the canisters and hurling them back at the plant. The thought of them risking injury, perhaps even their lives, made her stomach churn.

It's like a young war, she thought. This wasn't some far-off conflict she'd read about in the papers. This was happening right outside her door, involving people she knew and cared about.

That night seemed endless. Sleep was impossible with the constant noise and the lingering tear gas. She paced, alternating between peeking out the windows and covering her ears to block out the sounds of conflict.

As dawn broke again, she realized with a start that the fighting hadn't stopped. If anything, it had intensified. The "night of nights" she had witnessed was stretching into days of unrest and violence.

Standing at her window once more, watching young guardsmen and angry strikers clash in the streets she'd walked all her life, the neighbor felt a profound sense of disbelief.

How had it come to this?

How had her quiet neighborhood become a war zone?

She knew this was something she would never forget—the image of those young guardsmen, the broken glass everywhere, the lingering smell of gas. All of it would be seared into her memory.

CHAPTER 37

1984
WORKING-CLASS HERO

Jim calls me into his office three days later for an update—and an opportunity. He sits back and props his feet on the desk, puffing on a cigarette as I lay out excerpts from my interviews with survivors of the 1934 Auto-Lite strike. He skims the notes, grunting approval.

"Okay, this could be interesting—keep going."

He grabs a manila folder from his desk and tosses it toward me. It slides across the surface, stopping just shy of my elbow.

"Since you seem to be getting your teeth into this old strike story, here's a new one for you to look into."

I open the folder and leaf through the clippings. They're recent—articles from *The Sword* and the wire services about an impending strike at the AP Parts plant on Matzinger Road.

I sigh and set the folder down. "You trying to pigeonhole me into labor stories, Jim? I'm a little young to be *The Sword's* official strike historian."

He smirks. "Listen, kid, you're the one digging into the past. Thought you might like to see what's happening in the present."

I consider what he's saying. The Auto-Lite strike of 1934 had been a defining moment in Toledo's labor history—a brutal battle between workers, strikebreakers, and the

National Guard, culminating in gunfire, deaths, and national headlines. Fifty years later, AP Parts was shaping up to be a different fight, but the stakes weren't so different: workers trying to hold on to their jobs and dignity, a company trying to cut costs, and an economy that made compromise difficult.

"All right," I say. "I'll look into it. But if I see one more picket line, I might start charging the UAW rent for space in my notebook."

Jim chuckles. "Welcome to the real world."

I gather up the clippings and leave his office. As I walk back to my desk, I wonder—what is it about labor disputes that makes me uneasy? The history fascinates me, sure. The politics are messy, the stakes high. But there's something else. Something personal.

Maybe it's my dad, who spent most of his life on the Jeep line, coming home quiet and exhausted, never talking much about the work but never missing a shift. Maybe it's because I spent my teenage years wanting nothing more than to escape Toledo—and now here I am, neck-deep in the stories of the workers I once thought I'd never become.

I flip open my notebook to a blank page and create a new heading: AP Parts Strike—1984. *The more things change, the more they stay the same.*

Looks like I'm becoming the Strike Guy.

The Auto-Lite commemoration pieces are simmering on the back burner. The interviews will run the day before the June 3 commemoration, and my report will appear in the June 4 edition. That leaves me a narrow window to shift focus and dig into the AP Parts situation. Jim wants a few news pieces lined up before I dive back into the 1934 coverage, and as much as I resent becoming *The Sword*'s resident labor reporter, I have to admit—there are intriguing parallels between the two strikes.

I spread the clippings across my desk and flip through them. AP Parts has been a mainstay in Toledo's industrial landscape since 1939. It makes exhaust systems and other automotive components, supplying major automakers like GM and Chrysler. The multinational conglomerate Questor bought the company in the 1970s, and ever since, tensions between management and the union have been building.

At the heart of the current dispute: wages, job security, and the increasingly antagonistic stance of company executives. UAW Local 14, representing the AP Parts employees, has been negotiating with management for months, but by this spring, talks had stalled. The company proposed wage freezes, benefit cuts, and a two-tier wage system for new hires—moves the union sees as an existential threat.

With inflation still biting and the sting of recent layoffs fresh in workers' minds, an overwhelming majority of the rank-and-file rejected management's last offer in late April. A strike seemed inevitable—and now it's here.

I jot down notes. I want to track down union leadership, plant workers, and anyone on the management side willing to talk. The city has seen its fair share of labor battles over the years, but with the Reagan administration's crackdown on organized labor, workers everywhere are on edge. With AP Parts workers walking out, the company might take a hard line, hoping to break the union altogether.

That's a far cry from 1934, when organized labor was still fighting for its very existence—but the through line is clear: when workers push back, power pushes harder.

Labor disputes aren't my dream beat, but I know a good story when I see one. If I play this right, the AP Parts strike won't just be another union-management standoff—it'll be a modern reflection of the same struggles that fueled the Auto-Lite strike fifty years ago.

And if there's one thing I've learned in this business, it's that history has a way of repeating itself.

I'm halfway through the stack of info when the phone on my desk rings. The shrill tone cuts through the newsroom hum, and I answer without thinking.

"Gray speaking."

"Gray?" Kirby's voice sounds thin, hesitant—not her usual confident tone. "Can you come down to the archives? Now, please?"

My stomach tightens. "Are you okay?"

"Just come, please." The urgency in her voice leaves no room for questions.

I bolt from my desk, grabbing my coat on the way out. The quick trip downstairs feels longer than usual, tension building with every step. When I arrive, Kirby is waiting inside the archive doorway, looking shaken. Her arms are folded across her chest, eyes darting toward the entrance behind me.

I step closer, speaking low. "What's going on?"

She leans in, lowering her voice. "There was a guy here. He asked a lot of questions about you—what stories you're working on, whether you've requested anything about the UAW."

My pulse quickens. "What did you tell him?"

She shakes her head. "Nothing. But he wasn't here to do research. He didn't look at a single file. He stood there, trying to intimidate me. He knew things, Gray. Personal things. Like where I live."

I glance toward the archive's empty tables, a creeping unease settling over me. "Did he threaten you?"

"No," she says, biting her lip. "But the way he looked at me . . . it was a threat without words."

"You've never seen him before?"

"No. But he looked—official somehow. Short hair, glasses, dressed well. He wore a UAW pin, but it felt like a prop. Something about him felt off."

I exhale, anger and guilt mixing in my gut. "I shouldn't have dragged you into this."

Kirby's gaze sharpens. "You didn't drag me anywhere. I chose to help you, remember?"

"Yeah, but you didn't sign up for harassment. Maybe you should step back—at least for now."

Her eyes flash. "No way. If someone's going to these lengths, it means you're getting close to something real. I'm not backing out because they're trying to scare me."

I pause, admiration mixing with anxiety. "Okay. But promise me you'll be careful. And if this guy shows up again, you call security first—then me."

She nods, glancing toward the entrance. "Do you think he's from the union?"

"I don't know—but it means we need to find out."

Kirby hesitates, then manages a faint smile. "Good thing I like puzzles."

Despite my worry, I smile back. "Don't forget—this puzzle might bite."

"I'll remember," she says, the steel returning to her voice. "Now go write your damn story. I'll be fine."

But as I walk back toward the elevator, the unease remains, stronger than ever. Whoever's pulling strings behind the scenes—UAW or someone else—they're willing to threaten Kirby, and that makes this personal. More personal than I ever intended.

CHAPTER 38

MAY 1934

THE COLUMNIST

The columnist stepped off the train, his colossal frame causing the platform to creak under his weight. At six feet tall and pushing 220 pounds, with a mop of unruly hair and a pipe clenched between his teeth, he looked every inch the archetypal newsman of the 1930s.

He arrived in Toledo with the weight of his reputation preceding him. A journalist with a deep conviction for social justice, he had built his name through sharp wit and fearless reporting. A Harvard-educated intellectual who had once been a sportswriter, he had long since pivoted to championing the struggles of working people. He was a founder of the American Newspaper Guild and had spent years railing against the indifference of the powerful.

Now, in 1934, he had come to Toledo to see firsthand what was happening at the Electric Auto-Lite plant.

He wasn't the type to sit in a hotel room filing sterile dispatches from a safe distance. He believed in getting close—close enough to smell the tear gas, close enough to hear the fear in a striker's voice.

When he stepped onto the picket lines, it was clear he was no typical newsman. Barrel-chested and broad-shouldered, he commanded attention. But it wasn't just his size—it was his empathy. He spoke to the workers not as an outsider, but as someone who believed in their cause.

The morning the National Guard arrived, the atmosphere around the plant gates crackled with tension. The strikers, thousands strong, had held the line for weeks. Their numbers had swelled with unemployed workers and unionists from across the city. Inside the plant, scabs and managers huddled behind locked doors, protected by hired guards and company loyalists.

The city police had already shown where their loyalties lay—clubs and tear gas had made that clear. But now, with the arrival of the Guard, the stakes had risen. Everyone knew what it meant. The state had picked a side.

The columnist stood among the workers, listening to their stories. He had seen this before—industry-backed government forces brought in to crush labor uprisings, always under the guise of restoring order. He had no illusions about what was coming. But he resolved to witness it.

As he moved through the crowd, a commotion near the plant gates caught his attention. Company guards were facing off against a vocal group of strikers. The tension was rising fast. The columnist pushed his way closer.

A shout went up. The crowd surged. The columnist found himself caught in the middle, his bulk buffeted by the angry mass of humanity. He clutched his notebook to his chest, trying to stay upright.

Then, from behind, a National Guardsman—no older than twenty—spotted him. Maybe the young soldier mistook him for an agitator. Maybe his size made him a target. Whatever the reason, the guardsman lowered his rifle, fixed his bayonet, and jabbed it into the columnist's back.

The big man lurched forward, nearly losing his balance. The blade only grazed him, but the insult was clear. A stunned silence followed. Then the columnist turned, his face a mask of disbelief and rising anger. He was a writer, a man of words—but here, the message had been delivered in cold steel.

The guardsman braced for another thrust.

The columnist didn't give him the chance. He took off, his massive frame moving faster than anyone expected. Later, witnesses would chuckle about it—the sight of one of America's most respected journalists sprinting away from a boy with a bayonet. But in the moment, it was anything but funny. The columnist knew how quickly these things could turn. He'd seen it before. He knew the line between a show of force and outright bloodshed was razor thin.

After retreating, embarrassed but unharmed, he turned his attention back to the scene. The confrontation was escalating. A worker, face twisted with rage, hurled a rock toward the plant gates. It missed its target but shattered the window of a nearby car.

The sound broke the last thread of restraint.

Chaos erupted.

The columnist was caught in the middle again, his instincts warring with his sense of self-preservation. He watched as workers clashed with police and guardsmen, their cries for justice drowned out by the crack of batons and the hiss of tear gas.

He retreated to a safer vantage point, eyes watering, notebook in hand. In his mind, he was already composing the opening lines of his next column:

> In the shadow of smokestacks and broken dreams, the workers of Toledo have drawn a line in the sand. They stand not just for themselves, but for every man and woman who has ever been ground under the heel of industrial might. And let me tell you, dear reader, it's a sight to behold.

Back at his hotel, his suit torn and stained, the columnist sat down at his typewriter. His notebook held the raw material of injustice and hope. He knew his words would reach millions.

The clack of keys filled the room.

> It seems to me that what we witnessed today in Toledo is nothing less than a battle for the soul of America. On one side, we have men and women who ask for nothing more than the dignity of a fair day's pay for a fair day's work. On the other, we have those who would squeeze every last drop of profit from the sweat and blood of their fellow citizens.

He paused, puffing on his pipe.

> The question we must ask ourselves, dear reader, is this: What kind of nation do we wish to be? One where the many toil in misery for the benefit of the few, or one where prosperity is shared by all who contribute to its creation?

In the days that followed, the columnist became a familiar figure on the picket lines. His imposing presence and quick wit made him a favorite among the strikers. He faced tear gas and threats, dodged flying rocks and swinging batons—all in pursuit of the truth.

And through it all, he kept writing. His words became a beacon of hope for those fighting for justice—and a stinging rebuke to those who would deny it.

Because in the end, he knew: the pen was mightier than the sword.

Or even the bayonet of a nervous young guardsman.

CHAPTER 39
1984
HISTORY REPEATING

I arrive at the AP Parts plant to find the scene already chaotic. Thousands of workers have flooded the streets, defying the court injunction that limited picketers to six per gate. They're here in solidarity, furious over the company's use of nonunion labor to break the strike. The night air is thick with shouts, the glow of streetlights casting jagged shadows over the mass of bodies pressing against the barricades. Riot police stand in tight formation, their shields reflecting the dim industrial glare.

I park a few blocks away, the air humid and heavy with the scent of burnt rubber. The rhythmic thud of boots, the low rumble of voices, and the occasional bark of a megaphone create an uneasy soundtrack. I grab my notepad, stuff it in my jacket, and step into the street, the bricks uneven beneath my feet.

Even from a distance, I can see the flashing blue and red lights reflecting off the factory's steel façade. The rally has transformed into something much larger—a battle between Toledo's working class and the forces trying to break them.

The crowd is dense and volatile, banners and fists raised, voices raw from chanting. I recognize faces from other union stories—Jeep workers, guys from Hydramatic, Teledyne, even a few retired autoworkers who fought for these jobs decades ago. They're here in defiance of the injunction. That was never going to hold. Limiting picketers to twenty-five didn't work in 1934; squeezing it down to six in 1984 is laughable.

The police presence is overwhelming. Officers in riot gear form a wall between the workers and the plant, faces obscured by visors, hands gripping batons and tear gas launchers. Behind them, private security—"Knuckles," the workers call them—stand with arms crossed, black jackets bearing AP Parts patches. Hired muscle.

I push through the crowd, catching snippets of conversation:

"They wanna gut our wages—five bucks an hour, gone. No more thirty-and-out pension. They want us working till we die."

"That ain't bargaining. It's a fucking declaration of war."

"They're inside right now, those scab bastards, hiding behind cops."

Then, without warning, the air erupts.

Tear gas canisters arc overhead, white trails slicing the black sky. One lands near me with a dull thunk, hissing out a noxious cloud. Shouts turn to screams as the crowd surges back—then forward again. Police wade in, swinging riot sticks. Shields smash against bodies. Rocks fly in return, bouncing off helmets, clattering against car hoods. A cruiser lurches as someone slams a chunk of pavement into the windshield.

The crowd doesn't back down. A Jeep worker grabs a tear gas canister and hurls it back. The air is chaos—shouting, the crack of batons, the sound of glass shattering.

I spot a woman—mid-forties, bomber jacket with a union patch—arms locked around another picketer as they stumble from the gas cloud. She looks at me, eyes watering, teeth clenched.

"You getting this down?"

I wave my notebook. This strike is about survival as much as wages. Fifty years ago, workers stood in this city against the National Guard. Now, they're here again—fighting tear gas, riot sticks, and corporate greed.

I turn, trying to find another vantage point, just as the cops move in. Batons swing. A dozen workers are dragged toward waiting cruisers. Police will escort the scabs out of the plant at shift's end, shields raised. But the workers? They'll go home bloodied, arrested—or not at all.

Then it happens.

Something whizzes past my head—fast. I don't process it until I hear the sharp, splintering crack behind me. I spin. A tear gas canister has slammed into a telephone pole, inches from where I was standing.

My pulse pounds. That was close. Too close.

I step toward the pole, blinking through the gas—and then I see it. Just below the fresh dent from the canister's impact, a dark hole gapes in the wood.

A bullet.

A bullet embedded in the pole.

Wait. Was it only the canister I heard? Or was someone shooting at me?

My breath comes faster. Was someone trying to kill me?

The thought hits harder than the gas. I stagger back, scanning rooftops, police lines, shadows. But there's no way to tell. No way to know if it was a stray shot—or something more deliberate.

I came here to cover a labor battle.

Maybe I've walked into a different war altogether.

The adrenaline doesn't wear off until I'm back behind the wheel, hands trembling against the cracked vinyl of the steering wheel. Tear gas clings to my jacket. My throat is raw. My head buzzes with the concussion of riot sticks and yelling—and whatever the hell flew past my head.

Was it a bullet?

I keep playing it back. The way it sliced through the air. The crack as it hit the pole. The bullet left behind.

That wasn't a ricochet.

That was a shot.

Someone intended it for me.

I stare out the windshield, watching a garbage truck rumble past like nothing happened. Like the street wasn't on fire fifteen minutes ago. I pull my notebook from my coat. It's damp with sweat, smudged from gas, but my shorthand is still legible. I flip back a few pages—union locals, strike leaders, out-of-town organizers.

Someone wants me to stop writing this story.

But who?

The obvious answer is the UAW. I've been sniffing around their refusal to back the Auto-Lite commemoration. They've been icy. Hostile. One guy flat-out warned me to "let sleeping dogs lie." Could they see me as a threat to their sanitized legacy?

Or was it someone else?

My gut says this is bigger than the union. This shows organization. Reach. Someone who knows how to make problems disappear.

Like Ferner. Like Feldman.

And if I don't play this smart—maybe like me.

The coffee is even worse than usual this morning. I sip it anyway, staring at the half-finished article in my typewriter. I rub my temples.

How do you write about a protest when you're pretty sure someone tried to kill you during it?

I crack my knuckles and pick up where I left off:

> The streets outside AP Parts last night were filled with tear gas, shouts, and history repeating itself.

It wasn't a protest—it was a reckoning. Fifty years after the Battle of Toledo, workers once again faced off against the institutions that claim to protect them. The company hid behind private security. The state sent riot cops. And the people—well, they did what Toledo's always done when it's pushed too far. They fought back.

I pause.

Do I mention the shot?

Not yet. Not here. I'm not ready to accuse anyone without proof. And if I'm going to drop that kind of bomb, it has to be in the right story.

I file the piece, grab the carbon copy, and slide it into my bag.

That's when Kirby shows up beside my desk, clutching a manila folder. Her brow furrows when she sees me.

"Whoa, Gray. You look like hell."

"Thanks," I mutter. "Just doing my job."

"Doing it while getting shot at now?"

My head snaps up. "What did you say?"

"There's a bullet hole in your story, Gray." She holds out the folder. "A photo someone dropped off anonymously this morning. That's you. And someone circled what looks like a bullet lodged in the pole."

"What makes you think it's a bullet hole?"

She flips the photo over. On the back, scrawled in all caps:

I WON'T MISS NEXT TIME.

I stare at the image.

Kirby lowers her voice. "Gray, I think it's time we stopped assuming this is just about labor history."

I nod slowly. "I think someone doesn't want me to connect the dots."

She meets my gaze, steady and unflinching. "Then we better connect them faster."

CHAPTER 40
MAY 1934
THE FARMER

The air was thick with tension as the crowd of strikers and supporters swelled to six thousand strong outside the Auto-Lite plant on the evening of May 24. The arrival of nine hundred Ohio National Guardsmen early that morning had only intensified the anger and determination of the workers fighting for their rights.

Among the sea of faces was a stocky young farmer from nearby Millbury. He wasn't an Auto-Lite worker, but he had come to stand with them. He stood near the front of the crowd, heart pounding as he watched the line of young guardsmen—many not much older than himself—hands shaking as they gripped their rifles.

As the sun set, the mood grew more volatile. Taunts and jeers erupted from the crowd, punctuated by the occasional bottle hurled toward the soldiers. The guardsmen responded with volleys of tear gas, but the crowd, now well-practiced in dealing with such tactics, picked up the canisters and threw them back.

The farmer found himself caught in the surging mass of humanity. He stumbled upon a loose brick and, almost without thinking, hefted it in his hand. He hesitated—the weight of his potential action heavy in his palm—then, with a surge of adrenaline, he hurled it toward the line of guardsmen.

Time seemed to slow as the brick arced through the air. He watched, breath caught in his throat, as it struck a young guardsman square on the helmet with a resounding clang. The man went down hard, his helmet flying off his head and rolling into the gutter.

For a heartbeat, everything was still.

Then chaos erupted.

The crack of gunfire split the air—sharp, terrifying. At first, the farmer thought they were firing warning shots. But then came the screams. Real screams. And he realized with horror that some of the guardsmen were shooting into the crowd.

Close to him, a man clutched his chest, eyes wide with disbelief. Blood bloomed on his shirt as he collapsed. Nearby, another man—barely more than a boy—cried out as a bullet tore through his body.

The crowd recoiled in horror, then surged forward in rage. People rushed to the fallen, hands frantic, trying to stem the flow of blood.

"Medic! We need a medic!" someone shouted, their voice nearly lost in the cacophony of gunfire, screams, and the thunderous roar of the enraged crowd.

The farmer knelt beside the first man, pressing his hands against the wound. "Stay with us, buddy," he pleaded, voice shaking. "Help's coming. You're gonna be okay."

But as he looked into the man's eyes, he saw the light fading. The man gasped, tried to speak, then coughed up blood. The farmer held his hand, helpless, as the life drained from a man he'd never met.

A few yards away, the other man lay motionless, his boyish face frozen in surprise. A woman knelt beside him, sobbing, trying in vain to revive him.

The scene had devolved into utter chaos. The guardsmen—many of them shaken—continued to fire. Some strikers fled in terror. Others advanced in fury, hurling bricks, bottles, anything they could find.

The farmer, hands slick with blood, stood in a daze. These men—alive moments ago—were gone. Their lives snuffed out in an instant of senseless violence.

The smell of gunpowder and tear gas hung heavy in the air. Floodlights cast harsh shadows across a nightmarish landscape of writhing bodies and flashing muzzles. The sound was deafening—gunshots, screams, the roar of the crowd.

As word of the killings spread, the mood shifted from shock to fury. Workers who had come to protest peacefully now found themselves in a war zone. Many grabbed whatever they could use as weapons, faces contorted with grief and rage.

"Murderers!" the cry rose from a thousand throats. "They're killing us! Fight back!"

The guardsmen, many just boys from nearby towns, looked overwhelmed. Some fired wild shots into the air. Others stood frozen, unsure of what to do.

In the midst of the chaos, acts of bravery and compassion stood out. A group of workers formed a human chain to evacuate the wounded, passing them hand to hand to safety. Others tore off shirts to make bandages, doing what they could to save lives.

The farmer joined them, fear replaced by grim determination. He helped carry a wounded woman to a porch turned into a makeshift first aid station. The steps were slick with blood.

The battle raged through the night. The guardsmen, running low on tear gas, began throwing rocks and bottles back at the crowd. The strikers hurled unexploded canisters back at the troops. It was surreal—soldiers and civilians locked in a deadly street fight.

As dawn broke on May 25, the full extent of the violence became clear. Besides the two men who died at the scene, at least fifteen others had suffered bullet wounds. Dozens more were injured by bricks, gas canisters, or just caught in the general melee. The area around the Auto-Lite plant looked like a battlefield—strewn with debris, stained with blood.

CHAPTER 41
1984
BULLET STRIKES THE HELMET'S HEAD

Mom is stirring a pot of chili on the stovetop when I come in. She doesn't turn around.

"You're still determined to dig into old things," she says quietly.

I lean against the counter. "It's important."

She grips the spoon tighter.

"Important things still get people hurt," she says, "especially the ones who think they're smarter than the fire they're poking."

Her voice wobbles.

"I grew up with nothing," she says. "Nothing but borrowed land and promises that got washed away with the rain. And now you're out here, chasing after trouble like it owes you something."

I don't know what to say to that. She turns, eyes shining.

"I don't want to lose you," she says, "even if I never knew how to hold on right."

For the first time, I see it—not anger. Not control.

Fear. Pure and simple.

Dad is in his usual spot—the recliner in the living room, lit by a side lamp, a copy of *Time* magazine between his fingers. The TV murmurs in the background, some forgettable news program he isn't watching. He doesn't turn his head when I sit down on the couch across from him. Just stares at the screen, eyes dull and tired.

I've been trying to get information from him about the Auto-Lite strike ever since I got this assignment. I know he was there. I know he saw it. And now, after everything—after Sidney Feldman's murder, after the cryptic recollections from survivors—I need him to tell me what he knows.

I clear my throat. "Dad."

Nothing.

"I need your help."

After a long pause, he turns to me, taking a slow drag from his pipe. "With what?"

I hold out the photo—grainy, blurred at the edges. I point to the figure holding a brick in the corner, half-obscured by shadow and smoke.

"Was this you? Were you there that day?"

He doesn't move closer. Just stares at the photo, jaw tight.

"I've spent most of my life trying to forget what that day smelled like," he says.

I let the silence stretch as he gathers his thoughts.

His voice drops. "I was a scared kid who thought throwing a brick would make the world better. Then the rifles fired, and everything changed."

I sit forward, elbows on my knees. "So you were at Auto-Lite? At the strike?"

His lips tighten. "I already told you. I was just a kid."

"You were twenty. That's not a kid."

His mouth twitches, but he says nothing. The silence between us grows heavy.

"You saw what happened when the National Guard opened fire."

A long sigh escapes him, smoke curling from his lips. He rubs his temple like he's warding off a headache. Then, when I think he's going to shut me out again, he whispers, "I didn't just see it."

Something in his tone makes my stomach drop. "What do you mean?"

He doesn't look at me. Just stares ahead—past the television, past the room, past fifty years of silence.

"I threw a brick," he says. His voice is hoarse, raw, like the words are tearing something loose inside him.

I feel my breath catch. "What?"

"I wasn't part of it. Not really. I was . . . " He hesitates. "We all went down there. Me and a few guys from the neighborhood. We weren't union men. But we heard about the strike, the rallies, the fights with the cops. We wanted to see it for ourselves."

I wait. I don't dare interrupt.

"There were thousands of people by then. Strikers, their families, people like me who came to watch. And the Guardsmen, lined up with their rifles, looking scared as hell. They'd been out there for days. We knew they had orders to break it up if things got bad." He drags a hand down his face. "Then someone threw a rock. I don't know who started it. But it was like a match hitting gasoline. The crowd surged. People shouting, pushing forward. I picked up a brick."

His fingers tremble where they rest on his knee.

"I don't know why I did it," he murmurs. "I wasn't thinking. I got caught up in it. I hurled it as hard as I could. Hit a soldier on his helmet. Knocked him back." He swallows hard. "And then they started shooting."

A chill spreads through me.

"They didn't hesitate. Just opened fire. People started screaming, running. I saw a woman go down. Blood on the pavement. A guy beside me dropped like a sack of potatoes."

He squeezes his eyes shut. "I held him as the life drained from him. And then I ran. I ran, and I didn't look back."

His breath is ragged. He taps out his pipe with shaking fingers.

"I read about it the next day in the paper," he says. "Two dead. More than a dozen wounded. And all I could think was—I started it." His voice cracks. "If I hadn't thrown that brick—"

"Dad—"

He rocks his head back and forth. "I killed them, Gray. I killed those people."

I move to the edge of my seat. "No." My voice is steady. "You didn't."

He lets out a bitter laugh. "I might as well have."

I don't know what to say. I stare at him—the man who's been a ghost in his own house for as long as I can remember. The man who buried himself in silence and guilt for fifty damn years.

I take a shaky breath. "Dad, they were going to fire anyway. You didn't pull the trigger."

His red-rimmed eyes meet mine. "Maybe not. But I gave them an excuse."

I want to tell him he's wrong, that he was just a kid caught in the storm of history. But I know it won't help. He's carried this weight for fifty years. My words won't change that.

Instead, I reach out and place a hand on his arm. He flinches—then stills.

We sit like that for a long time. The past pressing down on both of us.

But for the first time, the silence between us isn't empty.

It's full—of pain, of truth, of something that almost feels like understanding.

CHAPTER 42
MAY 1934
THE GUARDSMAN

The sun hung low and angry over Toledo, pressing its heat through the woolen uniform that clung to the guardsman's skin like a damp second layer. His collar rubbed his neck raw, and the helmet squeezed his temples until his head throbbed. He shifted his weight, rifle slung awkwardly over his shoulder, and tried not to think about how badly he wanted to scratch that itch. Behind him, the Auto-Lite factory loomed like a brick fortress, its windows shattered and gaping. In front of him, the crowd seethed.

He shouldn't have been here.

Three weeks ago, he'd been in Lima, Ohio, sitting at the kitchen table while his mother folded laundry with hands reddened from the washboard. The notice had come in the mail—a dollar a day for National Guard drills, double if called to active duty. His father's cough had rattled louder that week, carving hollows under his eyes. The guardsman hadn't even finished filling out the form before his mother whispered, "Thank God," like it was a prayer.

Now, standing in this sweaty Toledo hellscape, he wondered if God had heard her.

The training had been a joke: three days of marching in a field outside Lima, an hour spent fumbling with an unfamiliar rifle. The sergeant barked about "crowd control" and "maintaining order," but the words meant nothing. The guardsman had stared at the weapon in his hands, its weight foreign and sinister, and thought about trigonometry exams and the cap-and-gown rental fee his mother couldn't afford.

Tonight was supposed to be his high school graduation.

Instead, he was here—a faceless cog in a line of faceless cogs, all of them sweating through government-issued wool.

A bottle shattered somewhere to his left. The crowd roared, a sound like a wounded animal, and he flinched.

"Hold the line!" someone shouted. He wasn't sure who.

The strikers pressed closer, faces streaked with soot and rage. Men in patched overalls, women in faded dresses, kids no older than him clutching signs that read A LIVING WAGE and WE FEED AMERICA—WHY STARVE US? Their voices tangled into a chant he couldn't make out, but he felt it in his ribs—a low, trembling vibration.

A rock sailed over his head. He ducked, helmet slipping sideways.

"Steady!" the commander barked. He righted his helmet, fingers trembling.

The brick came out of nowhere.

It struck his helmet with a hollow clang, knocking him sideways. Pain spider-webbed through his skull, and the world blurred into streaks of sky and asphalt. When his vision cleared, he was on the ground, rifle clutched to his chest. He looked up—and there he was: a young man, a farm boy who could still be in his teens, frozen at the edge of the crowd, arm still cocked from the throw. Their eyes met. The boy's face went slack with guilt.

The guardsman's rifle was in his hands before he realized he'd moved it. He aimed at the boy, the barrel wavering like a compass needle hunting north. The kid didn't run. Didn't even blink. He stood there, face pale, hands raised in surrender or supplication.

Don't, the boy mouthed.

The guardsman's finger hovered over the trigger. His breath came in shallow gasps. He'd never shot at anything but tin cans—and even then, he'd missed most of the time.

A crack split the air.

Not his rifle. Someone else's.

Three more shots followed—sharp, final. The crowd screamed. The guardsman spun, scanning the line—*Who fired? Who fired?*—but the men beside him looked as confused as he felt. He glimpsed someone—not a guardsman, someone in a shirt and tie—with a rifle in his hand. Then he was gone.

When the guardsman turned back, the boy was gone too, swallowed by the chaos.

Bodies moved in his periphery. A man crumpled, clutching his leg. Another dropped without a sound, a dark bloom spreading across his chest. The strikers surged forward, then back, like a tide reversing. A woman wailed, high and keening, as others dragged the fallen into the shelter of a burnt-out truck.

"Fire warning shots! In the air! Damn it, IN THE AIR!" The commander's voice tore through the noise, half-desperate, half-enraged.

The guardsman laughed—a sharp, jagged sound he didn't recognize as his own. *Warning shots?* Someone hadn't gotten the memo.

He raised his rifle skyward and pulled the trigger. The recoil punched his shoulder, and the shot tore a hole in the clouds. Around him, other guardsmen followed suit—pop-pop-pop—a staccato rhythm that did nothing to calm the storm below. The crowd scattered, then regrouped, hurling bricks and curses with renewed fury. A shard of glass grazed his cheek. He tasted blood.

He didn't know how long it lasted. Minutes? Hours? The sun dipped lower, staining the sky the color of a bruise. The air reeked of gunpowder and sweat and something sweet and metallic he refused to name.

When the order came to fall back, he moved like a sleepwalker. His uniform was drenched, his hands raw from gripping the rifle. As they retreated toward the factory gates, he glanced over his shoulder.

The strikers clustered around their wounded, shirts ripped into bandages, hands pressed to bleeding flesh. A man in a preacher's collar knelt beside a body, praying aloud. The guardsman looked away.

On the truck ride back to camp, no one spoke. The men stared at their boots, at their hands, at anything but each other. The guardsman pressed his forehead to the window, watching Toledo blur past. Somewhere, his mother would be setting the table, counting the dollars he'd send home. Somewhere, a classroom sat empty, diplomas gathering dust on a principal's desk.

That night, in a tent that stank of mildew and gun oil, he wrote a letter he'd never send:

> Dear God,
> Get me out of here.
> I'll do anything.

He folded the paper small enough to fit in his pocket, where it rubbed against the shell casing he'd kept from the first bullet he ever fired—during training.

Sleep didn't come. When he closed his eyes, he saw the boy's face.

Don't.

He wondered if the kid had made it home.

Then he wondered if he ever would.

CHAPTER 43
1984
LAWYERS, GUNS, AND MONEY

I sit down in George Slaughter's opulent living room on River Road, the air thick with the scent of leather-bound books and polished mahogany—a stark contrast to the homes of the workers I've visited. Sunlight filters through stained-glass windows, casting kaleidoscope shadows over walls lined with framed accolades: a lifetime of defending the underdog, of battles fought in courtrooms and congressional hearings. At eighty-one, Slaughter still carries himself like the litigator who stared down McCarthyism, his gaze sharp behind wire-rimmed glasses. But there's a weariness in the way he settles into his wingback chair, as if the ghosts of Toledo's past cling to his shoulders.

"Mr. Slaughter," I begin, adjusting my tape recorder on the coffee table between us, "thank you for agreeing to talk about the Auto-Lite strike."

Slaughter chuckles, his voice steady despite his age. "Ah, yes. That was a hell of a time. Only a year before, I'd transitioned from corporate law to labor law when the Auto-Lite workers approached me for help. In the 1920s, I'd done a bit of work for Clarence Flanagan—considered him a friend, in fact. I knew taking their case would burn bridges with some powerful people, but it was the right thing to do. Those workers were fighting for dignity, and I couldn't turn my back on them."

"You've mentioned in articles over the years that Communists and Socialists were involved in supporting the strike. What role did they play?"

Slaughter's face darkens as he considers his response. "The American Workers Party was deeply involved," he says. "Their leaders had been organizing unemployed workers through the Lucas County Unemployed League long before Auto-Lite went on strike. When things heated up, they stepped in to bolster numbers on the picket lines."

He sighs. "But there were agitators too—Communists and Socialists who wanted turmoil and violence to see what would happen. My feeling is that they hoped for revolutionary conditions to advance their cause."

I purse my lips but stay quiet as Slaughter continues.

"They weren't wrong about one thing," he says grimly. "The conditions during the Depression bred revolution-like sentiments everywhere—in Toledo, but also across America. Hundreds of people were sleeping out on courthouse lawns because they had nowhere else to go. City employees weren't even being paid real wages—they were given scrip instead."

He gestures toward my notebook. "It felt like anarchy. A total breakdown of order. And people recognized this strike could spark something bigger—a real workers' revolution."

Slaughter is blunt. "The sheriff couldn't control anything. His deputies were overwhelmed—outside Auto-Lite, and inside courtrooms too. Lawlessness reigned. Even basic order seemed impossible."

Outside, the wind slaps against the house, rattling loose storm shutters. I imagine the courthouse lawn packed with bodies, fists raised against the rain, against the government, against despair itself.

George raps his glass on the table, snapping me back.

I review my notes and ask, "Looking back now—fifty years later—what do you think made Toledo such fertile ground for this kind of upheaval?"

Slaughter smiles and gazes out the window. "It wasn't planned. It wasn't calculated. It was an accident that it happened here first." His voice, earlier soft, turns firm. "If it could happen here, it could happen anywhere."

"What stood out to you most from that time?"

Slaughter's eyes narrow. He leans forward, voice dropping to a conspiratorial whisper. "The fear, Gray. You could smell it." He taps his nose. "Like ozone before a storm."

I furrow my brow. "Fear from the strikers?"

He barks a laugh, sharp and sudden. "Hell no! From the bigwigs. Flanagan, the Auto-Lite brass, even that souse Judge Windsor." Slaughter mimics holding a gavel, his hand trembling. " 'This isn't a courtroom, Slaughter,' " he slurs, imitating Windsor. " 'It's a zoo, and I'm the zookeeper.' Can you believe that horseshit?"

"He said that to you?" I lean in, incredulous.

"Right to my face," Slaughter says, a glint of old anger in his eyes.

He pauses, eyes distant. "When Judge Windsor issued that injunction limiting picketing to twenty-five people at each entrance, we knew it was an attempt to strangle the strike. The workers were outraged—and with justification. Charles Pepper, one of the union organizers, defied the injunction outright. He told the strikers that if they were going to jail him for breaking it, they'd have to jail all of them."

I take notes as Slaughter continues. "Hundreds of strikers and supporters crammed into every available space in the courtroom that day. Workers, families, Communists, Socialists, teachers, unemployed folks from all over Toledo.

It felt like half the city had descended on that courthouse lawn.”

“What was the atmosphere like in court?”

Slaughter settles into his chair, a smile tugging at his lips. “Chaotic,” he says. “The judge was drunk—everyone knew it—and he couldn’t control the crowd. People were shouting obscenities, cracking jokes at his expense. It was lawlessness in every sense.”

He gestures toward a book on his shelf. “One of Auto-Lite’s attorneys even accused us of being Bolsheviks trying to overthrow America,” he adds with a wry grin. “Said law and order had disappeared.”

“But let me tell you—when Charles Pepper stood up in that packed courthouse . . . ” He pauses, lost in the memory. “You should’ve seen Windsor’s face. White as a sheet.”

“What did Pepper say?”

I scribble as Slaughter recounts how Pepper had taken the stand and pleaded guilty to violating the injunction.

“Pepper stood there and admitted his guilt. But then all the other workers stood up and shouted: ‘Your honor! If he’s guilty, we’re all guilty!’ ”

It’s fascinating to hear different versions of the same story. I’d spoken to Pepper earlier—his version matched Slaughter’s, though he added that Slaughter had told him to pull out his handkerchief as a signal to the others.

“The judge didn’t know what to do,” Slaughter says with a chuckle. “He realized he couldn’t throw them all in jail. In the end, he dismissed the entire case.”

“That must have been an incredible moment for you.”

“Incredible?” Slaughter scoffs, reaching for his bourbon. “It was terrifying and beautiful. Like watching the world turn upside down.” He takes a sip, ice clinking. “But that’s Toledo for you. Always on the brink of something. Never quite getting there.”

I cock my head. “What do you mean?”

Slaughter fixes me with a penetrating stare. "You're young, Gray. You see the rot in this city, but you don't know how deep it goes." He gestures toward the window. "Toledo's been shooting itself in the foot since before you were born. Hell, since before I was born."

"What do you mean?"

"Take the 1800s. While Chicago was becoming a railroad hub, we were digging canals like it was going out of style." He strokes his chin. "Then we missed the boat on automobiles—stuck on making bicycles until it was almost too late."

For once, I've encountered someone more cynical about Toledo than me. Strangely, I feel a flicker of defensiveness.

"But we adapted, right? The Jeep plant," I begin, but Slaughter cuts me off.

"The Jeep plant," he repeats, his tone sharp. "And now what? We're watching jobs disappear faster than Stuart could down a bottle of hooch." He sits back in his chair, and for the first time, he looks every one of his eighty-one years. "We cling to the past like it's a life raft, Gray. But it's an anchor. And it's dragging us down."

His words hit like a punch to the gut. I think of the boarded-up storefronts downtown, the quiet desperation in my parents' voices when they talk about the future.

"So what's the answer?"

Slaughter's expression softens. "You want to fix Toledo? Start by admitting it's broken. Study the actual history—not the Chamber of Commerce version." He catches my eye, gaze intense. "And for God's sake, quit waiting for the next big thing to save us. We've got to save ourselves."

My mind is racing. Slaughter's pessimism is contagious, but there's a kernel of truth in it I can't ignore. As I gather my notes, a question nags at me.

"Mr. Slaughter, after everything you've seen—the strike, McCarthyism, all of it—do you still have hope for Toledo?"

He's quiet for a long time, staring into his glass. When he looks up, there's a fierce light in his eyes.

"Hope? Hope is for amateurs. What we need is grit. The same kind those strikers had in '34." He points a finger at me. "You've got fire in you, Gray. Use it. But remember—this city eats idealists for breakfast. Arm yourself with the truth, or you'll end up another footnote."

He looks into the distance. "You know, Gray, after the strike, we thought we'd changed everything. Thought Toledo would become a beacon for workers' rights across the country."

"But it did, didn't it? The strike was a turning point—"

He waves his hand and grimaces. "A turning point, sure. But to where?" His gaze sharpens. "Look around you, kid. Take a good look. What do you see?"

I hesitate, caught between honesty and loyalty to my hometown. "I see . . . challenges. But also potential."

Slaughter snorts. "Potential. That's Toledo's curse, you know. Always at the edge of something great, never quite getting there." He takes a sip of bourbon, then adds in a low voice, "Reminds me of someone I used to know."

The weight in his words makes me pause. I sense he's not talking about the city anymore.

"Mr. Slaughter, do you regret—"

"Regrets are a luxury, Gray," he interrupts, his tone sharp. "What matters is what you do next." He gestures toward the window. "This city—it's at another turning point. The question is, who's going to steer it this time?"

I feel a sudden pressure in my chest, as if Slaughter's words carry a challenge aimed directly at me.

"And you think it should be someone who understands Toledo's history?" I ask.

Slaughter's eyes glitter. "History, yes. But even more important—someone who can see past it." He leans forward, voice low. "There are people in this town, Gray, powerful people. People who'd rather keep Toledo locked in the past. Makes it easier to control."

The implication hangs in the air between us. I think of the stories I've been chasing, the whispers of corruption I've heard.

"Mr. Slaughter, are you saying—"

He holds up a hand, stopping me. "I'm not saying anything, kid. That's your job." He sits back, looking exhausted. "Remember, the truth isn't always in what people say. Sometimes, it's in what they don't say."

As I drive home later, Slaughter's words echo in my mind. I realize he's given me much more than a history lesson.

He's handed me a torch—and a warning.

The question is: Am I ready to carry it?

CHAPTER 44
1934
THE PRESIDENT, THE MEDIATOR, AND THE TORCHBEARERS

May 25

A harsh light from the rising sun illuminated the aftermath of the previous night's violence over Toledo. The streets near the Electric Auto-Lite factory were littered with debris—spent tear gas canisters, shattered glass, and remnants of makeshift barricades. The air was thick with the acrid smell of smoke, a grim reminder of the chaos that had unfolded. The factory gate hung open. A tear in the fence flapped against the pole like a loose shirt sleeve. The clock above the entrance was cracked. The minute hand was gone. The hour hand pointed somewhere between four and five, then stopped. Nobody looked up at it.

Across the street, a woman stood in silence outside a bakery, staring at shattered shop windows. The owner, broom in hand, sighed as he swept glass shards into neat piles. "God help us if this goes on much longer," he muttered.

Outside the factory gates, the National Guardsmen, weary from the night's confrontations, maintained a vigilant watch. Sweat and grime stained their uniforms. The workers, too, bore the marks of battle—bruised knuckles, bandaged heads, and a simmering anger that threatened to ignite.

News of the deaths of two men had spread like wildfire. The two strikers had become martyrs overnight, their names rallying cries for a movement teetering between despair and defiance.

A middle-aged press operator, his sleeve still crusted with dried blood, repeated the names to anyone who'd listen. "They can't have died for nothing," he said, voice hoarse, eyes red-rimmed from tear gas and grief.

The stringer spotted the man from Earl Street near the back of the crowd outside the Safety Building—collar turned up, hands uncovered, face bruised yellow and green.

The man wasn't shouting. He wasn't even holding a sign. Just standing there, shoulders hunched, eyes fixed on nothing.

"Didn't expect to see you here," the stringer said quietly.

The man didn't look over. "Didn't expect to be here."

"You walked out?"

"Two days ago. Didn't want to wait until someone else made the choice for me."

The stringer glanced at his coat—a tear near the sleeve, dried blood on the cuff.

"Was it worth it?"

The man finally looked at him. "Ask me when we win."

May 26

In the bloodshed's wake, pressure mounted on all sides to find a resolution. President Franklin Roosevelt, increasingly alarmed, sent a skilled negotiator—a former judge and son of a former president—to Toledo. Known for his calm demeanor and impartiality, the mediator sought to bridge the chasm between strikers and management.

He convened meetings at a neutral hotel, away from the factory's shadow. Representatives from AFL Federal Local

18384, Auto-Lite management, and city officials gathered around a large oak table, the weight of recent events pressing heavily upon them.

The union's demands were clear: a 10 percent wage increase, union recognition, and improved working conditions. Auto-Lite's representatives, faces etched with fatigue, countered with offers that fell short. The chasm seemed insurmountable, but the mediator's steady hand kept the dialogue alive.

A union delegate, a short man with steel-rimmed glasses, spoke with quiet intensity. "We aren't asking for luxury. We want dignity. Fair pay for honest work."

An Auto-Lite manager fidgeted with his cufflinks. The mediator steepled his fingers. "Gentlemen, we are here to find common ground. Shall we proceed?"

Negotiations continued in fits and starts. Voices rose, then fell into weary silence as each side retreated, regrouped, and returned.

May 28

As talks dragged on, unrest simmered across Toledo. The Lucas County Unemployed League rallied support. In dingy union halls, fiery speeches echoed off peeling plaster walls. The prospect of a general strike loomed.

At the Central Labor Council's packed headquarters, workers from a dozen industries debated fiercely. A small, fiery factory worker stood on a chair, gripping it for strength. "We either stand with them now or wait till they come for us next!" she shouted. The crowd erupted, pounding fists on tables.

By May 29, sixty-eight of the city's 103 unions had voted in favor of a general strike. The threat of a citywide shutdown cast a long shadow over the negotiating table.

May 29

The atmosphere grew more volatile. Picket lines swelled with workers from other industries. The National Guard, once a deterrent, now inflamed passions.

At the factory entrance, an older guardsman watched the crowd with weary eyes. A younger recruit beside him asked, "Do you think we'll have to shoot again?" The old man shook his head. "Pray we never do."

Inside, Auto-Lite management was frantic. The vice president paced outside his office, demanding assurances from the governor. Local authorities passed secretive orders. Preparations for martial law had begun—though no one dared speak the words aloud.

May 31

Union leaders drafted urgent telegrams to Roosevelt in the cramped back room of the union hall, amid cigarette smoke and coffee cups. An older secretary finished one appeal with a flourish: "We trust you will not abandon the working people of Toledo in our hour of greatest need."

That evening, a union leader stood before a packed hall. "If we have no resolution soon, the council will call a general strike. Toledo stands ready to shut down."

Desperation bred boldness. The Central Labor Council sent an urgent appeal to Roosevelt, seeking federal intervention. The Committee of Twenty-Three set June 2 as the date for a final decision. By then, eighty-five unions had pledged support.

June 1

News arrived of an unexpected victory: Electricians had negotiated a 20 percent wage increase. The deal was ratified overnight, injecting cautious optimism into the labor community.

At a corner newsstand, two Auto-Lite picketers read the headline. "If they can win, so can we," one said.

The mediator seized on the momentum, pushing talks late into the night. Outside, a massive torchlight procession snaked through downtown—twenty thousand protestors marching in silence. Flames flickered against drawn faces, reflecting their quiet resolve.

June 2

In the early hours, negotiations bore fruit. A tentative agreement was reached: a 5 percent wage increase, a minimum wage of thirty-five cents an hour, and union recognition.

At the union hall, workers gathered to hear the terms. A young woman clutched her husband's arm. Silence followed the reading—tense, expectant. Then someone said, "It's something, isn't it? It's a start." Relief washed over tired faces. The vote passed—not unanimously, but decisively.

Later that day, the proposal was presented to the strikers. The assembly hall buzzed with murmurs. Leaders acknowledged the progress and the cost. The vote ratified the agreement. Subdued relief, not jubilation, greeted the decision.

June 3

The strike officially ended.

Workers returned to the factory, their faces a mosaic of weariness, pride, and lingering resentment. The machinery roared back to life, but the echoes of the past weeks lingered in the clatter and hum.

At the gates, National Guardsmen packed up without fanfare. The city exhaled. Tension began to ebb.

In the press room, a boy from Department Two looked around, expecting everything to feel different. An older worker squeezed his shoulder. "It might not feel like much right now, but we've planted a seed here."

Outside, a woman watched her husband pass through the gates. Relief mingled with apprehension. "They didn't give us everything," she whispered, "but at least they heard us this time."

Victory was incomplete.

But something important had shifted.

CHAPTER 45
1984
IT WAS FIFTY YEARS AGO TODAY

I adjust my tie as I approach the Lucas County Courthouse on a cool day in early June. The plaza is already filling with people—a mix of older faces weathered by time and younger activists carrying signs and banners.

Nostalgia and renewed purpose charge the air. As I walk, I catch snatches of conversation:

"Can you believe it's been fifty years?" an elderly man says to his companion. "Feels like yesterday we were out there on the picket lines."

"Yeah, and we're still fighting the same battles," his friend replies with a weary chuckle.

Near the podium, I spot a familiar face—Ted Selander, one of the original strike participants and something of a local legend. Now in his seventies, he stands tall despite the years, his eyes sharp as he surveys the crowd.

"Mr. Selander," I call out, approaching. "Gray Wheeler from *The Sword*. Mind if I ask a few questions before the ceremony starts?"

Selander turns, a smile creasing his face. "Sure thing, son. What do you want to know?"

"What does it mean to you, being here fifty years later?"

His eyes grow distant. "It means we didn't fight for nothing," he says. "Look around. These people remember. They're still carrying the torch we lit back in '34."

As we talk, the plaza fills. I notice a group of UAW officials in union jackets. Nearby, a cluster of younger activists wear T-shirts that read "The Struggle Continues" and "Remember Auto-Lite."

The ceremony begins with the strains of a union song drifting over the crowd. I recognize the melody of "Solidarity Forever." Voices join in—some wavering with age, others strong and clear.

Off to the side, I spot someone I didn't expect.

My dad.

He's standing near the edge of the crowd, hands in his coat pockets, brow furrowed like he's trying to remember something he never quite lived.

I didn't ask him to come. I figured he wouldn't.

But here he is.

I move toward him. He nods, eyes fixed on the makeshift stage.

"I didn't know you were coming," I say.

"I wasn't sure either," he replies. "Until this morning."

A long pause.

"I always thought the ones who raised hell were troublemakers," he says, almost to himself. "But I've been reading the stuff you've been writing."

He doesn't look at me.

"You got this one right."

The ceremony continues. Someone reads the names of the dead. The mayor stumbles over one of them.

"The Auto-Lite strike was more than an industrial dispute," he declares. "It was a turning point that shaped the very soul of our city."

Then Ted Selander takes the podium. The crowd hushes.

"Fifty years ago," he begins, voice strong despite his age, "we stood on these very streets, fighting for our rights—for our dignity as workers. We faced tear gas, bullets, and clubs. But we stood firm because we knew our cause was righteous."

He pauses, gaze sweeping the crowd.

"Some say our fight is over. That we won our battles long ago. But I say to you—the struggle continues. Look around at the factories closing, at the jobs being shipped overseas. We may have won in '34, but there are always new battles to fight."

I notice tears in the eyes of many older attendees, memories stirred by Selander's words.

Next come speakers from various unions and activist groups. A young woman from the UAW speaks passionately about the need for continued solidarity in the face of plant closures and outsourcing. An older Teamster reminisces about how the Auto-Lite strike inspired workers across the country.

Between speeches, I circulate through the crowd, gathering quotes and impressions. I speak to Mary Thornton, the daughter of a striker.

"I remember my mother cooking enormous pots of soup," Mary says, eyes misty. "She'd take it down to the picket lines to feed the strikers. We had little, but everyone shared what they had."

As the afternoon wears on, the mood shifts—from commemoration to renewed commitment. Speakers draw parallels between the Auto-Lite strike and today's labor struggles.

A local organizer takes the stage, voice ringing out over the plaza.

"The spirit of Auto-Lite lives on! Today, we face new challenges—globalization, automation, anti-union legislation. But like our predecessors in 1934, we will stand united. We will fight for our rights!"

The crowd erupts in cheers, fists raised in solidarity. I feel a shiver run down my spine. History isn't just being remembered—it's being reawakened.

As the ceremony draws to a close, Selander returns to the podium.

"Fifty years ago," he says, voice thick with emotion, "we showed the world what solidarity means. We proved that when workers stand together, we are a force that cannot be ignored."

He pauses, looking out over the sea of faces.

"To the young people here today, I say this: Learn from our struggle. Carry it forward. The fight for justice is never truly over."

Applause bursts from the crowd. As people begin to disperse, I see small groups forming—older strikers and their families talking with younger activists. The past and present of Toledo's labor movement are intertwining before my eyes.

I approach one such group, where a gray-haired woman is speaking to a young man in a "Workers Unite" T-shirt.

"Excuse me," I say. "I'm Gray Wheeler from *The Sword*. Would you mind sharing your thoughts on today's event?"

The woman smiles. "I'm Margaret Dawson. My father was on the picket lines in '34. I grew up hearing stories about the strike—about how it changed everything for working people in Toledo."

The young man nods. "And that's why we're still fighting today. I'm Mike. I work at the Jeep plant, and we're facing our own struggles now. Hearing about Auto-Lite gives us strength. Knowing that workers stood up and won before."

As I jot down their words, I feel the weight of the story I have to tell. This isn't just about remembering a historical event. It's about a living, breathing movement that connects generations.

The wind picks up. I zip my coat.

My father stands beside me the whole time.

He doesn't say another word.

He doesn't need to.

PART 3

CHAPTER 46

1984

HAPPINESS IS A WARM RIFLE

No rest for the wicked. I file the Auto-Lite commemoration piece and grab a sandwich I promptly forget to eat. The newspaper archive beckons—a fluorescent-lit cave where answers go to nap.

Kirby's already there when I arrive, cross-legged on the floor beside a stack of dusty boxes marked "Feldman—Misc. 1930s." She looks up from a folder, brow furrowed—not worried, just absorbed. I've come to recognize the expression.

"These boxes are a disaster," she says. "Three decades of files, no index, and a bonus layer of mildew. Maybe you should've left them at your place."

I sit beside her and peel open the next box. "Anything interesting?"

"Depends how you feel about union newsletters and water-damaged city council minutes."

We work quietly. The only sounds are the scrape of paper and Kirby muttering at bad handwriting.

Then she stops.

"Hey. Gray. Look at this."

She holds out a black-and-white photo, warped at the edges. It shows a mass of workers in motion, flanked by uniformed men forming a line with bayonets forward. In the corner, a small cluster of men are standing near the factory gates, separate from the crowd. All wear rough work clothes—except one.

I take it from her and hold it up under the fluorescent light.

The image is grainy but unmistakable. It shows the chaos outside the Auto-Lite factory. A contingent of National Guardsmen are standing with bayonets pointed at the crowd. On the left, a group of men stands behind the Guardsmen at the factory doors. They're all in shabby coveralls—except for one young man in a shirt and tie. While the others have their hands at their sides, this man holds a rifle across his chest, his expression grim.

I tilt the photo toward the light. "Who's this?"

A tall man. Shirt and tie. Hair slicked back. Holding a rifle like it belongs there.

I flip the photo over. On the back, in Feldman's neat cursive:

May 24, 1934. Elm & Champlain. Owen Sinclair—confirmed.

I say the name aloud. "Owen Sinclair."

Kirby shakes her head. "Ring any bells?"

"Not off the top of my head."

I run a thumb along the edge of the photo. The paper is stiff with age, but the ink is clear. Sinclair. Holding a rifle. In the middle of the bloodiest labor standoff Toledo ever saw.

"Could've been security?"

"He doesn't look like security," Kirby says. "And why would Feldman write it like that—'confirmed'?"

I nod. "You don't confirm someone unless they're important."

We stare at the image a moment longer.

Then I say, "I think it's time to figure out who Owen Sinclair was."

Kirby reaches for her satchel. "I'll check the stacks. You pull the city directories."

She scratches her chin. "Why does that sound familiar? Wait a minute, I remember—that clipping I found right back when you were first looking into Auto-Lite. This guy was Clarence Flanagan's son-in-law."

"Oh yeah. I guess that explains him being at Auto-Lite, but what's with the rifle?"

We dive into the physical archives, combing through folders permeated with dust and old glue. There are a few profiles on Sinclair—press releases from companies he chaired in the '50s, social pages from the '60s showing him at charity galas, a glowing 1978 feature where he donates to a hospital.

All clean. Too clean. The same language over and over: "Reclusive industrialist." "Quiet philanthropist."

Kirby shakes her head. "It's all spin. But look—here's something interesting. Every one of these companies changed names or merged a year after Sinclair joined the board."

"Shell game," I mutter. "Hide the money. Hide the trail."

I nod. "Which is why I think we need to check corporate records. Business directories. Property holdings. Sinclair's empire might be in the stacks over at the library. Let's meet there tomorrow."

I tuck the photo into a folder.

Until today, the Auto-Lite story was about the past.

Now it feels like someone just walked out of it.

CHAPTER 47

MAY 1934

THE SON-IN-LAW

The streets outside the Auto-Lite plant churn with bodies. Tear gas clouds the air, and the sounds of shattering glass and shouting voices echo down the alleyways. The picket lines have become battlegrounds. But the son-in-law stands above it all, watching from the second-floor window of the company office.

He adjusts his tie, though sweat darkens the collar of his crisp shirt. Below him, chaos reigns. The workers—filthy and furious. The Guard—hesitating. No one in control. No one strong enough to end this.

Behind him, the tycoon paces like a penned bull.

"These bastards won't back down."

The son-in-law straightens his shoulders, the weight of expectation settling across them like a mantle.

"Then we make them," he says.

The tycoon glares, sizing him up like a man appraising a tool he's not sure he can trust.

"You think you're ready to handle this?"

The younger man's jaw tightens. *This is why I married your daughter, old man,* he thinks. *Not for love. Not even for comfort. For legacy. For power. For the future I deserve.*

"I know what needs to be done."

The tycoon believes he does. That's what troubles him.

He'd had him investigated, back when his daughter first brought him around for Sunday roast and soft smiles. Too poised. Too polished. Knew exactly when to speak—and when silence worked better.

His parents had died young in a house fire. There'd been talk of an orphanage, then a church-run boarding house in Ottawa. The details were thin, but not clean. The file said he'd been quiet. Watchful. One line stuck with the tycoon: *"He does not respond when provoked."* Not that he didn't feel it— just that he didn't react until he chose to.

He'd liked the fire he saw in him back then. Relentless. Clear-eyed. Smarter than the other second sons sniffing around his money. Someone to carry the legacy forward.

But lately, the coldness worried him. Not the calculation— that he understood. But the lack of pause. The sense that the ledger mattered more than the cost.

The tycoon had taught him to move the pieces. But he hadn't taught him how to stop the game.

Now he wondered if he should have.

The tycoon snorts and turns away. The son-in-law slips out before things sour further, heart pounding with sharp, hot clarity.

That night, as workers clash with police and National Guard soldiers, the son-in-law moves unseen through the factory's shadowed halls. No one questions him. No one even sees him. He's another ghost in the machinery.

At the loading dock, he crouches behind stacked crates. The rifle in his hands feels heavier than expected. Colder.

He sets his sights down the broken alleyway where strikers chant and shove against the Guard line.

They think they can win by shouting, he thinks. *They think the company will fold under noise and numbers.*

He knows better.

Victory requires blood. A little. Just enough.

He raises the rifle. His hands do not shake.

Through the iron sights, he picks a target—a man shouting and waving a flag. In front of him, a National Guardsman stumbles and falls as a brick thrown by a young farmer bounces off his helmet. If he fires now, it will look like the Guardsman fired the shot: An idea made flesh. He exhales and squeezes the trigger.

The man jerks backward, collapsing onto the pavement like a puppet with cut strings.

The crowd panics. Sinclair doesn't hesitate. He fires again, hitting a woman trying to pull her friend to safety.

Then he swings the rifle toward the Guards' position and fires into the bricks two feet from their helmets.

The reaction is immediate.

"We're under fire! Return fire! RETURN FIRE!" a lieutenant screams.

The National Guard unleashes hell. Bullets rip through the night air, shattering windows, tearing into flesh. The crowd scatters in a tide of screams and blood.

The son-in-law watches without blinking. This is how the world is won. Not with speeches. With force.

He has no sons to inherit what he's building. But he has the city—the structures, the secrets, the silence—etched deeper than any bloodline. A man can live forever if he controls what is remembered and what is forgotten.

He slips back into the factory unnoticed. No one sees the son-in-law who started a massacre.

No one—except the crouched figure across the street, a camera clicking once, twice. A mechanical witness to murder.

By the time city officials arrive, the son-in-law is seated behind the tycoon's desk, a drink in hand, his expression cool and untroubled.

History will remember this as necessary.

If it remembers it at all.

CHAPTER 48
1984
ANOTHER BRICK IN THE WALL

The basement smells like damp paper and old laundry. I flip on the fluorescent light and drop my bag on the floor.

The photo's still in my pocket. I pull it out, smooth the crease, and stare at the man with the rifle.

Half-turned, blurred by distance — but there's no mistaking the posture. The confidence. The ownership of the moment.

Owen Sinclair.

I don't know who he is yet. But I know this: He wasn't supposed to be holding a rifle. He wasn't supposed to be there at all.

I clear a patch of wood paneling on the far wall. Strip off two tacked-up Waite High yearbook pages and a faded Rolling Stone cover with Jim Morrison — the one titled *"He's Hot. He's Sexy. He's Dead."* The tape peels with a soft rip.

On the desk, I spread out everything I've gathered: Sidney's list. The UAW leaflets. Clippings from the morgue files. A torn page from my notebook: *White Tower—Thursday—"He fired first."*

I tack them up, one at a time. No order yet—just shapes. Threads waiting for anchors.

Then I open a drawer in the laundry nook and find a spool of red yarn. I don't remember what it was originally for. Probably Christmas.

I run a line from the 1934 police report to Feldman's obituary. From Feldman's final column to Ferner's press pass. A note connecting Sinclair's photo to a map of the Vistula district—the Auto-Lite factory and surrounding streets. The yarn pulls gently under tension, like it knows how much weight it's meant to carry.

The Wall breathes.

Footsteps creak above. Then my mother's voice from the top of the stairs.

"What are you doing up so early — or is it late? You redecorating?"

"Organizing," I call back.

She doesn't ask what. The light switches off. Her footsteps fade.

I sit on the edge of the bed, notebook in hand. I stare at the photo again. The man in the tie and pressed shirt stands just behind the line of Guardsmen, holding the rifle like it belongs there. Not like a threat. Not like a prop. Like a tool. Like something he's used before.

He's not shouting. Not flinching. Just watching.

I lean closer, tracing the faint outline of his jaw.

"Not a soldier. Not a striker. Not a bystander," I murmur.

Something about that rifle—the way it's held, not swung—keeps echoing in my head.

I don't know who pulled the trigger in 1934. But I know the man in the tie didn't look like a bystander.

I flip the photo over again. Feldman's handwriting: Confirmed.

A chill runs through me.

You don't confirm someone unless they matter.

And this man matters.

My hand drifts to the phone.

I'm still too wired to sleep, and there's only one person I know who answers at this hour without complaint.

I dial Larry's hospital line from the basement extension, phone cord wrapped around my wrist like a tether.

He picks up fast.

"You're up late," he says. "Working on your murder conspiracy?"

"Sort of."

"Are you still working on this with that girl from the archives? What was her name, Kiki?"

"Kirby, yes."

"Have you done anything more than 'research' together?"

"Moving right along, Larry!"

"A man stuck in a hospital bed can't help but live vicariously through his friends."

I shake my head, staring at the Wall.

"Listen, I need a favor. I found something. A photo."

"What kind of photo?"

"Auto-Lite strike. National Guard, early crowd. In the corner, there's a guy—not in uniform. Shirt, tie, rifle in hand. Doesn't match anyone else in the frame."

Larry pauses. "So what, you think it's staged?"

"No. He wasn't part of the Guard or the workers. He's standing apart. Like he belonged, but not with either side."

"Name?"

"Owen Sinclair. It's written on the back in Feldman's handwriting. '*Confirmed.*' "

Larry goes quiet. I can hear the hum of hospital equipment through the line.

"Sinclair . . . " he says slowly. "Doesn't ring any bells for me. Not in a union context, anyway."

"I was hoping it would. It feels important. The way the name's written—like Feldman wanted to make sure no one missed it."

"You got anything else? Title, company, role?"

"Turns out he was old man Flanagan's son-in-law—explains the fact that he was there, but not why he was carrying a rifle. Kirby and I are going to check city directories, property records. Maybe old Chamber of Commerce bulletins. He would've been in management. Or something above that."

Larry exhales. "Sounds like one of those names people don't say out loud. The kind you only find in ink and footnotes."

"That's what I'm afraid of."

"Well, send me what you've got. I'll ask around. A couple of the old homicide guys here still trade stories over bad coffee. Someone might've crossed paths with a Sinclair."

"Appreciate it."

"And Gray?"

"Yeah?"

"Be careful where you pull. Guys like that don't always leave loose ends. Sometimes they cut them off."

Twelve hours later, the phone rings again—this time while I'm at the office, pouring a stale cup of newsroom coffee.

"Larry?"

"Yeah." His voice is tight. "I've been working the phones all morning."

I sit down. "Talk to me. Have you found something?"

"No, which is stranger than finding something. I asked about Sinclair. Got nada. Which is weird as hell. A guy with that kind of money? That kind of influence? There should be lawsuits. Business filings. Dirty laundry."

"But there's nothing."

"More than nothing," he says. "It's too clean. Like someone scrubbed it. And not just from public records. Some departments I called didn't even know who I was talking about."

My stomach tightens.

Larry continues, "But while I was digging, I hit something else. Carl Madison."

I blink. "Who's that?"

"Ex-cop. Was involved in some . . . questionable shit down in Cleveland in the late '60s. Dirty money, disappeared evidence. Got kicked off the force, on the QT. Then started doing 'security work' for private clients in the '70s."

"Let me guess," I say. "Sinclair?"

"I can't prove a direct connection. But Madison's name pops up in a bunch of places Sinclair's companies owned. Real estate deals, contractor records. Always third-party, but I'm telling you—it's him."

"Is he still active?"

"He's a ghost now. Last confirmed sighting was in '82—some muscle job in Dayton. Since then, zip."

"But you think Sinclair still has him on the payroll."

"I think it's worse than that," Larry says. "I think he's been cleaning up after Sinclair for decades."

I go still. "You mean—"

"Yeah. A guy who knows how to make someone disappear and never leave a fingerprint. Do you think Ferner and Feldman died because they tripped over the wrong story? You're not the first, Gray. You're just the latest."

I run a hand through my hair. "So, what do I do?"

Larry sighs. "You find everything you can, fast. You publish before they can shut you up. And you watch your back."

CHAPTER 49
1984
IT'S ONLY WORDS

The next morning, Kirby and I meet at the main city library. Not *The Sword*'s musty archives—the public building on Michigan Street with sun-faded blinds and carpet that smells like old dust.

Kirby's already staked out a table in the back corner. She has a legal pad, a stack of Toledo city directories, and a half-drunk cup of coffee that smells burnt. I slide into the seat across from her.

"I've got three decades of chamber bulletins and zoning records," she says, nodding to the pile beside her. "Let's see if this Sinclair guy ever left a footprint."

We divide the years and start reading.

For a while, it's nothing. Names that don't match. Property transfers with no context. A few companies with bland names like Midland Partners and Great Lakes Consolidated, registered to PO boxes or now-defunct addresses.

But after an hour, I pause over a typed entry in the 1959 city directory:

"Owen Sinclair—Municipal Relations Liaison—Electric Auto-Lite Co."

I nudge the book toward Kirby. "He worked for Auto-Lite."

She squints at the title. "Municipal Relations? That's not factory-floor. That's power lunches and handshakes."

I write it down.

A few minutes later, she finds something in a zoning commission meeting from the late '60s: a variance approval for a new industrial complex under a holding company called South Ridge Development. One of the signatories?

O. Sinclair.

"Could be a coincidence," she says.

"Could be a pattern," I reply.

We keep going.

Kirby leads us to the public records section like she's casing the place. "We'll want city business directories," she whispers. "Maybe tax assessor archives, real estate filings, any of the cross-indexes by company name, address, and officer."

I blink. "You say that like you've done this before."

She grins. "Archivists are librarians with secrets."

We get to work.

For the next hour, we're buried in reference books. Kirby flips through city directories like a blackjack dealer on speed. I trace property transfers on yellowing ledger sheets, cross-referencing names that might be shell companies. And slowly—maddeningly—a pattern emerges.

A company called Midwestern Equities bought a half-dozen properties in East Toledo in 1950. That company merged with Great Lakes Trust in 1956. Then Great Lakes Trust divested into Second Growth Holdings in the early '60s. Guess who was listed as a director on all three?

Owen Sinclair.

"He never stays on the paperwork for long," Kirby says, circling each entry. "But he's always in the first round. He gets things moving. Then vanishes."

"Like a shark cutting through water," I say. "Never breaking the surface."

I pull out a plat book and start marking dots. "Look at the locations. They all cluster near former factory sites—Auto-Lite, Willys, that abandoned chemical plant on Front Street."

Kirby squints. "Industrial real estate. Cheap during the collapse. High potential value in a rebound."

"And ideal places to launder cash or hide . . . anything."

"What about this one?" she says, pointing to "Rockridge Security." "It shows up in a half-dozen contractor permits for 'guard services' in these buildings. Hired by Second Growth Holdings."

I flip through a separate directory, trying to connect Rockridge to a person. It takes fifteen minutes and three indexes, but finally I hit it.

"Here," I say, jabbing the page. "Carl Madison. Listed as Rockridge's 'operations manager' in 1975."

Kirby studies the entry. "So Sinclair's company hires Madison's company . . . which is basically Madison."

I grab my notebook and start sketching. At the center: Sinclair. Lines branch out to each company, with dotted lines connecting them to Madison. I underline two addresses that repeat across multiple filings.

Kirby watches, quiet.

I say, half to her, half to myself, "This is it. The infrastructure. How Sinclair kept everything off the radar—property, money, muscle."

She taps a note I'd jotted down earlier. "And if Ferner and Feldman were digging into this when they were killed . . ."

"Then we're next," I say.

The gravity of it lands like a weight between us. We've moved beyond theory. This isn't about a forgotten strike or a historic scandal anymore. This is about a man who's been constructing a shadow empire for fifty years—and eliminating anyone who pokes too hard.

Kirby breaks the silence. "We need to copy this. All of it."

We spend the next half hour feeding quarters into the ancient photocopier. My hands shake as I gather the pages into folders.

Outside, the sun is going down, casting long shadows across the marble floor. I catch our reflection in the glass door—two people weighed down with paper and half-formed fear.

"I'm going to write it all up," I say. "Every connection. Every thread. Before we even talk to Sinclair."

Kirby looks over. "Because if we don't make it to the end, someone needs to know what we found."

"Exactly."

By early afternoon, we've mapped out a dozen data points. None of them damning. But taken together, they hum with quiet pressure. Variances approved. Environmental citations dismissed. Shell companies registered, folded, reborn.

It's like Sinclair's signature is always one step off the page.

Kirby leans back, rubbing her eyes. "So this guy goes from being present at the worst labor massacre in Toledo's history to holding invisible power across half the city. And no one ever mentions him by name?"

"Not unless they're writing checks."

I glance at the scratch pad:

- Owen Sinclair—Photo 1934—Auto-Lite
- 1959: Municipal Liaison—Auto-Lite
- Zoning Approval—South Ridge Dev.
- Links to 3+ shell companies

None of this is conclusive. But it's no longer coincidence either.

We've found the shape of a shadow.

And it's moving.

Back at *The Sword*, Kirby digs through the business license archives while I cross-reference company officers from the zoning files.

We're on our third pot of newsroom coffee, and the fluorescent lights feel like they're peeling the skin off my eyes. But then Kirby makes a sound—not a word exactly, more like a breath caught mid-reaction.

She holds up a thin yellow folder.

"I just found a 1981 renewal form for South Ridge Development."

I perk up. "Still active?"

"Technically, yes. But here's the interesting part—look who signed off as managing officer."

She passes the page across the desk. I read the name.

Thomas J. Dellinger.

It takes a second to click.

Then I remember.

"He's on the board of the Toledo Port Authority," I say. "And the downtown redevelopment committee."

Kirby nods. "He gave a speech last month at the Portside ribbon-cutting. Remember? You called it urban taxidermy."

I don't smile.

This Dellinger guy isn't a ghost. He's a fixture. Civic pride, clean-shaven, coat-and-tie optimism.

And he's listed as managing officer of a holding company originally tied to Owen Sinclair.

I grab a notepad and flip back through my notes on Ferner's reporting.

"Wait—Ferner mentioned Dellinger," I say. "In one of the interview logs. Said he'd asked for comment and got stonewalled."

Kirby finds the sheet. "Here—Dellinger declined to comment on Ferner's allegations about shell companies buying up East Toledo properties on behalf of undisclosed investors."

I sit back.

The photo. The rifle. The hidden hand behind property deals and zoning gifts.

And now one of Sinclair's corporate descendants is sitting on a dais downtown, posing for the mayor's newsletter.

"It's not just history," I say.

Kirby doesn't answer. She doesn't have to.

We both know what this means. This isn't just about uncovering the past. It's about stopping the future from repeating it.

Back in the basement, I add a new corner to the Wall— Midwestern Equities, tied with twine to Sinclair and AP Parts. The yarn's starting to sag under its own weight.

CHAPTER 50

1984

THERE'S DANGER ON THE EDGE OF TOWN

I leave Kirby behind to close up the research room and walk out to my car just before sunset. The street is quiet. Too quiet. Everyone's gone home, or to bars, or into hiding.

My car's parked half a block away—same spot as this morning. Nothing looks out of place.

Until I open the door.

There's something on the seat. Just sitting there, bold as brass.

A ledger book.

I pick it up carefully, like it might explode.

It's one of those old red accounting journals—clothbound, thick paper, probably from the fifties or sixties. No label on the front. No name. Just a faint grease stain and the smell of dry ink.

I flip it open.

The pages are blank.

Every one of them.

Except the last.

On the final page, someone has written one thing in thick black marker:

"YOU'RE NOT THE FIRST—YOU WON'T BE THE LAST"

Beneath that, in smaller print—almost delicate:

"Ask Slaughter what happened to the others."

I slam the door shut and look around, but the street's empty.

Whoever left this wanted me to find it. Wanted me to know they were watching. And that George Slaughter has seen this kind of thing before.

Maybe more than once.

I drive home without the radio on.

The ledger stays on the seat beside me like a warning.

Or an invitation.

One that I will accept.

CHAPTER 51

1984

GHOST IN THE MACHINE

Slaughter's house is quiet, the kind of quiet that settles when a man has outlived most of the people who used to knock on his door.

I hold the red ledger under one arm as I step onto the porch. The last page still feels warm in my hand.

Ask Slaughter what happened to the others.

No return address. No explanation.

Just a warning disguised as advice.

I knock once. Then twice more, sharper. The door creaks open a minute later.

Slaughter stands there in a sweater that looks older than me, glasses perched low, eyes sharp behind them.

"Ah, Gray," he says. "I figured you'd be back eventually."

He looks me over once, then steps aside.

"I've read your pieces. You write like someone trying to stop a storm with an umbrella."

"I'll take that as a compliment."

He doesn't smile. Just gestures to a chair.

"Whatever you've found, it's not the worst of it," he says.

I set the ledger gently on the table between us. Open it to the final page. Slide it toward him.

He reads it once, then looks up at me.

"They're stirring the coals again," he says. "I wondered how long it would take."

"Why didn't you tell me about Owen Sinclair the first time I came?"

"You didn't ask the right questions," he chuckles.

"I didn't even know who he was until the other day," I admit. "But now it's like he's been hiding in every file, every dead end, every gap in the story."

Slaughter picks at a thread on the edge of his cardigan. "That's the trick with Sinclair. He doesn't show up in the history books, but he's in the footnotes of everything."

I wait.

He sighs. "Back in '34, he was only there because he was Flanagan's son-in-law. Officially a consultant. Unofficially, a fixer. A man who could make a problem vanish before anyone realized there was one. And after the strike? He didn't vanish—he expanded."

"Expanded how?"

"He learned what kind of chaos made people desperate. And what kind of desperation made money. So he turned chaos into a business model."

Slaughter pours another inch of bourbon and stares into his glass like it holds a memory.

"You know, I met Sinclair once," he says. "Not long after the strike. I was still green, still thinking the law was a scalpel, not a club."

"What happened?" I ask.

"He invited me to lunch. Said he admired my 'principled stance.' Wanted to talk about the future of the city."

He chuckles, bitter.

"Never once mentioned the strike. Not the dead men. Not the blood on Champlain Street. Just zoning, infrastructure, 'opportunities for growth.' "

He looks up, eyes sharp.

"But the way he said it? It wasn't about building. It was about erasing. He didn't want to fix Toledo. He wanted to own it."

He drains the glass.

"And I realized then—he wasn't a man who made deals. He made decisions. And if you weren't useful, you disappeared."

He gets up from his chair.

"Come with me, Gray."

I follow him into his study. He unlocks a bottom drawer and pulls out an old folder—already prepared. He's been expecting this visit. He flips it open with gnarled fingers and hands me a few yellowed pages.

"Take urban renewal. Ever hear of 'Toledo Tomorrow'?"

I nod. The postwar dream project. Norman Bel Geddes, the designer behind the Futurama exhibit at the 1939 World's Fair, had been commissioned to reimagine Toledo—sunken superhighways, five airports, leafy parks. A clean, modern city.

"Most of it never happened," I say.

George snorts. "Oh, it happened. Not the pretty parts. But the highways? The neighborhood demolitions? That was real. And Sinclair was in the room every time one of those maps changed. I saw the same names getting land grants before the ink was dry on zoning changes. Names tied to shell companies. You dig deep enough, you get back to a group of investors. You dig past that, you get to Woodchuck Holdings."

"Which is Sinclair."

"Bingo."

I thumb through the papers. Handwritten memos. Typed meeting summaries. Clippings. George is quiet while I read. The impact settles in.

Slums bulldozed. Highways slicing through Black neighborhoods. Segregated suburbs springing up like weeds.

"He picked his battlegrounds," George says. "Labor, housing, media. Played all sides, but only to win."

"And the race riots in '66?" I ask.

"His companies sold the city riot gear. And after the smoke cleared? His buddies picked up the damaged properties cheap. That was the game. Destroy, then buy what's left."

I look at him, notebook forgotten in my lap. "Why didn't anyone stop him?"

"Because he never left fingerprints. And when someone got close, they either lost their job—or much more."

I don't ask what "more" means. I'm already thinking of Feldman. Of Ferner.

George lets the silence sit before continuing.

"You need a historian's mind on this, Gray. Someone who knows the public story and can tell you where the holes are."

"Any suggestions?"

"Brad Winters. University of Toledo. Teaches contemporary history. Writes about urban policy and labor. Smart kid. Smarter than me."

I jot the name down.

"Tell him I sent you," George adds. "He'll know what that means."

As I stand to leave, George rises from his chair.

"You keep chasing this, Gray, you should know something—"

I wait.

"He's still out there. Not the ghost of Sinclair—I mean the man. And he doesn't just bury stories. He buries people."

My ears perk up. It's the same phrase my unnamed informant used.

"I know."

But I don't *really* know.

Not yet.

I do know I can't stop now.

CHAPTER 52
1984
I ONLY HEARD OF YOU

The University of Toledo campus is quiet under low gray skies, the kind that make concrete buildings feel heavier somehow. Kirby and I follow a path lined with maple trees toward the history department, her satchel slung over one shoulder, my notebook tucked under my coat like contraband.

We find professor Brad Winters in his office, exactly where Slaughter said he'd be: behind a cluttered desk, surrounded by more books than floor. He's tall, balding, with a frayed corduroy blazer that could tell a few stories on its own. He sizes us up like a primary source that might not be reliable. His white shirt is rumpled, his tie loose, and his glasses ride low on a nose clearly used to holding them.

"Wheeler," he says, looking up without rising. "And you are Ms. . . . ?"

"Kirby Peters," she says, extending a hand. "Research and trouble."

He smiles faintly. "A necessary combination."

He motions us inside. The office smells like Wite-Out, leather, and a hint of pipe tobacco—though I'm pretty sure smoking's been banned in here since the Nixon administration. Overstuffed shelves line every wall, folders jutting out like overambitious footnotes. Behind

Winters, a faded WPA poster for a labor rights campaign hangs next to a photo of five men with picket signs and steel-set jaws.

"So," he says, settling into his chair, "George thinks you're onto something big. Which means you've stumbled into something dangerous."

"That's what people keep telling me," I mutter.

Winters arches an eyebrow but doesn't press.

"We're following a thread," I begin. "Started with a photo we found in the Feldman boxes. 1934, Auto-Lite strike. Guardsmen holding the line. In the corner—a man in a tie, holding a rifle."

Winters raises his eyebrows.

"Name on the back: Owen Sinclair. Feldman wrote 'confirmed' beside it."

The professor exhales slowly. "That's a name I haven't heard out loud in a long time."

Kirby leans in. "You know it?"

"I do. Not from faculty mixers. Sinclair was one of those shadow men. Officially, he was listed as a liaison between management and the city. Unofficially, he was Clarence Flanagan's son-in-law. And after the strike, he quietly began accumulating control over much more than factory floor disputes."

He walks across the room and unlocks a filing cabinet. From the bottom drawer, he pulls a few binders.

Kirby opens the top folder and begins flipping through copies of property deeds, board appointments, and faded newspaper clippings. I recognize the pattern—names we've already traced. But here, they feel older. Rooted.

"After Flanagan sold the company, Sinclair stayed in Toledo," Winters continues. "He didn't want public power— he wanted influence. Real estate. Zoning. Contracts. He inserted himself into every committee that mattered without ever running for anything."

I'm flipping through my notes when Kirby pulls a folded page from her satchel and lays it on Winters's desk.

"I found this last night," she says. "It's a 1954 land transfer—South Ridge Development. One of Sinclair's fronts. But look at the second signature."

Winters adjusts his glasses. "Thomas Dellinger."

"Same guy who's now on the Port Authority board," she says. "He was listed as a junior partner back then."

I blink. "You found this on your own?"

She shrugs, but there's a spark in her eyes. "You were chasing ghosts. I figured someone should check the living."

Winters nods slowly. "That fits. Sinclair believed in legacy. And insulation. He didn't hold the reins—he just made sure everyone owed him something."

Kirby speaks softly. "Did anyone ever try to expose him?"

"Oh, a few. Journalists, junior council members, even a city auditor once. They didn't end up dead—not exactly. But careers collapsed. Families relocated. One man's house caught fire. The fire chief called it an accident, but nobody was buying it."

I glance at Kirby, who's gone very still.

"And Sinclair himself?"

"Retreated into the background in the '70s," Winters says. "His name stopped appearing. But his fingerprints? Still everywhere." He steeples his fingers. "I've studied a lot of power brokers in this town. Sinclair's different. Most people like him want their names on buildings. Sinclair? He wanted to erase the buildings—and the people—who got in his way."

"He's a through line for this city, Gray. Defense contracts in the '40s. Redlining in the '50s. Urban renewal in the '60s. Environmental deregulation in the '70s. Whenever the working class got organized or neighborhoods got too noisy, Sinclair found a way to 'reorganize' them."

"Can you prove it?"

"I can give you the breadcrumbs. You'll have to follow them."

He opens a binder and flips to an aerial map. "This is the Junction Avenue corridor. Pre-expressway. He bought up parcels through a series of shell companies before the I-75 route was announced. Made a killing when the state bought him out."

"Money was only part of it," Winters says, turning the page. "It was about shaping who lived where—and who didn't. The redlining in the '50s? Sinclair backed the local banks that refused home loans to Black families in the North End. The schools in those zones declined. Property values dropped. He bought up the land at a discount, then lobbied to have the schools closed due to underenrollment."

Another binder. "Here—1954. Sinclair's behind the push to kill the Civic Unity Committee. Behind the scenes, he funded every initiative to keep the Vistula neighborhood segregated."

He flips again. "1963: A wave of industrial closures. People blamed automation, but these memos," he taps a sheaf of stapled pages, "show Sinclair consolidating factories under a holding company, then selling their equipment overseas for cash. Workers thought their jobs had evaporated. In fact, they'd been exported."

"And when people pushed back?" Winters says. "He moved faster. He funded neighborhood associations to infiltrate activist groups. Paid for 'community leaders' who would toe his line. When that failed, he turned to intimidation. Lawsuits. Firings. In one case, a 'spontaneous' fire at a print shop producing anti-development flyers."

And another. "The Tiedtke's fire. 'Accidental,' they called it. But two weeks before, the property transferred to a company called Allen Bray Holdings. Registered in Delaware. One of Woodchuck's first subsidiaries."

I whistle low. "That was him."

"He always used cutouts. People like *The Sword*'s publisher, developers, councilmen. They thought they were in charge. They weren't."

He pauses, tapping a page with a name circled: *Potter, Mayor John.*

"Is this about the race riot?" I ask.

During the Long Hot Summer of 1967, violence flared across the city. At Monroe and Tenth streets, police apprehended nine individuals carrying gasoline, bottles, and rag wicks—components for makeshift firebombs. A firebomb was believed to have caused a $10,000 blaze at the Kellermeyer Chemical Company. The riots lasted five days. Eighty arson fires. One hundred eighty arrests. Five hundred National Guardsmen on standby.

"Sinclair advised Potter personally," Winters says. "Urged him to take a hard-line stance. Then turned around and sold the city riot gear through one of his dummy military surplus suppliers."

I shake my head. "Holy shit."

"He played both ends against the middle. Controlled the problem and sold the solution."

Winters lowers his voice.

"And here's the kicker—he did it all while erasing his own footprints. Any time someone tried to expose him, the story never ran. Or the source disappeared."

A chill slides down my spine.

Winters closes the binder.

"Look, I'm not naïve. I've published on powerful people before. But Sinclair? Every time I tried to write about him, something got in the way. One time, when I knew I was onto something, I got a photo in the mail—my fiancée's house, her bedroom window circled. Suddenly, publishing that piece didn't seem so important."

He looks at me, steady.

"He doesn't just kill stories. He kills the curiosity that fuels them."

"There's a pattern," he continues. "Every time power changed hands—new mayor, new paper editor, new union president—Sinclair already had a man waiting. With a check. Or a threat."

"And if neither worked?" I ask.

"People disappeared."

We sit in silence, the weight of the room pressing in.

Finally, I ask, "Do you think he's behind what's happening now?"

Winters doesn't blink. "If he's alive? Almost certainly. If he's not? Then someone's still carrying out his blueprint."

Kirby closes the folder. "We're going to print it. All of it. Name, history, connections."

Winters smiles—not with joy, but with a kind of grim admiration.

"Then you'd better be damn sure," he says. "And you'd better move fast. Because if he even suspects you're close . . . "

He doesn't finish the sentence.

I stand, gripping my notes. "Thanks, Professor."

He gives me a look that's somewhere between admiration and pity. "Be careful, you two. This isn't just history. This is now."

I'm halfway down the hall, still reeling, when I hear footsteps behind me.

"Hey!" Professor Winters calls, striding out with a folder in hand. "Wait—there's something else you should see."

We follow him back into the office. He sits and opens a slim manila file, sliding out a single page. A copy of a typed letter, yellowing with age, marked CONFIDENTIAL. The letterhead reads:

Toledo-Labor-Management-Citizens Committee
Dated: 1965

"It's unsigned," Winters says. "But it's a smoking gun."

I scan it. Bureaucratic language, sterile—until the last paragraph. That's where it talks about *"removing troublesome community leaders"* and *"discouraging labor unrest through targeted pressure."* In the margin, a note scrawled in pencil:

See OS.

"OS. Owen Sinclair," I murmur.

"This letter was part of a cache found in a city councilman's estate sale in the '70s. Most people didn't know what to make of it. I kept copies."

Kirby says, "So this guy—he's been at the center of every dirty deal in Toledo since the Depression?"

"More or less," Winters replies. "Urban renewal, race suppression, environmental sabotage, political manipulation. He didn't just survive every shift in power—he steered those shifts."

Kirby exhales slowly. "You could write an entire book."

"I'm trying to write a newspaper story," I mutter. "But now I feel like I'm chasing Moriarty."

Winters gives a small smile. "Don't flatter him too much. He's not a genius—he's ruthless, well-connected, and unburdened by conscience."

He clears his throat.

"You're going to need more than newspaper clippings and paranoid footnotes to nail him. You need proof, current proof. Connect the old to the new. The Ferner and Feldman deaths. The shell companies. The enforcer. You need something indisputable."

Kirby leans forward. "We already started. There's a name—Carl Madison. Shows up on the periphery of Sinclair's real estate ventures. Disappeared in the '70s. Might still be his hatchet man."

Winters gives a low whistle. "Then you're doing more than digging up bones, are you? You're stirring the hornet's nest."

His face grows stern as he looks at me.

"If you go forward with this, you won't be able to undo it. Sinclair won't just sue you or smear you. He'll erase you."

"I know," I breathe.

Kirby gives me a look that's somewhere between admiration and worry. "We're not turning back now."

Winters stands and extends a hand. "I'll help however I can. You need documents, references, footnotes that hold up under scrutiny—I've got them. But for God's sake, be careful."

"You're doing more than chasing ghosts," he says as we leave. "You're poking the living ones who think they're still untouchable."

I don't respond. But I glance at Kirby, and she meets my gaze with a look that says: *Let them come.*

We step outside into the cool night air, and I feel a shiver ripple through me—and it's not the weather.

Kirby pulls her coat tighter. "You okay?"

"No. But I'm ready."

We walk back toward the car in silence. The wind cuts harder now—not bitter, just sharp. Enough to make you feel alive. And a little hunted.

Kirby glances sideways at me. "That was worse than I expected."

I nod. "It always is."

We cross the brick-paved quad, gray sky above us, bare branches overhead like bones.

"I've worked archives most of my adult life," she says. "I've read about men like Sinclair. I just never thought I'd walk into the middle of one of their stories."

"You didn't walk in," I say. "You helped write the map."

She gives a small shake of her head, but I see the fire behind her eyes. Not fear—not quite. Something more dangerous.

Purpose.

"Do we have enough?" she asks.

I look down at the notepad, crammed with Winters's citations, folder numbers, cross-referenced board positions, and dates of vanished men.

"We're close. But it needs shape. We need to tie this to Ferner. To Feldman. To Dellinger."

We reach the car. She pauses before getting in.

"Gray . . . if we do this, there's no half-measure. No walk-back. If Sinclair's alive—or if someone's carrying this for him—it won't be idle threats next time."

Kirby eyes me. "So, what now?"

Even I can hear the doubt in my voice as I reply. "We thread all this together—Sinclair, Woodchuck, the deaths, the history. And we publish. We get the story out before someone buries it. Or us."

Kirby reaches over and takes my arm. "You said *us*."

"Sure—we're in this together now, aren't we? I couldn't have done this without you."

She gives me a look I don't quite understand—but I think about it that night, when I'm trying to get to sleep.

CHAPTER 53

1984

SHARE THEIR HOLLOW GLOW

Back at AP Parts, the air hangs heavy and wet—thick as soup. Even the picket signs sag under their weight. It's been weeks now since the first fists flew and the first batons cracked skulls.

Weeks filled with eviction notices, repo men, and electric bills gone unpaid.

Weeks of promises fraying into desperation.

Management hasn't budged. They pulled out of negotiations after the police crackdown, blamed the union for the violence. Now private security guards linger around the gates, mirrored sunglasses and blank stares.

There are rumors of night shifts starting up inside—scabs sneaking in through back entrances. The strike isn't being fought anymore.

It's being smothered.

A dozen diehards march in front of the plant gates, their signs bleached and curling under the relentless humidity.

FAIR CONTRACT NOW
AP PARTS UNFAIR

Some of the cardboard placards droop so badly they're barely legible.

Danny McCullough is still here. He looks like he's aged ten years in the past few weeks. He's sweating profusely. His hands hang like dead weight at his sides.

He catches sight of me and gives a tired nod.

"You again," he says, voice raspy from heat and shouting.

"I wanted to see how things were holding up."

He snorts, wipes his forehead with the back of his sleeve. "Holding up? Kid, we're melting out here. Melting and starving."

I ask if there's been any progress—any hint the company might blink.

He shakes his head, slow and weary. "They're digging in. Got all the time in the world. Meanwhile, we're out here trying to stretch nickels into meals."

He gestures toward a group huddled under a makeshift shade tarp—tattered banners strung between two cracked poles. A baby cries weakly from somewhere in the cluster.

"They know how this ends," Danny says, voice flat. "Starve us out. Break us. Make us turn on each other."

Behind him, the factory walls shimmer in the heat haze—cold, blank, and utterly indifferent.

I keep writing in my notebook even though the ink smears from the sweat dripping off my hand. It feels stupid. Insulting, almost. Like trying to chronicle a slow death in bullet points.

Danny clasps my shoulder before I leave, his grip dry and shaking.

"Print what you want," he says. "Won't make a damn difference."

I drive away with my shirt clinging to my back and the sun hammering the roof of the Hornet.

In my rearview mirror, the picket line wavers like a dying mirage.

This isn't a strike anymore—it's a siege. And summer's already won.

I drive north, back to the newspaper, leaving the sagging picket signs behind me.

But the rot that's killing AP Parts doesn't stop at their gates.

It runs through this whole damn city.

And its roots run straight back to Sinclair.

CHAPTER 54

1984

MY EYES HAVE SEEN YOU

Back at *The Sword* archive room, I flick on the light. It buzzes overhead with an angry hum, casting its usual jaundiced glow on rows of filing cabinets and steel shelves, all groaning under the weight of yellowing clippings.

I glance at Kirby. She's already pulling open the drawer labeled "M," rifling through folders with practiced efficiency. She's not waiting for me to give directions anymore.

Part of me loves that.

I take a seat at the dusty side desk, stretch my legs, and mutter, "Let's see if the ghost left any footprints."

We divide the work. I start with the 1970s. Kirby tackles the 1960s. We're looking for any mention of Carl Madison—private security, real estate, labor suppression. Anything with Sinclair's stink on it.

It takes thirty minutes before Kirby lets out a low "huh."

She turns, holding up a clipping from 1972: "Labor Dispute Turns Violent at Westgate Mall Site."

It's about a construction project that turned into a standoff between union picketers and nonunion labor. Buried three paragraphs down is this nugget: "Security for the site was provided by Madison Protective Services, a private firm led by former TPD officer Carl Madison."

I sit up straighter. "That's him."

Kirby flips the article toward me. "He was more than Sinclair's goon. He was public-facing. Or at least, he used to be."

"Until he vanished."

Kirby keeps digging. "Let's see how long he stayed visible."

Fifteen minutes later: another clipping from 1974. Madison's firm is listed as security for a contested land development project on the Maumee waterfront. The article mentions complaints about intimidation tactics and calls to the city ethics board.

Nothing ever came of it.

After that—nothing.

From 1975 onward, Madison disappears. No listings. No news. No city contracts.

Silence.

"He ghosts himself," Kirby mutters. "Just like Larry said."

I frown. "Sinclair told him to go dark. He must've still been working—just not under his own name."

We sit back, the silence between us stretching. Outside, dusk is falling fast, the faint outline of the city's decay pressing in through the windows.

"We need more," I say. "Records. Shell companies. Property transfers."

Kirby stands, stretches, and looks at me with that glint in her eye. "We need to go back to the main library."

I grin despite myself. "You read my mind."

An hour later, we're back in familiar territory: the library's business records section.

This time, though, we're not chasing shadows from the '30s—we're hunting names.

We start with Carl Madison. I dig into old personnel records, the paper trail brittle and thin. Madison wasn't your average dirty cop. He started straight—decorations for bravery, a couple of commendations from the mayor's office.

Then the complaints started stacking up. Excessive force. Intimidation. A kid in the Old South End who wound up in the hospital after a "routine stop."

Officially, Madison resigned. Unofficially, he was cut loose—too rough even for a department that wasn't known for being soft on protestors.

Sinclair found him six months later. Offered him a job. Offered him purpose.

Offered him something the badge never could.

Kirby, meanwhile, requests the old city business registries and corporate formation records from the 1970s. We sit side by side at a long wooden table, flipping through brittle pages that smell like dust and bureaucracy.

"You said Sinclair has shell companies," she says. "Let's start with any that used Woodchuck as a parent entity."

"Hey, wait a minute!" I say. "I remember something from grade school history. In 1900, when the Toledo Zoo opened, someone donated a woodchuck—the zoo's very first animal."

"At least there's something to chuckle about in the middle of all this," Kirby says.

Within twenty minutes, we've got a short list of subsidiaries, most of them sounding like bad Bond villain covers: Toledo Development Holdings, Great Lakes Logistics, Midwest Realty Associates, and one with an Orwellian name: Civic Renewal LLC.

Kirby cross-checks "Civic Renewal" against security firm contracts.

"Bingo," she says, tapping the page. "In 1976, Civic Renewal lists a security subcontractor: Madison Group Solutions. That has to be him."

"No address, no phone number," I mutter, squinting. "Only a PO box."

"But it's there," she says. "He never quit. He rebranded and hid behind Sinclair's curtain."

I run a hand down my face. "So what now? We follow the companies?"

Kirby thinks. "We could pull property deeds tied to Civic Renewal or the other shells. We might find something recent—an office, a holding. A place Madison might still check in."

I tap the folder with the clipped articles. "Or we go old-school and talk to people who remember him. Real estate guys. Cops from back then."

Kirby gives me a look. "You mean put your face out there again?"

"Not my face," I say. "Yours."

She raises an eyebrow.

"I'm the one in the crosshairs. But you? You're the girl with glasses asking questions for a college paper."

She frowns. "You want me to lie?"

"No," I say. "I want you to ask questions like you don't know what they mean. Let them underestimate you."

She considers that, then nods. "I've done it before."

We sit back, staring at the accumulated files.

One name leads to another. One thread to another.

Sinclair. Madison. Woodchuck. Civic Renewal. It's all there—hidden in plain sight, under layers of time and silence.

Kirby looks closely at me. "You know what this is, don't you?"

I look up at her.

"This is the real story," she says. "Not just two murders. Not just the 1934 strike. This is fifty years of corruption, stitched together with money, fear, and silence."

I feel the full weight of it settle on my shoulders.

"And we're going to rip every stitch out."

CHAPTER 55

1934 TO THE 1980S

BLUEPRINT FOR SILENCE

History remembers the noise—the marches, the strikes, the broken windows and shouted demands. But Sinclair understood something most men never did:

Power isn't built in noise. It's built in silence.

Behind doors that never open. In meetings that never make headlines. In names that disappear from ballots, payrolls, and grave markers.

It thrives in shadows, where names fade and deeds wear other men's faces.

In the city he helped shape, the loud were buried—and the quiet inherited the earth.

1934: The Strike and Aftermath

The strike broke the company, just as Sinclair had predicted. Auto-Lite's share price crumbled in the panic. Insurance costs spiked. Board members whispered about dissolving the brand.

Sinclair didn't shout.

He signed papers.

Through a web of front companies, he acquired battered shares at a fraction of their worth. When the dust settled, the name over the factory gates changed. The workers didn't notice—and didn't care. They were too busy trying to feed their families.

The factories still belched smoke. The paychecks still came.

But the owners had changed.

And Sinclair owned them all.

1953: The Blacklist

The Red Scare swept the country. Sinclair rode it like a wave.

He didn't care about Communism. Ideology was a tool, nothing more. What mattered was weakening the unions that still clung to old grievances.

Behind closed doors, he financed whisper campaigns. Loyal politicians launched investigations. Names appeared on blacklists: loud organizers, troublemakers, lawyers like George Slaughter—men who had once marched against companies like his.

They were accused, discredited, discarded.

Strikes faded into history books. Business flourished.

And through it all, Sinclair's name never surfaced.

1962: The Committee

The city needed "civic cooperation," or so the papers said. The Toledo Labor-Management-Citizens Committee was born—a partnership between businessmen and "responsible" labor leaders.

Sinclair smiled as the radicals were shut out. Only the pliant remained—the ones who knew their place.

The committee helped broker contracts that kept wages flat and strikes off the front page. Factories stayed open. Profits soared.

The working poor learned to settle for survival instead of dignity.

1973: The Renewal

Progress demanded sacrifices.

Sinclair was happy to offer them.

Urban renewal plans gutted entire neighborhoods under the Toledo Tomorrow banner. Families who had lived for generations on the same streets watched bulldozers erase their histories.

Land was cheap. Sinclair bought in bulk through shell companies. Shiny office parks and bland apartment complexes rose from the rubble.

None of them bore his name.

But all of them paid him tribute.

1978: The Last Silence

Some battles were fought with bullets. Others with dotted lines.

Sinclair and his allies leaned on banks and city officials, reinforcing the invisible boundaries that divided the city. Loans were denied. Districts crumbled. Hope shriveled block by block.

Neighborhoods were boxed in.

And so were the people who lived there.

Sinclair didn't need guards or guns anymore.

He had maps and mortgages.

1984: The Ghost

Sinclair sat behind Flanagan's old desk, a drink in his liver-spotted hand, staring out over the city he had built.

There would be no sons to inherit it. No bloodline to carry his name.

Only buildings and broken promises stitched into the streets.

His empire had no plaques, no parades, no name carved in stone.

That was how it survived.

And somewhere out there, he knew, a photograph still existed—a flicker of truth that refused to stay buried.

He raised his glass to the window.

The skyline stared back, silent as a graveyard.

And Sinclair, the architect of silence, waited for history to forget him.

CHAPTER 56

1984

WHERE DOES THAT HIGHWAY GO TO?

We're back in *The Sword*'s ill-lit archive room, the afternoon sun struggling to break through the wire-mesh glass. Kirby and I sit opposite each other at the long, battered table, our notebooks spread out like maps of a battlefield.

We're two hours into the archive crawl when I lean back and rub my eyes. Kirby doesn't stop scanning.

"You ever think about leaving Toledo?" I ask.

She doesn't answer right away. Just slides another clipping under the lamp. "I did leave."

I glance at her. "Grad school?"

"Yeah. Columbus. Thought I'd stay there, maybe find a job in a university library. Something tidy. Climate-controlled. Nobody shouting in the margins." She slides the clipping aside. Reaches for another.

"What happened?"

She shrugs. "Life. Marriage. Then un-marriage."

I wait.

"He got tenure in Michigan. I got tired of apologizing for having a career. When it ended, I looked at the map and drove in the direction that didn't make me sick."

"Toledo?"

"Didn't say it worked."

That gets a small laugh out of me. She smiles, faintly.

"I guess I figured if I was going to start over, I might as well be somewhere I didn't owe anyone anything."

I nod slowly. She doesn't notice. Or maybe she just lets me think she doesn't.

"Okay," I say, tapping my pen on the list we've compiled. "We've got three addresses linked to Madison: one in West Toledo that burned down in '79, a PO box registered through a security firm in Sylvania, and this rental property on Bancroft that shows up in tax records but never had a listed resident."

Kirby chimes in. "Every one of them is tied to a Sinclair shell company dormant since the mid-'70s. You think Madison's still in the area?"

"I think someone like him doesn't go far," I say. "Not unless he's told to."

Kirby flips through her notes. "Here's what I found in the paper's morgue. Madison worked private security on two strikes in the late '70s—both ended in violence. The articles don't name him, but eyewitnesses describe the same man: tall, wiry, crew cut, aggressive."

"He's a ghost," I mutter. "No interviews. No charges. No photo on file."

Kirby looks up, eyes steady. "So we call the people who were there."

We divide the list. Former strike organizers. A retired labor reporter in Detroit. A guy who used to work at the security firm Sinclair hired. One by one, we dial numbers off yellowed Rolodex cards and phone book entries we pulled from the library's back shelf.

We're burning through the names. Phones in hand, note cards pinned along the carpet like a scatter of fallen soldiers. Most people don't remember Carl Madison.

Those who do wish they didn't.

Kirby picks up the next name on our list: the labor reporter.

He answers on the third ring. "Hello?"

"Mr. Achenbach? This is Gray Wheeler from *The Toledo Sword*. I'm looking into a man named Carl Madison. You covered the Crosswell Rubber strike back in '78?"

There's a long pause.

"You're digging into Madison?" he says finally. "Whoa. I haven't heard that name in years."

"So, you remember him?"

"Like a bad dream. He didn't just run security—he ran intimidation. Workers' tires slashed. Dogs poisoned. One guy got beat so bad he lost hearing in one ear. Madison was never touched. Cops always said there wasn't enough evidence."

"And you think he was working for . . . ?"

"Somebody bigger. I always suspected organized crime or a company board, but we never proved it. If you're on his trail, watch your back."

I thank him and hang up.

Kirby's already on the line with someone else. I only catch snippets: "—yeah, from the Tiedtke's fire—yes, I know it sounds crazy—do you have any photos?"

She hangs up and turns to me, eyes wide. "Someone says they saw Madison with a Sinclair associate a few months before the Tiedtke's fire. Nothing official, but the timing lines up. And he's got a photo."

We look at each other. We don't speak for a few seconds, letting it all settle in.

I finally break it.

"Every path we chase leads back to Sinclair."

"We're not chasing a story anymore," Kirby says. "We're chasing a system. A whole damn machine."

Outside, the light is fading—streaks of orange slicing across the brick walls of downtown.

But in here, the momentum is building.

We're not done yet.

Not even close.

CHAPTER 57

1984

THE NIGHT SHIFT

The drive back is quiet. Not the tense kind—just worn out. After seven hours in the archives, three crumbling city directories, and one cracked-open storage box full of business licenses, our brains are too fried to talk.

Kirby rides with one leg tucked under her, half-facing me. She's still holding the file folder from the library like it's radioactive—or sacred.

As I pull into the narrow drive beside my parents' split-level house, she finally speaks.

"You really live here?"

"Technically. Temporarily."

"This is the subterranean wing."

"I'm honored."

We enter onto a landing and head down into the basement. One of those design quirks of '60s split-level homes—an entrance that lets you sneak in without passing through the living room. Or worse, seeing (and being seen by) my mother in curlers and slippers.

The basement smells like dust and detergent. A dehumidifier hums in the corner.

"This way," I say, flicking on the fluorescents.

She follows. I motion toward the far wall, where I've already thumbtacked a few photos—the 1934 aerial of

Auto-Lite, a blown-up map of Champlain Street, a snapshot of Ferner's handwriting.

"This," I say, "is where the real story lives."

Kirby walks up to the Wall and runs her hand over the surface like she's reading Braille.

"You haven't even started yet."

"That's where you come in."

I hand her a roll of red yarn and a box of thumbtacks. "You do the honors."

She gives me a look. "You want me to define a criminal empire with craft supplies?"

"Yes."

We work in silence for a while. She pins names— Midwestern Equities, Owens Realty Trust, Guard reports, AP Parts, Auto-Lite, Sinclair. I draw lines. Some stick. Some don't. The connections shift as fast as the string.

At some point, she kicks off her shoes. Folds one leg up on the stool. Drinks half a root beer I'd forgotten I had. The fluorescents flicker.

"This is completely insane," she says—but she doesn't stop working.

Later—much later—I catch her watching me as I pin a blurry photo of a man in a fedora standing at the corner of Elm and Champlain.

"What?" I say.

"You don't blink when you're focused," she says. "It's weird."

I nod once. "You breathe through your teeth when you're writing."

She flushes a little. "I do not."

"Do too."

She throws a thumbtack at me. It misses by a mile. We're both smiling now—but not fully.

There's a moment. Not long. Just . . . longer than it should be.

Neither of us moves.

The red string between us is taut.

I wake up to the sound of birds and the faint rattle of pipes.

Kirby's in my bed, curled up with the sheet half-slid off her shoulder. Her back is to me. The light makes patterns on the ceiling.

My mouth tastes like dust and root beer.

I sit up slowly. My shirt is on the chair. Her jacket is folded over the radiator.

There's a tension in the room—not uncomfortable. Just unspoken.

She shifts. "Do you have any coffee?"

"Not that you'd want to drink."

She sits up, pulling the sheet tighter. "Okay. Then I'll take silence and plausible deniability."

We both laugh. Awkward. Careful.

Neither of us says anything else.

CHAPTER 58
1984
FREEZE FRAME

Later that day, we're halfway through a second pot of newsroom coffee—burnt and bitter, arguably no better than the instant I could've offered at home—when the call comes.

Kirby grabs the receiver, then waves me over. "It's your guy. The one with the photo."

I take the phone.

"This is Gray."

A voice crackles over the line, low and wary. "Name's Bennett. Told your friend I might have something. If you want to see it, you come to me."

"Where?"

He gives me an address. I grab my coat before the receiver's even back in its cradle.

"Want backup?" Kirby asks.

"Not yet," I say. "If I'm not back in two hours, check the coroner's reports."

Kirby rolls her eyes but doesn't laugh. "I'm coming with you."

The air is sticky with late spring heat as I pull the Hornet into the parking lot of a bowling alley on the west side. It's noon, but the lot is half-empty—a place caught between shifts. Day drinkers not yet arrived, night bowlers still asleep. A pair of middle-aged men sit out front, chain-smoking beneath a Miller Lite sign, their eyes flicking toward us and then away again.

"This is the place," I say, rereading my note. *Noon. Look for the Mustang.* I spot it across the lot—an old fastback with primer spots on the rear quarter panel, sun-faded and unloved.

"Doesn't scream trustworthy," Kirby mutters.

"I've made worse judgment calls," I say, and open the door.

The man is already leaning against his car, sunglasses masking his expression. He looks like someone who's spent a lot of time not wanting to be noticed—nondescript jacket, baseball cap, the kind of posture that avoids security cameras. When I approach, he doesn't extend a hand.

"You Gray Wheeler?"

"Yes."

He glances at Kirby. I nod. "She's with me."

From his jacket, he pulls out a large manila envelope, grease-stained at one corner.

"You didn't get this from me."

I hesitate, then take it.

"What is it?" I ask.

"Proof," he says. "If you know what to look for."

"And this is . . . about Madison?" Kirby asks.

"It's what ties him to Sinclair. It's why they buried everything. I've been waiting for someone brave enough— maybe crazy enough—to take these guys on. Good luck."

He gives us a quick two-fingered salute—something I haven't seen since my Boy Scout days—then slides into the Mustang, starts the engine with a loud growl, and pulls out before I can even open the envelope.

Kirby and I climb back into the Hornet. I flip open the flap and pull out a black-and-white photo—grainy, with April 22, 1975, written on the border. A group of men stand outside what looks like a warehouse in North Toledo. At the edge of the group is a younger man with a buzz cut and a hard stare.

Same face from the clippings we'd found.

Carl Madison.

And standing beside him, almost in shadow, is Owen Sinclair.

Kirby whistles. "That's them."

"And this isn't decades-old labor stuff. This is post-Watergate, post–Kent State. They were still operating then."

Kirby studies the photo. "Where was this taken?"

"I don't know. But maybe we can figure it out. And if we do, maybe we find where Madison went next."

Back in my car, I flick the Hornet's fan to full blast, trying to cool my torso before the sweat soaks through my shirt. Kirby taps the folded photo against her thigh like a metronome.

"We're close," she murmurs.

We head back to *The Sword*. I turn on the cassette deck and the Doors' *LA Woman* album is playing. "The cars hiss by my window, like the waves down on the beach . . . "

Kirby wrinkles her nose. "What is this crap?"

"Sorry, I left my Cindi Lauper tape in my other car."

She gives me a dig in the ribs as I leave the Doors on. "I got this girl beside me but she's (pause) out of reach." Kirby looks down her glasses at me.

We head straight for the city library, pushing open the heavy glass doors into a space that smells of newsprint and polished wood. The same librarian from before gives us a tired smile.

I spread the photo out on the research table under one of the overhead lamps.

"We need building permits," I tell her. "Industrial warehouses near the docks, north end of town, sometime before 1974. Bonus if any of them changed hands through shell companies."

She gives me a look like I asked her to rebuild the Gutenberg press from memory. "Give me a few minutes."

Kirby digs into the microfiche while I pull old zoning reports. Half an hour later, we've got a name:

Toledo River Freight & Transfer Co. Dissolved in 1976.

But before that? It changed owners twice. The last listed owner: a holding firm with known ties to Sinclair's companies.

Kirby traces her finger down a page. "Here—Carl Madison filed a private security license through a front company the same year. Same neighborhood."

"So he didn't vanish," I say. "He went off-grid where no one would look."

We sit back. The pieces are clicking into place like tumblers in a lock.

"We've got a photo of the two of them together," Kirby says. "And now a property that ties them both to this part of town."

"We find out where Madison is now," I say, "and maybe—just maybe—we get to the bottom of what they're still hiding."

Kirby folds the photo and slips it into her file folder.

"Let's track him."

CHAPTER 59
1984
LEAN ON ME

We return to the office and I use Kirby's phone in the archive room.

Larry picks up on the second ring. His voice is ragged, like he's been sleeping.

"Detroit General, ICU."

"It's me."

"Wheeler. Tell me you're not in more trouble."

"I think we've found Carl Madison—and a direct connection to Sinclair. I've got a photo of the two of them together in '74."

Larry's silent for a beat. "Holy hell. You sure it's him?"

"Same face from the clippings. Sinclair had him posted outside a shell warehouse near the river. That building changed hands through a holding firm tied to Sinclair's other companies."

"And you're telling me this why?" he says, but I can hear him shifting upright in bed.

"Because I think Madison's still alive. And he's local. We want to find him. Maybe talk to him. Maybe more."

"You want to *talk* to the guy who tried to kill you outside the AP Parts protest?"

I flinch. "We don't know that was Madison—"

"Gray."

"Fine. Yeah, we think it was."

Larry exhales. "Then the hell you're just talking to him. This guy's not a messenger. He's a hammer."

Kirby gives me a look. I hold up a hand.

"We're not stupid," I say into the receiver. "We're not going to knock on his door."

"No, you're going to find out if he has a door at all," Larry mutters. "You got an address?"

"Working on it. We traced him to that freight warehouse in the '70s. But he dropped off the map after that. No active license. No utilities in his name. He's gone full shadow."

Larry hums. "Let me make some calls."

"From your hospital bed?"

He snorts. "I'm not dead. Just temporarily fused to this mattress. And Detroit's got a few guys who still owe me favors."

"Police?"

"Let's say . . . retired associates with selective memories."

A pause.

"Give me twenty-four hours," he says. "You'll have a location—or a warning to run."

I hesitate. "What do we do if we find him?"

The line goes quiet.

"If you corner a rat, Wheeler, it won't beg—it's going to bite. If you're going to knock on Madison's door, you better be ready to finish the damn story."

I glance at Kirby. Her lips are pressed into a firm line. She's listening. Always listening.

Larry adds, "And for the love of God, don't go alone."

"I won't."

He exhales. "You've always been stubborn, but you're not stupid. Call me when you've got something more concrete."

Click.

I hang up, my fingers still on the receiver like it might say something else.

"Let me guess," Kirby says. "He told you not to go looking for the guy."

"He told me to bring a gun," I say, smiling.

She arches a brow. "Do you have one?"

I think about it.

"No," I say. "But I've got something better."

Kirby smiles. "Let me guess. Me?"

"Yep."

We sit, neither speaking, as the sun dips lower in the sky, the photo between us on the seat like a loaded weapon.

Time to hunt.

CHAPTER 60
1984
IT AIN'T SAFE ON THE STREETS

After Kirby leaves, I pack my notes, the backup tape, and my recorder into the bottom of my battered satchel and head out the side entrance of *The Sword*. The air's heavy with humidity, like a thunderstorm is lurking just out of sight.

Something's off. Has been all day.

I tell myself I'm being paranoid.

But as I walk the two blocks to my car, I notice the sedan again. Brown. Unremarkable.

Too unremarkable.

It pulls away from the curb as I pass, idles at the corner, and then—when I make a sudden turn down an alley instead of heading straight—it creeps past and stops, engine running.

I flatten myself against the wall, heart pounding.

Okay, Gray. Time to stop playing gumshoe and start thinking like a survivor.

I cut behind the hardware store, into a narrow alley that lets out on Front Street, then jog up toward the next intersection. A diner still glows in the distance. I duck inside, order a black coffee I won't drink, and slip into the back booth.

I wait.

Ten minutes. Fifteen.

Nothing.

By the time I leave, I've almost convinced myself it was coincidence. A neighbor's car. An overactive imagination. Maybe Kirby spooked me.

But when I get in the Hornet and drive, I see the headlights again. Two cars back. Staying far enough behind to be plausible.

I test it. Take a left where I normally wouldn't. Then another. Then double back.

Still there.

My palms start to sweat on the wheel.

I head west, toward the industrial edge of town, where the streetlights grow farther apart and the pavement turns to patches. The factories out here are long abandoned—rusted hulks eaten by ivy and time.

I whip around a corner and pull the Hornet into the ruins of an old warehouse loading dock—something I scoped out months ago for a different story. Kill the engine. Lights off.

And wait.

The car cruises past at a crawl.

I glimpse the driver—a man in a cap, face shadowed. He doesn't stop. Doesn't look around. Just keeps driving.

I sit in silence, every sense on fire.

Whoever that was . . . they weren't sightseeing.

They were sending a message.

I'm not just being watched.

I'm being hunted.

I take the long way home to make sure I'm not being followed. As I pull into the driveway, my sister Elaine is coming out of the front door.

"Hey," I say.

"How's the investigation going?"

"Oh, you've heard."

"That's all Mom's been talking about. I know we've had our issues with Mom, but she's seriously worried about you."

"I've told her there's nothing to worry about."

Elaine shrugs. "Sure. But you know Mom. Take care."

"Say hi to Doug and the kids for me."

She gives me the thumbs up as she gets in her car and drives away.

CHAPTER 61

1984

YOU MIGHT GET WHAT YOU'RE AFTER

The next morning, the archive room phone rings as I'm scribbling notes into my notebook, cross-referencing property records with a city map spread out across the table like a war planner's chart. Kirby looks up from the desk where she's flipping through old city directories, her hair tied back, eyes rimmed with exhaustion.

I snatch the phone off the receiver.

"Yeah?"

"It's me." Larry's voice is rough but direct.

"You got something?"

"Depends how you define 'something.' Madison's off the radar, but one of my guys from organized crime flagged a pattern."

I sit up straighter. "Go on."

"He's not living under his real name. But he's been showing up—without fanfare—on security gigs for private clients. Corporate interests. Mostly in northern Ohio and southern Michigan. Places where no one asks for a badge number, just a pair of fists."

"So he's still working."

"Sort of. My guy swears he saw Madison two weeks ago near a rail yard in Rossford. Warehouse job, off the books, real hush-hush. Said he was driving an old brown Chrysler and walking with a limp."

Kirby stands, drifting closer. I cover the receiver and mouth: *Rossford.*

"Anything else?"

"Yeah," Larry says, his voice dipping. "He's got connections to a halfway house downtown. Place called St. Alban's. Used to be a front for parolee housing. Real bottom-of-the-barrel stuff. A guy like Madison wouldn't live there—but he might stash something. Or someone."

"You think he's got backup?"

"I think," Larry says, "that if you go sniffing around the wrong door, you won't get another chance to call me back."

I rub the side of my face. "I'm not giving this up."

"I know. Be careful, buddy. You've got Sinclair's attack dog sniffing you now. And he bites."

I hesitate.

"Thanks, Larry."

"Hey," he adds. "Take Kirby. She's smarter than you."

I smile. "I know."

Click.

He hangs up.

An hour later, Kirby and I park half a block from St. Alban's. The building slumps like a boxer after a bad round—concrete flaking, windows smeared with grime. A chain-link fence sags on one side, and a busted neon sign buzzes to life at dusk: ROOMS WEEKLY. CASH ONLY.

"We're not exactly headed to the Four Seasons," Kirby mutters.

"No. But someone who doesn't want to be found might pass through here."

I tuck the photo of Madison into my coat pocket. It's dog-eared now—a ghost's portrait.

Kirby eyes the front entrance. "What's the plan?"

"Split up. You check the back lot, see if that Chrysler's parked anywhere. I'll try the front desk. Maybe someone remembers his face."

"I'll circle around. Don't get murdered."

"I'll do my best."

Inside, the lobby reeks of mildew and Pine-Sol. A man in a wife beater watches a small TV behind the counter, his cigarette balanced on the edge of an ashtray blooming with lipstick-ringed butts.

I take my time approaching.

"Evening."

The man looks me over like I've already annoyed him. "You checking in?"

"No. Looking for someone. Maybe he stayed here." I slide the photo across the counter. "Seen this guy?"

He stares at it. Blinks once. Then twice.

"Never seen him."

"You sure? Older guy. Walks with a limp. Might go by another name."

He slides the photo back. "I said no."

His tone carries weight.

"Got it."

But as I turn, I catch the flicker of something in his eyes.

Recognition.

And fear.

Outside, Kirby meets me at the corner of the building.

"There's a brown Chrysler parked in the alley. Matches the description."

I exhale. "Then he's here. Or he was."

She raises a brow. "What now?"

I glance back at the grim little motel and feel the pressure building in my ribs.

"We watch. Tomorrow morning, I'll come back. Maybe offer a bribe. Maybe something stronger."

Kirby eyes me. "You mean charm?"

I smirk. "Or desperation."

She crosses her arms. "We're going to need a better plan."

"I know." I glance once more at the photo. "But we're getting close."

CHAPTER 62
1984
KILLER ON THE ROAD

The rain hasn't let up all evening. It's turned the streets of Toledo into slick ribbons, and the air smells like rust and gasoline. I hunch lower in the Hornet's seat, watching the abandoned warehouse across the street. Kirby sits next to me, binoculars up, scanning the boarded-up windows.

"We're sure he's here?" she whispers.

"Larry's guy tracked him here two nights ago. Same brown Chrysler's still in the lot."

Kirby shifts in her seat. "You think Larry tipped the cops?"

"I called him from the archive room before we left," I say. "Told him where we'd be. He said he'd pass the word along. If they can come, they will."

"And if they can't?"

I glance at her, heart hammering harder than I let on. "Then it's just us."

She offers a tight smile. "Typical."

The rain patters against the windshield, a steady, hypnotic sound. We wait. Five minutes. Ten. My fingers drum the steering wheel until Kirby elbows me, sharp.

"Movement."

I jerk upright. A figure slips out from the side door of the warehouse, hunched against the rain. Even under the weak streetlamp, the shape is unmistakable—tall, wiry, with a hard, fast stride.

Madison.

"That's him," I mutter.

He moves toward the Chrysler, scanning the street with quick, predator eyes. Something about the way he carries himself—like he's expecting trouble—sets my nerves screaming.

"We can't let him leave," Kirby says, already reaching for the door handle.

"Wait," I hiss, but she's already moving.

I grab my satchel, heart thudding against my ribs, and follow.

We slip into the shadows across the street, boots splashing through puddles. Madison pops the trunk of his car and tosses something inside—a duffel bag, heavy. He glances around again, then heads back toward the warehouse.

We hurry to intercept him before he disappears inside.

"Madison!" I shout.

He freezes. Spins. Hand darting under his coat.

For a terrifying second, I think he's reaching for a gun.

Kirby raises her hands. "We only want to talk."

Madison snarls. "No, you don't."

And then he charges.

I try to dodge, but he slams into me shoulder-first, sending me sprawling across the wet asphalt. Pain shoots up my arm. Kirby yells something, but Madison barrels past her too, sprinting toward the loading dock.

I stagger upright, adrenaline drowning the pain.

"Get after him!" Kirby shouts.

We chase him into the skeleton of the warehouse—dark, dripping, full of rusted debris and the stench of mildew. Madison is fast for a man pushing sixty, but he limps slightly, favoring his left leg. We stay close, weaving between broken pallets and fallen beams.

He bolts for a side exit.

And that's when the sirens wail—sharp, rising over the rain.

Relief slams through me so hard my knees nearly give.

Larry came through.

Flashing blue lights cut through the gloom outside. Tires screech against wet pavement. Shouts echo through the ruins.

"Freeze! Police!"

Madison skids to a stop near the back door, trapped between the approaching cops, guns drawn, and us. His head swivels, calculating, desperate.

For a second, I see it—the man Sinclair relied on. Muscle, teeth, and bad intent wrapped in a human frame.

He hesitates . . . then drops to his knees, hands behind his head.

Officers swarm him, shouting commands, cuffing him hard enough to make him grunt.

He doesn't fight.

And for a moment, a flicker—I see it. Not rage. Not pride. Fear.

Not fear of jail—fear of becoming useless.

Fear of being discarded by the only man who ever saw him as more than muscle.

Kirby and I stand frozen for a beat, catching our breath.

"You okay?" she asks, touching my arm.

"I will be," I say, wincing at the growing throb in my shoulder.

An officer jogs over. "You Wheeler?"

"Yeah."

"Stay put. We'll need statements. But you did good."

I nod, feeling numb.

My eyes stay locked on Madison as they drag him toward a waiting squad car. Even cuffed, even soaked and beaten down, he radiates menace.

But I don't see a thug.

I see a man who thought he was fighting for something bigger than himself. A man who traded his conscience for a sense of order—and somewhere along the way, forgot the difference between protecting and crushing.

Kirby exhales a shaky breath. "That was too close."

I watch the rain hammer the broken roof of the warehouse, the police lights painting everything in frantic, blinking color.

"This isn't over," I whisper.

Kirby glances at me. "No," she says. "But it's the beginning of the end."

CHAPTER 63

1984

AFTER THE GOLD RUSH

The storm's letting up, but Toledo still sweats secrets under the slick shine of rain. I rest my hand on the side of a police cruiser, the blue lights painting the wet pavement in quick, anxious pulses. Officers move in and out of the warehouse, securing the scene, calling out codes. Kirby stands beside me, arms crossed, jaw tight.

A uniform approaches, businesslike but respectful. "Mr. Wheeler? We've got Madison in custody. He won't be walking away from this one."

I keep my voice level. "What are the charges?"

"Attempted assault, possession of an unregistered firearm, and intimidation. Plus, there's talk of reopening several cold cases—union-related incidents from the '70s and '80s. The DA's office is already making calls."

Kirby puffs out her cheeks. "So it sticks?"

"For now," the officer says. "But guys like this don't always stay down. Not if they've got money behind them."

That lands harder than I want to admit. I watch the warehouse door swing shut behind two detectives.

"They found this stuff in his van," the officer adds. "Maps. Surveillance photos. Newspaper clippings. A knife. Looks like he was tracking both of you."

Kirby and I exchange a glance. She says nothing, but her hand curls into a fist at her side.

I step away, fishing out my little spiral notebook. It's soaked at the corners, but the number's still legible. I duck under an awning, find a payphone, and dial.

"Gray?" Larry's voice comes through with that Florida grit and a scratch of fatigue.

"We got him," I say. "Madison's in custody. The cops are locking it down."

"Good," Larry says, then lowers his voice. "Be careful. Sinclair's not a man who lets things go unanswered."

"I know," I say, eyes scanning the warehouse across the street. "But we're close now. This ends soon."

I hang up and head back toward Kirby. She doesn't ask what Larry said. She gives me a look that says: *Let's go.*

The ride back is quiet. Toledo's streetlights flicker in the fogged windows, casting long streaks across the dash. Downtown is dark, but something's shifting beneath it.

It's as if the city's waiting to exhale.

Kirby comes back with me to the house. My parents are in bed, and we head straight downstairs. I'll introduce them to Kirby at some point—but not tonight.

There's more work to be done.

We've got Madison.

Now it's time to lay it all out—thread by thread.

Madison's name gets a thick black marker line through it. Not gone, but neutralized.

For now.

It's time to finish the Wall.

CHAPTER 64
1984
WHEN THE LEVEE BREAKS

Back at my parents' house, the fluorescent tube buzzes overhead, washing the room in its usual green-tinged glow. It's like living under aquarium lighting. My bedroom down here has long since stopped looking like a place where someone sleeps. Half the floor's gone to stacked documents. The bed's buried under boxes.

And the Wall feels like it's all that matters anymore.

My mother hates it. She doesn't understand the importance of the Wall. Yesterday she stood in the doorway, arms crossed, laundry basket sagging against her hip.

"This isn't healthy, Gray," she said, voice tight. "It looks like a madman's workshop down here. Like you're building something that'll fall apart and take you with it."

For once, there was no real anger behind it—only fear that the center won't hold.

Maybe it never did.

Kirby drops her coat over the chair, pulls her hair up with one hand, and starts rearranging the printouts we've pinned. Dates. Names. A copy of the Sinclair photo. A zoning map in red pencil.

I step closer to the Wall. Photos, memos, receipts, Post-it notes, union newsletters, EPA reports, anonymous letters, torn clippings. The whole chaotic map of Sinclair's shadow empire, strung together in red thread like a bloodline.

My eyes lock on a grainy photograph of Carl Madison taken during a strike in '74. I run a fingertip along the thread that leads from him to a folded document: Sinclair's investment disclosure—hidden in a business registry Kirby found two weeks ago. A shell company, layered under two more. But it traces back.

"Madison was there—and Sinclair funded the company that broke the strike."

I remember the interview. The old union man, too scared to go on record. *"He didn't carry a gun, but we all knew who was giving the orders."*

I tack a fresh note beneath an aerial photo of the old Elgin Plant: Environmental violations—EPA reports suppressed. That line only makes sense if you follow the money trail. And I did. All the way to Sinclair's real estate arm. Kirby pulled the city council minutes. The fines were waived.

The Wall quivers in the air current from the AC vent. It's alive now. A breathing archive of fifty years of quiet violence and systemic rot, staring back at us—strings crisscrossing, notes pinned like battle scars.

I stand in front of the Wall, red yarn crisscrossing like veins through the city's history.

One thread runs from Auto-Lite to South Ridge Development. Another from the 1934 strike to the 1967 riots.

And at the center of it all, like a spider in a web: Owen Sinclair.

Not a name in headlines. Not a face on plaques.

But always there.

I step back, heart pounding.

"This isn't a story about a strike," I whisper. "It's a story about a man who never stopped pulling the strings."

I look at the photo again. The rifle. The tie. The calm.

He didn't just survive the strike.

He won it.

I'm sitting on the edge of the bed, legal pad in my lap, trying to finish the last connecting pieces before we send it all to print. The yarn crosses itself so many times now I can't trace a line without hitting a dozen others. It looks less like a map and more like a web—one that finally caught something.

Toledo hadn't fallen by accident. It had been hollowed out, sold off, bricked over and renamed until even the ghosts couldn't find their way home. Men like Sinclair made more than fortunes.

They created ruins.

And they left the wreckage behind for people like us to sweep up—too late and too tired to save what mattered.

Kirby joins me at the Wall, scanning it like a battlefield. I can feel her brain clicking into place beside mine, triangulating from memory.

Then she stops. Frowns. Steps closer.

"Wait," she says. "Where's the photo from Feldman's box—the one with Sinclair holding the rifle?"

I follow her finger to the string—it's there, intact, still leading to the City Trust transcript and the 1948 zoning refile. But the image it all branches from is missing. Just a clean square of empty cork, one tack left behind.

My stomach drops.

I check the table. The floor. The folders.

It's gone.

Kirby's face darkens. "You didn't take it somewhere to copy?"

I shake my head. "We haven't done that yet."

My spine tightens.

"I didn't move it," I say quietly.

"Neither did I."

We search the floor. The bed. The desk. Nothing.

For a second, we both just stare at the blank spot, like it's looking back.

"They were here," she says. "Whoever left the note. They were in here."

The thread connecting Sinclair to the 1934 killings just snapped.

And whoever took that photo knew exactly what they were doing.

I don't answer. I can't. My jaw's already set and aching. Not only have I dragged Kirby into this—but my parents as well.

She turns to me, steadier than I expect. "Then we don't wait."

I hand her a legal pad. "You take the timeline. I'll take Sinclair's rise."

"No quotes?"

"No need. Everyone who could give one is either dead, bought, or too afraid to open their door."

She nods once and drops into the desk chair.

I take the floor. For the first time in weeks, we're not chasing—we're shaping.

"What's the lede?" she asks. "Because it's not just 'man with gun.' That's history. This is about legacy."

"Legacy built on blood," I say. "Sinclair wasn't just present—he steered it. And he never let go."

Kirby nods, pacing. She talks with her hands when she's working—quick, sharp gestures that trace the air between thoughts.

I watch her more than I should. The way her mind clicks forward. The way she catches something just before I do and waits to see if I'll get there.

"Start with the bodies," she says. "Ferner. Feldman. Show the cost. Then rewind."

"Then we give them 1934. The strike. The rifle. The first thread Sinclair pulled."

We talk fast for an hour. Maybe two. At some point she takes my chair and I sit on the floor, our knees almost touching.

Papers pile up between us. Diagrams scrawled in Sharpie. Half a dozen headlines circled and scratched out.

We argue over the middle section—how much to speculate, how much to let the evidence speak.

"Don't go soft," she says. "If you're afraid to say it, it's not the story."

"I'm not afraid."

She looks at me.

I'm not sure either of us breathes for a second.

Then I say, quieter, "I just don't want it to be sloppy."

"You're not sloppy," she says. "You're scared. Me too."

I nod. "Good. Means we're still alive."

She smiles—just enough to shift the air between us.

I don't know who leans in first. But we're closer now. Not touching. Not quite.

The clock ticks. The Wall looms behind her, red threads crossing like veins.

She breaks the moment, reaches for another page.

"We'll need three pull quotes. One from Slaughter, one from Winters, one from Feldman's file. Something that punches."

"You mean something they can't ignore."

She looks at me again. "No. Something they can't bury."

We keep writing.

Side by side. Two voices. One story.

The rest of the night folds into quiet urgency—papers rustling, the scratch of pens, the clack of my ancient typewriter's return lever. Kirby reads aloud when she needs to hear the rhythm. I rework paragraphs in the margins. We break once to heat canned soup. Neither of us tastes it.

Around 2 a.m., she leans back, rubs her eyes. "We have enough for the first piece. The timeline, the connections, the photo trail, the investment shell—it's all here."

I tap my pencil twice against the desk. "It's too clean. We need to leave in some smoke. A little static."

She frowns. "To protect us?"

"No. To make it harder to erase."

She understands. Doesn't reply. Just turns back to the draft.

At 4:30, we finish.

I slide the pages into an envelope, seal it with tape, and write JIM in block letters across the front.

Kirby sits cross-legged on the floor, her hair a little undone now, staring at the Wall.

"It's not perfect," she says.

"No," I say. "But it's true."

She doesn't move. I don't either.

The AC kicks on again. The red thread sways slightly—like it's waiting for the story to leave the room.

CHAPTER 65
1984
UNDER PRESSURE

The newsroom at *The Sword* crackles with tension. Phones ring. Typewriters clatter like distant machine guns. The smell of ink clings to everything, and the floor hums with the vibration of the presses running below.

I sit at my desk, surrounded by chaos, though I'm oblivious to it. In front of me: notes, clippings, photos—decades of secrets that have clawed their way into the light.

Kirby stands beside me, the final draft of our exposé in her hands. She doesn't speak right away—just reads. When she finishes, she sets the pages down like she's placing a weapon on a table.

"This is it, Gray," she says, voice steady but sharp. "We've got everything. The witnesses. The paper trail. The photo. It's time."

My eyes are locked on a black-and-white photo—Carl Madison and Owen Sinclair, younger, arms crossed in front of an old brick building. One smiling. One not.

"It's time the public knew what he did," I say.

As I reach for the phone to alert the production desk, mine rings.

Jim's tone is tight. "Gray. Come to my office. Now."

I shoot Kirby a look.

"Go."

I head upstairs, heartbeat loud in my ears. His door is ajar. When I walk in, he's pacing. A copy of our draft sits open on his desk, red ink scrawled across it. He doesn't sit.

He speaks without expression. "Sinclair's lawyers have hit us with a cease and desist. They're threatening an injunction. Libel. Defamation. You name it."

"Let them," I say. "Everything in that piece is fact-checked. We've got sources, documents, visuals—"

"Yes. And if any of it so much as wobbles under pressure, they'll bury us in court fees before it ever gets to trial."

I stare at him, waiting.

"You want me to kill it?" I ask.

He exhales, sitting on the edge of the desk. He looks exhausted. Older than he did yesterday.

"You ever wonder why this paper never touched the Auto-Lite aftermath?" he says, not looking up.

"I asked Feldman about it once. He told me, 'The silence is a story too, but it won't keep the lights on.' "

He flips through a few pages of the draft.

"Things went quiet for a reason, Gray. Not because we didn't have leads. Not because we didn't care. Just . . . pressure. Quiet, consistent pressure. Pull this quote. Drop that paragraph. No names, no memos. Just the air getting thinner around a story until you can't breathe it anymore.

"I want to know how sure you are. Not about your sources. About yourself. Because if this goes out and Sinclair fires back—and he will—it's not only your byline on the line. It's the paper. The staff. Everything."

I let the silence stretch.

"I'm sure," I say. "This is the story. The whole city's been breathing his poison for fifty years. This is how we purge it."

He looks at me then—just for a second.

"This is going to raise hell. You ready for that?"

I nod.

Jim slides the pages back. "Then so am I." He holds my gaze. "Let's run it."

Sinclair's office issues a statement by evening: "Viciously false." "Politically motivated." "We will be pursuing all legal remedies."

But it's too late.

The truth is out.

I walk out with my heart pounding but steady.

Back at my desk, Kirby doesn't need to ask. She sees it in my face. We go over everything one more time. I make a quick call to our lawyer in Chicago, who gives us the green light.

We send the story to print.

By midmorning, the presses roar like thunder. I watch from the stairwell window as stacks of papers roll off the belts and vanish into bins for bundling. On the front page, bold and unflinching:

THE HIDDEN EMPIRE: UNMASKING SINCLAIR'S SHADOW OVER TOLEDO

Byline: Gray Wheeler and Kirby Peters

The story hits the streets like a grenade. Protesters fill downtown. Students walk out of UT classes. Retirees who remember the Auto-Lite strike line up outside City Hall holding yellowed clippings and homemade signs.

Inside the newsroom, we watch the phones ring off the hook. City officials scramble. The mayor calls for a full investigation. Sinclair's name is plastered across evening news bulletins in Cleveland, Chicago, and D. C.

Kirby sits on the corner of my desk, arms crossed, watching the newsroom swirl like a storm around us.

"We did it," she says—and this time, the smile stays on her face.

I nod. My voice is quiet, but certain. "It's only the beginning."

I gulp, feeling the responsibility of every person who trusted me with their truth. Feldman. Ferner. Even Larry, calling from his hospital room, tells me:

"You hit the heart of it."

I don't feel triumphant.

I feel responsible.

CHAPTER 66
1984
CAN'T SEEM TO FACE UP TO THE FACTS

By the second day, the newsroom is still running on adrenaline. Phones don't stop ringing. Kirby's been fielding calls from reporters in Cleveland, Detroit—even *The Washington Post*. Jim keeps stepping into his office and slamming the door hard enough to rattle the glass, then coming out and telling us to "stay the hell off record until legal says otherwise."

Sinclair's lawyers move fast. They file a formal defamation complaint in Lucas County Circuit Court, claiming "malicious intent" and "reckless disregard for the truth." They want an immediate injunction to stop the paper from distributing reprints and syndication rights.

Our legal team files a counter motion before lunch.

"Classic suppression tactic," our lawyer says over the speakerphone, calm as ever. "It won't hold. But they want to intimidate you."

Jim doesn't blink. "Let 'em try."

Outside, the story spreads like fire.

At City Hall, a crowd gathers demanding answers. Someone's taped our article to the mayor's office door. Protesters chant for transparency, for a federal investigation, for Sinclair's arrest. Others stand in silence, holding copies of *The Sword* like they're cradling a verdict.

By afternoon, the dominoes begin to fall.

City Council president Irene Cavanaugh calls a press conference. It doesn't go well.

"We were unaware of the extent of Mr. Sinclair's business involvement—" she begins, but someone from the crowd shouts, "You've taken donations from his shell companies for ten years!"

The rest unravels in heckling and shouted demands for resignation.

By nightfall, two council members named in the article as accepting Sinclair-linked contributions every year since 1976 announce they've stepped down.

The city council is in disarray. Sinclair's lawyers are foaming. And the mayor's press secretary issues a statement so bland it might as well have been written in flour.

At home that night, my mother shuffles into the kitchen in her slippers and stares at me over her glasses. She sets down a folded copy of *The Sword*.

Her voice is flat. "You're going to get sued."

"Perhaps."

"Well, don't ask us to pay for it. Paid out enough for that degree of yours."

In the basement, I spend an hour pinning maps and photocopies from Sidney's box along the east side of the paneling. His handwriting curls between the threads like veins under skin.

The Wall feels different now. Lighter, somehow. Not empty—but quieter.

For the first time, it doesn't feel like I'm shouting into a void.

It feels like the city's shouting back.

CHAPTER 67

1984

DUST IN THE WIND

The cemetery is still damp from last night's rain, the grass soft underfoot and drops falling from the trees as I walk between headstones. Spring here always carries that strange tension—half growth, half decay.

I find Feldman's plot near the back, under a broad, listing maple. The headstone is modest: a name, dates, and a carving of a notepad and pen in the corner. I never asked his family if they added that. I'd like to think they did.

Sydney Feldman
1914-1984
"Truth is what survives the noise"

I crouch and wipe a slick of moisture from the base. No flowers. I didn't bring any either.

All I have is the paper.

I pull a copy of *The Sword* from my coat pocket—yesterday's edition, folded and re-folded, the edges already soft. I smooth it out and set it against the base of the stone. The headline catches in the wind.

"It ran, Sidney," I say aloud. My voice sounds too loud out here, so I lower it. "We got him. Or started to. Madison's in custody. Sinclair's scrambling. They're threatening lawsuits, sure, but people are paying attention."

I sit back in the wet grass, arms resting on my knees.

"You were right. About the photo. About the pattern. About the way the city protects its own rot if no one looks too hard."

I pause. The breeze shifts.

"I kept wondering why you didn't tell me everything outright. Why you made me dig. But I get it now. You weren't hiding the story. You were making sure someone else believed in it enough to finish it."

A crow calls in the distance. Another joins it.

"I wish you could've seen it. The calls. The protests. The letters pouring in. I wish I could tell you it's over. But I know it's not."

I glance down at the folded paper. The ink's bleeding where it touches the damp granite.

"I'll keep going. That's the deal, right? When someone hands you the thread, you don't drop it."

I stand, brushing dew from my coat.

"You lit a fuse," I say. "I simply followed the spark."

I start walking back through the rows, the city stretching quiet beyond the cemetery gates. Gray sky overhead. Damp earth below.

And somewhere between, voices that never got silenced after all.

CHAPTER 68
1984
THE EMPIRE STRIKES BACK

The phone call comes just after dawn. I'm still lying on the mattress in the basement, half-dressed, the static of the old radio playing in the garage filling the air like nervous breath.

When I hear Kirby's voice, it's tight with something deeper than fear.

"Gray, someone smashed my window. Last night. I think it was meant for you."

I'm already pulling on my coat. "Are you okay?"

"I wasn't there. Stayed at my sister's. But the rock came through the living room. Glass everywhere. It—it had a note."

She hesitates. Then: "It said, 'Print again and you bleed.' "

The words chill me more than the morning air. The blood drains from my face. I'm already out the door, the Hornet coughing to life, speeding through Toledo's half-frozen streets—thinking only of her safety.

And of the Wall.

By the time I get there, police tape flaps in the breeze and a patrol car idles outside. Glass crunches underfoot as I approach. A few shards still cling to the shattered frame like teeth after a fistfight.

Kirby meets me at the door, arms folded tight across her chest. Her eyes are fierce, but I can see the shake in her hands.

"They knew where to find me," she says.

"They know who wrote the story," I reply.

We stand inside. She shows me the note. It's on newsprint, the letters clipped and pasted like something out of a bad detective novel.

But the threat is real.

The police response is tired. A report. A shrug. No real sense that anyone will follow up. Another line on another form. It's like watching a door close in slow motion.

"That wasn't much use," Kirby says quietly as the officers leave.

We clean up the worst of it in silence—sweeping the glass, pulling the curtains tight. I board up the hole with a piece of plywood from the garage while Kirby stands in the doorway, arms still folded. She hasn't said much since.

Afterward, we sit in the living room, the silence thick.

"They know," Kirby finally says.

"They knew before. Now they want us to know they know."

We're both thinking the same thing: This wasn't random. This wasn't bored teenagers or a drunk driver knocking over a mailbox.

This was precision.

"This is about the story," I say. "About Sinclair."

"They waited until it ran." Kirby's voice is low, tense. "That's not a coincidence."

I run a hand through my hair, still buzzing with leftover adrenaline. "We need to go further. We thought we had enough—about the shell companies, the strike, the bribes. But this proves it. We hit a nerve."

She's nodding, but her eyes are distant. "So what do we do now? They won't stop."

I nod. "Then we don't either." I look down at the stack of clippings on the table. "We keep going. We dig until the next piece falls into place. We find something they can't deny. Something that ties Sinclair directly to the shootings in '34."

Kirby looks at me, wary but resolute. "You think we missed something?"

"I think we missed the last thread."

Silence stretches. Then she stands. "Then let's find it."

Later, when I return to the basement, the Wall is there staring at me, waiting like a giant unsolved equation.

And for the first time since the exposé ran, I feel like we're not just reacting anymore.

We're hunting.

CHAPTER 69

1984

TURN OUT THE LIGHTS

The knock at my office door is soft—almost polite. Kirby glances up from the pile of municipal records she's been sorting.

"Expecting someone?" she asks.

I shake my head and get up.

It's a courier—middle-aged, denim jacket, union bumper sticker on his clipboard. "Delivery for Gray Wheeler."

I sign without a word. He walks off without waiting for a tip.

No return address. No postage. Just my name on a plain manila envelope.

Kirby's at my side in a second. "What is it?"

I tear the seal and pull out a single typed note.

Mr. Wheeler,

I have seen your story. I am willing to speak with you—but only once, and on my terms.

If you are serious about the truth, meet me at the Auto-Lite ruins.

Thursday night. 10 p.m.

Come alone.

—O. S.

I read it again, then hand it to Kirby.

She scans it, then looks up. "Sinclair."

"Yeah."

We stand in silence. It's the first contact from the man we've spent months chasing.

Kirby folds the paper in half. "You're not going alone."

"If I show up with someone else, he won't talk. You know that."

"So what? You think he'll confess? Just hand it to you because you showed up?"

"No. But maybe he'll slip. Maybe I'll see something in him that tells the final piece of the story. Or maybe it's a setup. But either way—I need to go."

She doesn't like it. I don't blame her.

"I'll have a backup plan," I say. "Police on standby. Recorder running. Maybe even Larry on the line."

Kirby looks over my desk and picks up a photo—George Slaughter in his younger years, standing in front of the courthouse.

"You already have your witness," she says. "George confirmed Sinclair's name in the photo. Brad Winters backed it up. So why meet with him?"

"Because he thinks he still controls the story," I say quietly. "But he doesn't. And he needs to feel that."

She turns back to me. "Then you'd better make damn sure he doesn't pull the trigger either."

I nod.

We don't speak again for a few minutes. We just look at each other, at everything that's brought us to this moment.

"I'm going," I say. "But we finish the second story first. Before Thursday. Everything on the record. Everything in print. So if I don't come back—"

"You will," she says. "Because you're not going alone. Even if it looks that way."

I glance at her, confused.

She just nods once and walks back to her desk.
The story's not done. Not yet.
But we're almost there.

CHAPTER 70
1984
THE TIME TO HESITATE IS THROUGH

The next morning, the city feels different. Not safer. Just quieter—like the hour after a thunderstorm, when the air is still charged but everything's pretending to be calm.

I spend the day making calls I don't expect returned. A few sources are suddenly unreachable. One old city clerk I talked to weeks ago has apparently retired early. No forwarding address. No phone.

Sinclair's reach isn't subtle anymore.

It's surgical.

By afternoon, the newsroom has settled into its usual low hum, but I'm barely there. I check in with Jim, hand over some follow-up notes, and try not to look over my shoulder. Kirby and I are planning our next move in hushed tones by the coffee machine like kids plotting a jailbreak.

"Slaughter was right. He sent a message. A location, too."

Kirby frowns. "Why The old Auto-Lite factory?"

"He wants it to mean something. Or maybe he wants me off balance. Either way, it's theatrical. He's picking the stage."

She chews her lip. "You sure you should go?"

"No. But I have to."

We agree on precautions. I'll leave notes behind. Call from a payphone beforehand. Record the meeting if I can. We sketch it all out like it matters—like it will somehow keep the worst from happening.

That night, I go back to the basement and stare at the Wall. Everything's there: Sinclair's companies, Madison's arrest, the EPA violations, the payoffs, the faces of the dead.

Even the missing photo—a blank space that glares like an open wound.

But there's one thing still missing: a direct reckoning.

It doesn't matter what I've written if he keeps hiding behind silence and lawyers and threats. If I want the story to end right, I have to finish it myself.

Sinclair wants control. He built a kingdom on shadows, intimidation, and fear. He thinks he can summon me to the ruins of his empire and still dictate terms.

Tomorrow, I'll find out what he's really afraid of.

CHAPTER 71

1984

THIS IS THE END

The factory is a gutted skeleton of industry. Roof half gone, graffiti scrawled across the brick like a dying man cursing in his own blood. The air inside is thick with mildew and memory. I step across the debris-strewn floor, boots crunching on shattered glass, old rivets, brittle plastic. Rusted girders loom overhead like the ribs of a collapsed beast.

There's a clatter behind me. I spin.

Not Sinclair. Not yet.

From behind a bank of rusted machinery, a figure emerges. Big. Neck like a stump. Gloves. Steel flashlight in his hand. Eyes like someone who enjoys the work.

He's here to soften me up. To scare me off. Or worse.

"You're the writer," he says. No question mark.

"Depends. You the welcoming committee?"

He smiles. Then he lunges.

I duck the first blow, but he moves like a freight train. The second catches my ribs. I go down hard. Wind knocked clean. The world spins. I taste blood.

He hauls me up by the collar. My ribs bark in protest. The flashlight raises again.

"Don't make this harder," he growls. "He said no witnesses."

But before the blow can fall, a jagged clang shatters the air.

The thug howls and staggers sideways, clutching his ribs. Kirby stands behind him, breathing hard, both hands wrapped around a rusted length of pipe. Her knuckles are white.

I scramble to my feet as the attacker pivots toward her, fury twisting his face.

"Come on then!" Kirby shouts, lifting the pipe again like she's ready to go down swinging.

I drive a shoulder into him, and together we bring the bastard down. He hits the concrete with a thud that echoes through the factory bones.

Kirby drops the pipe, her hands shaking.

"You followed me," I pant.

"You're an idiot," she says, voice trembling. "Of course I followed you."

Before I can answer, a slow clap cuts through the room. We both look up.

Owen Sinclair steps from the shadows of the second-floor catwalk, his footsteps deliberate, his face carved from stone. He's older now, grayer, but there's no mistaking the confidence. The cold calculation in his eyes.

He steps into the light. Immaculate. Cold. Like he belongs in a boardroom, not the ruins of his origin story.

"You always did have a flair for the dramatic, Wheeler."

"So do you," I grunt, wiping blood from my mouth. "Only yours ends in bodies."

He looks down at the thug, groaning. "Don't be too hard on him. He's old school."

"Like you."

Sinclair smiles. "You've published one piece. You think that matters? You think any of this will stick without a confession?"

Kirby steps up beside me. "We're not done. The rest is coming."

"And what exactly do you think you're going to prove?" he says. "That a scared young man made a choice in 1934 and lived with it for fifty years? That I protected the only city I ever cared about from falling into chaos? That I did what your beloved institutions were too cowardly to do?"

I step closer. "You fired the shot. You started the massacre."

His eyes narrow. "I ended an uprising. I stopped a contagion."

"You murdered people. You buried the truth."

He shrugs. "And yet here we are. All these years later, and you still had to dig through ashes just to find me."

"And now the world will see what was in the fire."

We stare each other down. Breath hard. Blood drying.

I take a step closer, fists clenched, throat tight. "You didn't just bury strangers. You buried families. You buried mine."

Sinclair raises an eyebrow. "How sentimental."

"My father." My voice hardens. "He was there, on Champlain Street. Thought he saw a Guardsman fire the first shot. Thought the brick he threw started it all. He carried that for fifty years – the guilt, the silence. It hollowed him out. It wrecked him. And all this time, it was you."

Sinclair lets out a small, amused exhale. "You think I knew his name? You think I gave a damn who happened to be standing in the wrong place that day?"

Sinclair steps closer, voice low now, poisonous. "You want a villain for your little exposé? Fine. Make me the monster. But don't forget – your father chose to throw that brick. Just like I chose to fire that shot. One of us built something from it. The other got crushed by it."

He straightens his cuffs like this is a boardroom, not a ruin.

"That's the difference between you and me, Wheeler. I use history. You drown in it."

Sirens in the distance. Kirby must've called them while I was getting the hell beat out of me.

Sinclair hears them too. He smiles one last time. He glances at the crumbling factory walls, ivy creeping like veins through stone. For a moment, he seems to consider the weight of it all.

"History never cared about the individual," he says at last. "Only the outcomes."

"You've made a lot of noise, Wheeler," he says. "Let's see if you can live long enough to enjoy it."

Then he steps backward into the shadows. Gone.

We stand there for a moment in the ruin's silence, the sirens still distant, but closing in.

Kirby slips her hand into mine, her grip steady despite the tremble I feel in my own fingers.

The red and blue lights flicker at the factory gates.

We walk out of the shadows, together. We survived the fire; now comes the reckoning.

CHAPTER 72
1984
ASHES TO ASHES

We don't speak for a long time.

The road away from the factory is black and empty, except for the long smear of our headlights over cracked pavement. I keep checking the rearview mirror, half-expecting Sinclair to rise out of the ruins like some wounded ghost. But there's only darkness, and the factory sinking behind us like a bad dream.

Kirby clutches the seatbelt across her chest, breathing shallowly. Her knuckles are still red from the pipe. I can feel the heat of adrenaline finally ebbing away, leaving behind the numb weight of survival.

"You okay?" I ask, not because I need the answer, but because the silence feels heavier than words.

She nods. "What about you?"

"I think I will be. Eventually."

A rustle of fabric as she leans back. Her voice is quiet but steady. "That was too close."

"Yeah."

Neither of us says more. There's nothing left to say about what just happened. Not yet.

We drive through the empty grid of Toledo's midnight streets, past crumbling storefronts and shuttered diners. The city feels spent, like it exhaled decades ago and forgot to breathe back in. Somewhere out there, the presses are still running. Our story is already in readers' hands.

I drop Kirby off at her place, and she lingers in the open doorway for a moment.

"Gray," she says, "do you think it'll change anything?"

I want to give her hope. I want to say yes, this will blow it all open. That Sinclair will be charged, his empire dismantled, truth redeemed. But I can't promise that.

"It already changed me," I say. "And you."

She gives a tired smile. "Then maybe that's enough for now."

I wait until she's inside. Then I drive.

Not home. Not yet.

The streets lead me, eventually, to Champlain Street.

I pull over and step out into the night air. The Auto-Lite memorial sits half-swallowed by weeds, the plaque dulled by time and exhaust fumes. I run a finger over the etched names of the men and women who died or were seriously injured.

Martyrs of a city that forgot them.

The ghosts feel quieter now. Like they saw what we did and decided, just maybe, it was enough.

A train rumbles in the distance. I close my eyes and breathe it in—steel and rust and memory.

The fire's out. But the ashes still speak.

Tomorrow, maybe I'll start writing again. Not about Sinclair. About something else.

Maybe this time, I won't be alone.

CHAPTER 73

1984

YET ANOTHER BRICK IN THE WALL

I don't sleep that night. I walk. Drive. Watch the city roll past in the dark, one broken streetlight at a time.

Sinclair let me go, but that doesn't mean I'm safe. Just that he's already lost.

The ruin still clings to me—oil on my boots, dust in my throat, his words grinding in my skull like gravel. "You've published one piece. You think that matters?"

I don't know what's coming next, but I know what I have to finish.

The basement is quiet. The hum of the fluorescent light is the same, but everything else feels different. Lighter. Like the air itself has shifted.

I stand in front of the Wall of Truth again, the red strings sagging in the humidity of early summer. A few corners have curled. Some tape has peeled back. It looks tired.

But it held.

The photo of Sinclair is still there, now surrounded by the final pieces: a map from Madison's car, the court filing from Madison's arrest, a copy of our article, folded and yellowing. The circle around Sinclair's face gives off a faint glow in the greenish light.

I reach up and unpin a photo. Then another. I don't tear them down. I catalog them. Sort them. Place each piece into a box marked with a Sharpie: ARCHIVE.

I can hear my mother's voice call from upstairs. "Dinner in twenty, if you're hungry."

"I'll be up soon," I call back.

The final thread I remove is the one connecting 1934 to 1984. It crosses the center of the Wall like a scar. I hold it in my fingers, form a loose coil, then drop it in the box.

I leave a few pins in place. I don't know why. Maybe I'm not done yet. Maybe I want to remember what it felt like to chase something this big.

As I kill the light, the room plunges into shadow, but I don't feel buried.

For the first time, I feel like I'm coming up for air.

Tomorrow, there'll be fallout. Statements. Trials. Maybe more silence.

But tonight, there's only the hum.

And the truth, still clinging to the walls.

Sinclair built factories. He built fear. He thought walls and silence would make him immortal.

But in the end, all he left behind was a byline he couldn't erase.

I stare at the final line for a long time before pulling the page from my typewriter.

The story's complete. The names are all there. Sinclair. Madison. Feldman. Ferner. A list of the living and the dead, tangled in fifty years of silence.

But the truth doesn't feel like a victory. It feels like a body you carry out of a fire, heavy, scorched, still smoking.

I've peeled back something the city didn't want uncovered. Not simply a conspiracy or a man, but a mindset. A machine that keeps turning, long after its architect is gone.

Sinclair built his empire on obedience. Madison enforced it with fists.

And the rest of us—journalists, union men, politicians—we looked the other way long enough for it to take root.

I take all the typed pages and stack them neatly in order.

And for the first time, I think about what will happen after it runs.

It won't change everything.

But it might stop one lie from becoming permanent.

And that has to be enough.

When I do arrive home, my father is at the kitchen table reading his *Time* magazine, fluorescent light humming softly overhead, the old Westinghouse clock ticking on the wall. I pour two glasses of Vernors and set them on the table. I haven't said a word since I walked in.

He glances up. "You back for good?"

I shrug. "For now."

Silence settles between us. Comfortable, but tight around the edges. The kind that accumulates when too much has gone unsaid for too long.

I push one of the glasses toward him. He takes it without looking. Sips.

"The exposé ran," I say. "Both parts."

He doesn't react, not right away. Then, without lowering the paper: "You said what needed saying?"

"Yeah."

He folds the page down, sets it beside the glass. "You make a lot of enemies?"

"A few."

An approving nod.

I take a breath. "I found out who fired the first shot. In '34."

That gets him. His eyes lift to mine, sharp beneath his weathered brow. "The Guard?"

"No."

He waits. Patient, but clenched.

"It was someone behind the Guard. A civilian. Part of the company. A man named Owen Sinclair."

The name hangs there like smoke.

"Sinclair . . . " he repeats. "Why the hell would he . . . ?"

"To escalate. To give the Guard an excuse to open fire. He was trying to break the strike. He figured a little blood would do it."

He stares at the table, fingers curled slightly on the Formica edge. I know what he's thinking. That day. The chaos. The panic. The Guardsman he hit with a brick.

"Wasn't him," I say quietly. "The Guardsman, the one you hit with the brick, he didn't shoot."

His jaw flexes. "I thought . . . for years . . . I thought maybe I killed the man who started it."

I shake my head. "You didn't. Sinclair did. You tried to stop it."

Something shifts in his face. Not relief, exactly. Something deeper. A loosening. Like a knot that's been drawn so tight for fifty years it forgot how to be anything else.

He lifts the glass again, holds it a moment.

"Bastard," he mutters. Not at me. Not even to me.

He takes a sip. Then another.

We sit there, not talking. Just breathing in the same quiet. And for once, that feels like enough.

CHAPTER 74

1984

GIVE US TIME TO WORK IT OUT

By the next week, the Sinclair headlines were already slipping into the background.

City leaders moved on. The paper moved on. People found other things to worry about.

AP Parts crept back onto the front page—another scuffle on the line, another broken promise.

I filed the stories. I told the truth. And the wheels kept turning, same as always.

The newsroom is quiet. Monday evening, after the rush. Phones silent. Typewriters idle. The sunlight leaking through the blinds makes everything look washed out, like a faded photograph.

I sit at my empty desk. Everything's packed in boxes. The investigation is over. The story is out. Sinclair is finished—or close enough. And yet—

I'm still here.

Kirby passes by with two mugs of coffee. She glides one down on my desk.

"You okay?"

"I think so."

She doesn't press, but sits across from me, sipping in silence. It's a comfortable pause—the kind you don't get with many people.

We haven't talked about what comes next—about us, about this city. It's all been about the story. But now the silence asks the question neither of us has dared to voice:

Stay or go?

Do I keep chasing my ghosts here in Toledo? Or do I finally do what I tried to do years ago—leave?

The decision hovers like steam off the coffee.

That's when I see it.

A plain white envelope sitting on top of my inbox. No markings, except for a postmark: Chicago, IL.

And in the top left corner, a faint logo: *The Chicago Reader.*

My hand rests on the envelope, but I don't open it. Not yet.

Kirby notices, raises an eyebrow. I don't say anything.

Outside, downtown Toledo glows with early evening light. Quiet. Restless. Watching.

"Big day tomorrow?" she asks.

I smile, but it doesn't reach my eyes. "Could be."

Then we receive the phone call from D. C.

Kirby takes the message while I'm out for coffee. When I return, she's standing next to my desk, arms crossed, trying very hard not to smirk.

"*The Washington Post* wants to reprint your story," she says, handing me a yellow slip with a number scribbled in red ink. "They want to talk to you first."

I blink at the note. "Reprint it?"

"With a national introduction. They want to run it as part of a series on American power brokers and buried histories."

The call lasts twelve minutes. The editor on the other end sounds sharp, practiced—but excited. She's read our exposé three times. She calls it "understated but explosive." She says it will land hard.

By the weekend, the piece appears in the national edition of *The Post*—home of Woodward and Bernstein, who brought down a president and inspired my career. Same headline. Same byline. New context.

They keep our words intact. But they add a preface:

> "What follows is one of the most thorough and disturbing accounts of localized power, systemic manipulation, and the long arm of mid-century American industry we've ever published. It is a reminder that some of the most consequential histories are not national—they are local, layered, and passed down like folklore until someone digs deep enough to exhume the truth."

Copies sell out by noon. National TV picks it up. NPR calls. Sinclair's legal team issues another statement. The US Department of Justice says it's "monitoring developments."

I hear from people I haven't spoken to in years. An old professor. A former roommate. Even my father leaves a clipping on the kitchen table without saying anything.

Kirby walks into the newsroom Monday morning holding a copy of *The Post*. She taps the front page.

"You made the national front page."

I shake my head. "We made the national front."

She grins. "So . . . what now?"

I glance at the phone. Then at the box marked ARCHIVE under my desk. I think about the Wall, now dismantled in the basement. Jim Morrison's haunting voice plays in my head, unbidden: "The future's uncertain and the end is always near."

"Now?" I say. "We find the next shadow."

ACKNOWLEDGEMENTS

I knew I had a novel in me ever since writing a serialized story for my school newspaper when I was about 12. Although I pursued a career in writing, life happened and I could never quite come up with either the idea or the time to let that novel out until recently, when my research uncovered the Auto-Lite strike, which turned out to be a signature moment in the history of both Toledo and the American labor movement. It started out as historical fiction based solely in 1934, but I found parallels in the story to the Toledo of my own youth, as well as struggles going on in the world today, so I added a timeline revolving around the 50th anniversary commemoration of the strike.

As always with this sort of undertaking, there are many people and sources that helped make this novel a reality. On the research side, I am indebted to Philip Korth and Margaret Beegle's monograph *I Remember Like Today*, which contains detailed interviews with many people who were involved in the Auto-Lite strike. I drew on many of the interviews to develop colour, atmosphere and a timeline for the 1934 events. A big thank you to Mike Ferner (who was involved in the actual 50th anniversary commemoration) and Brad Sommer (a Toledo historian), who generously made time to speak with me about their perspectives on both the strike and the commemoration (they have been immortalized by having characters named after them). My childhood friend Larry Lawson, the inspiration for the character Larry in the book, helped keep the police angles authentic. And thanks to publisher Mike Sager – who I met when I interviewed him for a podcast on the infamous Janet Cooke saga back in

2022 – for encouraging me to back myself and making me look and sound good.

The number of people who gave me tips and encouragement are too many to mention – you know who you are – but I want to make special mention of my 'beta readers' Tim Causbrook and Rod Best, who helped to keep things real and on track. And of course, the biggest thanks to my partner in crime, Roslyn, who has listened to me talk about writing this novel for more than 40 years, and whose skills and experience in English and crime fiction were invaluable in finding inconsistencies and helping the story to hang together. Ros, this would not have happened (on so many levels) without your love, help and support. Love you to the moon and back!

ABOUT THE AUTHOR

Ray Welling, PhD, grew up in Toledo, Ohio and earned a journalism degree at Northwestern University in Chicago. Later, he migrated to Australia, where he has worked as a journalist, editor, publisher, content director, writer, marketing manager, lecturer and podcaster. He lives in Sydney with his wife. *Byline for the Dead* is his first novel.

ABOUT THE PUBLISHER

The Sager Group was founded in 1984. In 2012 it was chartered as a multimedia content brand, with the intent of empowering those who create art—an umbrella beneath which makers can pursue, and profit from, their craft directly, without gatekeepers. TSG publishes books; ministers to artists and provides modest grants; and produces documentary, feature, and commercial films. By harnessing the means of production, The Sager Group helps artists help themselves. For more information, please see TheSagerGroup.net.

MORE BOOKS FROM THE SAGER GROUP

The Cheerleaders: A True Story by E. Jean Carroll

Flagrant Fouls: A Novel of Basketball, Murder and Despicable Acts by Richard O'Connor and Glenn Stout

Death of a Playmate: A True Story by Teresa Carpenter

The Detective: And Other True Stories by Walt Harrington

Mary in the Lavender Pumps: A True Story by Joyce Wadler

The Strange and Mysterious Death of Mrs. Jerry Lee Lewis by Richard Ben Cramer

Meeting Mozart: A Novel Drawn from the Secret Diaries of Lorenzo Da Ponte by Howard Jay Smith

Death Came Swiftly: Novel About the Tay Bridge Disaster of 1879 by Bill Abrams

A Boy and His Dog in Hell: And Other Stories by Mike Sager

Eat Wheaties: A Novel by Michael Kun

Goodbye, Sweetberry Park: A Novel by Josh Green

Lifeboat No. 8: Surviving the Titanic by Elizabeth Kaye

Hunting Marlon Brando: A True Story by Mike Sager

The Sing Sing Follies (A Maximum-Security Comedy): And Other True Stories by John H. Richardson

See our entire library at TheSagerGroup.net_

THE SAGER GROUP
Artifex Te Adiuva

www.ingramcontent.com/pod-product-compliance
Lightning Source LLC
Chambersburg PA
CBHW021442310726
48971CB00005B/1467